John S.G. Blair

HOW THEY
BROKE BAXTER

THE MANAGERS MOVE IN

John S.G. Blair

HOW THEY
BROKE BAXTER
THE MANAGERS MOVE IN

MEREO

Cirencester

Also by John S.G. Blair

History of St Andrews OTC

History of Medicine in St Andrews University.
Scottish Academic Press Ltd., Jan 1988.
ISBN 978-0707305257

Ten Tayside Doctors.
Scottish Academic Press; First Edition, Jan 1990.
ASIN: B002KDU0MI

Bridge of Earn Hospital: A History.
Bridge of Earn Hospital,1992.
ASIN: B0000COHZM

*In Arduis Fidelis: Centenary History of the
Royal Army Medical Corps, 1898-1998.*

Recollections of One Hundred Years of Service.
With Major General A.C. Ticehurst.
Scottish Academic Press Ltd, July 1998.
ISBN 978-0707307695.

The History of the Royal Perth Golfing Society.
Private. First Edition, 1997.
ASIN: B003VV24UE

The Conscript Doctors: Memories of National Service.
Pentland Press, 2001.
ASIN: B001MK83S8

The History of Medical Training in Dundee.

Published by Mereo

Mereo is an imprint of Memoirs Publishing

1A, The Wool Market, Cirencester, Gloucestershire GL7 2PR
Tel: 01285 640485 Email: info@mereobooks.com
www.memoirspublishing.com www.mereobooks.com

How They Broke Baxter: The Managers Move In

Book jacket design Ray Lipscombe

ISBN 978-1-86151-082-2

To Mr Kenneth Ward, former Network
Development Manager at Perth College, for his help
with my computing.

FOREWORD

I was surprised to find how interesting I found this novel, and how quickly I became absorbed in it. But perhaps it is not surprising that I could relate to it so well—for, though I come from a different field of academia, it is all so familiar to me. People who live in the "outside world"—outside the world of academia, universities and, I dare say, hospital politics, will probably find this goldfish bowl quite alien if not tedious; but I found myself reading this almost with a sense of nostalgia! What it tells me is that this novel should appeal to a wide range of people albeit in a narrow niche market—doctors, surgeons, even ex-professors of English like me! I think John Blair's book highlights the need to swim or sink in the world of academia or medicine—and I am sure his book will strike a strong sympathetic keynote with many who live in this suffocating, and competitive, world, which also serves such an important service to the community, be it education or surgery.

Doctors, surgeons, consultants, and medical staff in general, will clearly relate to this slice of modern medical history presented in dramatic form as a novel. Also, it is not inconceivable that the layman outside the medical profession will in fact find the book interesting, in view of its insights into a different world—for many are curious about the world of doctors and surgeons. Having read the book, I found myself (during my recent visit to a large hospital as a patient) watching with interest the expressions and manners of the medical staff as they passed one another in the corridors. Was that a sincere greeting, a dismissive nod, or a thinly disguised sneer? For this is a very competitive world of the survival of the fittest, where personal jealousies and the 'ganging up' by grudge-bearing senior (and junior!) practitioners against a surgeon who is always friendly and tries his best, and is a recognised achiever and brilliant in his field, attracting many private referrals, can make the victim's life a private hell, in the end obliging him to choose early retirement (and a sacrifice of pension) just to be rid of the unwanted burden. The book is also, as I said, a dramatized potted history of the NHS with all its convolutions of management since its early inception, tracing the impact of the changes wrought by the various governments, where people like Harold Wilson, Margaret Thatcher, and Robin Cook have had far-reaching effects on individuals ranging from nurses to consultants. The drive of the NHS managers, who are not in the front-line of medical care, to transform many Teaching Hospitals into self-governing bodies, or Trusts, can have disastrous effects on the practitioners that do the job. It is not surprising that many in their sixties have coronaries, or are obliged to endure a life characterised by 'heart-soreness', as our protagonist tells himself while driving home one night. The novel makes us aware that this is not limited to just one hospital. As the Regional Medical Officer says to our protagonist prior to his retirement: "You haven't had the easiest of lives in your neck of the woods. But if you knew about other places, they have the same. It's perhaps not much consolation, but it's true." Thanks to this novel we have the truth—from the horse's mouth!

Charles Muller
MA (Wales) PhD (London) DEd (SA) DLitt (UOFS)
Diadem Books   19/08/2013

CHAPTER 1

"Look," said Jim to Anne as he came to the breakfast table from the front door. "Look—here's a letter from Peter Millard."

Jim read it. Peter Millard was, like Jim, a surgeon in training. Peter had gone from their hospital to the United States for a year to do research. He passed the letter over to his wife. "He doesn't sound too happy. And he doesn't know what's happened about the jobs here."

A. Stanley Bennet M.D.
950 East59th Street
Dean of the Medical School.
Chicago, Illinois 6037.

May 6th 1965.

Dear Jim,

I've only two months to go here and I'm not sure how good my year has been. My research project went well to begin with but in the last couple of months the results aren't working out and I'm afraid I won't get a thesis out of it. I'll get a paper or maybe two papers, but that's all.

There's nothing more I can do. Our passage back is booked.

The clinical work has been good though and there's certainly enough of it. They do things quite differently from us in England and of course it's all private here—everyone pays except the very poorest... they all make big money. The senior resident as they call him is of the same sort of seniority as you and I are—he gets 1000 dollars for a big abdominal operation. What the consultants make must be colossal.

I'm a bit worried that there's no word about these 2 consultant jobs we are both expecting to come up at the end of this year. I wrote to my boss a while back to ask but he wrote to say nothing had been decided. I asked him again if he'd let me know but there's been no word. Could you let me know what's happening?...

"None of the rest of it sounds very cheerful either," said Anne. "Their apartment doesn't sound too wonderful and it must be awful having to be scared about the children or about people breaking in. You'll have to write to Peter. He doesn't know about the jobs. He could still stay there and get a job somewhere in America."

Peter Millard and Jim Baxter were both training to become surgeons in the National Health Service. They had been appointed on the same day to the most senior post for training—senior surgical registrar—in the neighbouring surgical units of their Teaching Hospital. The third unit—or "firm" as everyone called it—was the professor's—it had lecturers as well as registrars on its staff. It was where the academic research went on.

Peter was some years older than Jim. He had been in the War while Jim had done National Service after he qualified in medicine. It was perhaps because he was older that Peter had taken much more time to get his surgical qualification—Fellowship of the Royal College of Surgeons.

But to get promotion to the highest level—the one that really counted—to become a consultant—you had to write and have published four or five reports of rare cases, and research of some sort. These were your published papers which you included in your application for a job. It did not matter very much what they were about—unless you wanted a Teaching Hospital job. But you had to have them. And while Peter Millard was a very good practical surgeon he had only one paper to his name. He was what was called "not academic."

Jim Baxter had been lucky. He had got a place in the professor's research lab and had done enough—all in his spare time—to produce a thesis and have it accepted by his Medical School for the degree of Master of Surgery. This was one of the reasons why he was sure the prof would back him when he applied for a senior post—they had always seemed to get on well. He had got on well too with the senior lecturer—the prof's blue-eyed boy if ever there was one. He had his quota of published papers too.

But Peter Millard had not got on so well with the professor of surgery. He was the practical surgeon, not the laboratory researcher. He liked to spend the tiny amount of time off he had with his family. And a year ago he had found himself a senior registrar for four years—and with only one small paper to his name. So he had what most men of the time did—he went abroad to get another set of letters after his name. They were B.T.A.—they stood for "Been to America." There were so many senior registrars, so few consultant posts. Anything "extra" could help you at your interview. Peter hoped to return from the U.S.A. with a big research project all put together, in time for a new consultant post which he believed was coming up.

"Peter is in trouble," said Jim. "When he wrote to us after he got out there first he sounded fine. But this is a worry."

"When did he write last?" asked Anne.

"It must be about six months ago," said Jim. "No. He sent us a Christmas card."

"He doesn't know about the jobs?" asked Anne again.

"It doesn't sound as if he does. Why they've never told him, I can't understand."

For there was urgency in getting these medical papers written. The "jobs" Anne spoke about were two new, additional, consultant posts—one on each of the units Jim and Peter were working on—to bring the total number of seniors in them to three. The professor's firm—professors' firms always had more staff—already had three—himself and two senior lecturers. The senior lecturers counted as consultants and had made the big break between being a trainee on a short contract and being a senior on a permanent one. The new posts had been promised by the Area Health Authority—their employers in the N.H.S.— and it was in expectation of getting one of them on his return that was another big reason for Peter wanting to come back from the States. "I thought you said they weren't going to do anything about the jobs," said Anne.

"That was the latest. I must ask the chief if he has heard anything."

"If they don't do anything about them soon, you'll have to apply somewhere else again."

"I know."

"Maybe it's a pity you didn't try for that other job in the south."

"Well, look what happened before. It was all fixed for that local man."

"But you didn't have your thesis accepted then."

"No."

The thesis which had brought him his degree of Master of Surgery had made Jim hang on, because he thought it helped his chances of staying on in his Teaching Hospital.

"We'd have to move."

"Yes."

"The children would have to go to another school. We might find ourselves somewhere where there weren't any good schools nearby."

"I know. And we couldn't send them away. We couldn't afford to."

"I don't like boarding schools anyway," said Anne as she began to clear the table. "Remember the children we saw in Euston station that time coming back from boarding school? The brothers and sisters didn't know one another. They were all strangers."

As he drove into work, Jim went over the job problems as

he kept doing, over and over again. They filled his waking moments when he was not taken up with his hospital worries and excitements. He was well aware he was like too many young men in England in the National Health Service. He was well qualified. He was well trained. But he too was now in his fifth year as a senior registrar, and four years was the legal limit in that grade of job. The anniversary had just come and gone and a week later, the letter from the Regional Board had said "To allow you to compete for senior posts in the National Health Service, your period of employment as senior surgical registrar on Mr William Armsworth's Unit has been extended for one further year." If nothing came along soon—and he had had two unsuccessful interviews so far this year—he would have to think about emigrating. He had seen plenty of his contemporaries emigrate to find a permanent job. He might have to think about going into general practice, or as a last resort, joining the Army.

There were three medical staff dining rooms at the Teaching Hospital. The house doctors, newly qualified junior house officers and responsible for the hour-to-hour and minute-to-minute care of the patients, had their own as part of what was called their mess. It was elegant, traditional, with waitress service and meals of a high standard. It was looked after by one of the home sisters who saw to it that meals were available at any hour of day or night. The consultant staff also had their own dining room; through its doorway it looked elegant and wood panelled too.

Then there was the largest by far—the canteen for all the rest—senior house officers, registrars, lecturers, senior registrars; the only staff of non-consultant level who did not use it were the R.M.O., or Resident Medical Officer, and his opposite numbers, the Resident Surgical Officer and the Resident Obstetrician. These persons of critical importance in the running of the hospital enjoyed the luxury of the house doctors' mess.

The big canteen had no waitress service. You queued with your tray, ate off plastic-topped tables decorated with sauce bottles and salt and pepper pots, and carried your used cutlery to the big bins at the end of the room where you left them before you went back to your ward.

At the hospital canteen the talk was about two things only—apart from clinical cases and ordinary gossip—getting or not getting consultant jobs for the senior registrars, senior registrar promotion for the middle registrars, and registrar promotion for the more junior doctors; the other subject was passing or failing the higher qualifications—Fellowship of the Royal College of Surgeons or Membership of the Royal College of Physicians or of the Royal College of Obstetricians and Gynaecologists. Hard-luck stories abounded. The rare occasion when a successful candidate got one over an unpleasant examiner was told and re-told with glee.

"I had a letter from Peter Millard this morning," Jim said to Andrew Morton. Andrew Morton was his special friend—he was a lecturer on the medical professorial firm waiting on a senior lecturer's post promised soon.

"What did he say? His year must be just about up."

"Yes. But he says his research hasn't come to anything. So he feels he's wasted his year."

"Well," said Andrew, "my work in the States didn't come to all that."

"No, but you got an M.D. out of it later."

"Yes, much later. But Peter Millard should get something. The very fact he's been working in that good hospital won't do him any harm."

"I wonder if I should write and tell him about the rumours."

The rumours were that their employers were not going to go ahead with creating the new jobs.

"That's a bit difficult," said Andrew. "You don't really know they're not going to make up the jobs. He might think you were putting a fast one over him. If anyone is to advise him... well... it ought to be Robinson, his boss. In any case, he's so near coming back now he must have made his arrangements. His job there will have terminated and he might not get another one straight away. He'd have to get immigration and all that sort of thing."

Jim had a lot of time for Andrew's judgement. He'd been to the States, too. He was probably right, he thought. He wasn't all that of a close friend of Peter's, either. Yet he wasn't sure. The letter sounded like cry for help.

And then about a couple of weeks later, Mr Armsworth, Jim's chief, called him in to his room. "Baxter," he said, "I've good reason to believe they are definitely deferring these two new consultant posts for at least a year."

Jim's face fell.

"But I've also heard that Rollands of the Royal Reid at Reidham is going to retire at last. You remember he got an extension till he was 66. His job will come up in about three months. It would suit you. Of course, it's not certain."

The Baxters had another pair of friends they shared their hopes and fears with. These were their neighbours, the Macgregors. Ken, the husband, was a strong personality. His wife Mary was quiet and homely. He taught economics at the local Technical College and was a Scot from Glasgow committed to Socialism. Ken Macgregor used to tell Jim he was his link with the outside world.

"You medicals live in a goldfish bowl," Ken used to say. "You only meet other medicals. You're so taken up with your work that you don't have time for anything else. And even if you are somewhere outside and meet another medical, you start talking shop straight away."

"Or start talking about jobs," grinned Jim.

"Yes. It's sad how all you think about is your promotion to become a consultant. That's because there are far too many of you registrars used by the consultants to do their work for them while they go off and make money in their private nursing homes. If there were more of them and fewer of you, you wouldn't be so obsessed about your future. In a properly run society your seniors would be made to do much more and not just leave it to you lads."

"That's not entirely fair," Jim retorted. "They vary like all groups of people. Mr Armsworth's fair. He's much easier than Robinson, Peter's chief. You're just as bad—your world's your college."

"Yes, but I meet all sorts of people. And they're up and about, not lying in bed with tubes down their noses and needles up their veins. They answer back."

"Well, the students answer back."

"Yes, but they know fine how far they can go. They've got to please the bosses in that class system of yours. So do you."

When Ken heard the news about Millard and about the Reidham post the surprise made him suck his teeth in.

"You must write to your friend Millard now. He's still got time to make up his mind about coming back to Britain."

"He hasn't any time."

"Yes he has. He'd be better not to stay there. Their medical service is all based on profit like the rest of their society. Luckily ours isn't."

"Do you think I should write to him?" asked Jim.

"I do," replied Ken. "He's been trained to work here. Things aren't so bad. He'll get a job. From what you've told me about him, he wouldn't fit into their selfish hard commercial medicine. We need people like him. Tell him about those jobs, but tell him to come back."

Ken was equally sure that Jim must go all out for the Reidham post. "You've waited long enough," he said. "Both of you."

So Jim wrote to Peter Millard that evening. He told him about the decision not to create new consultant jobs. He suggested to Peter that he think seriously about looking for a job in the States, adding that he too was in two minds about what to do.

But Peter Millard did come back. And when he talked to Jim about his year in Chicago, it was a sad tale.

"It all went wrong when I couldn't get any results to my research project. I kept trying. My supervisor was helpful for a while, but then he seemed to lose interest."

"What about your clinical work?"

"I got very little. You see, Jim, I was paid as a research

worker, and I had no definite clinical attachment. I had to do casualty work. It was pretty awful. It paid all right, but we needed every dollar we could earn. You've no idea how expensive it is to live in Chicago—anywhere in the United States."

Once started, Peter went on and on. As he talked, he became more and more upset.

"I just don't know what to do, Jim. I just don't know what to do. I was so miserable there—so were we all—that we couldn't have stayed. And now I've come back to this—this news that they aren't going to make up our jobs. When you told me in your letter, I just about wept."

"What has Mr Robinson said?"

"Not much."

Peter's eyes looked like the eyes of children brought into casualty, Jim thought—a mixture of puzzlement and fear.

"There's nothing I can do. A woman we know said I should go into general practice—become a proper doctor!— but I'm too old. I've done nothing but surgery for years. People don't know about us in hospital. They know, or they think they know, about ordinary doctors. But they don't know about *us*. I'm frightened, Jim. I don't see myself getting a consultant job anywhere now. There's *nothing* else I can do. I can't transfer to another specialty. I'd have a go at general practice, I suppose." Peter looked as if he was going to cry—Peter, who had always been so bright and sure of himself.

"I don't know what to do. I'm so frightened I can't sleep." His fists clenched and his hands were shaking. Then he pulled himself together when a nurse came into their room with a question. Jim took the chance to escape. He walked back to his own wards, his own heart pounding. What Peter had said about the public not knowing about the stresses of hospital junior staff was true.

CHAPTER 2

"Thank you, Mr Baxter, that will be all. You must remember this is only an advisory appointments committee. Our decision must be ratified by the Regional Health Authority. We will let you know our decision as soon as possible."

With that the chairwoman dismissed him. He was fortunate, he knew, that he had to go back to hospital to do his chief's outpatient clinic, due to start in the next half hour. It would take his mind off his worry. His chief had been on the committee to appoint the consultant surgeon at the Royal Reid Hospital, and he had been glad of the reassuring smile he had given him at the end of the interview. It had been a long and difficult one. He felt utterly exhausted.

As he drove off to the Teaching Hospital, he thought back to the interview. There was the eagle-eyed lady chairman, a lawyer whose husband was a university big-wig. She had been nice. There was the professor of Surgery, one of his referees, with his senior lecturer beside him. For this appointment was unusual because it carried with it an honorary senior lecturer's post at the university, the Royal Reid being a hospital where students were taught. There was the friendly pathologist, Jack Jenkins, whom he knew well. There was the senior physician at the Royal Reid, Dr Sheridan, who asked fierce questions. There was the senior surgeon at the Reid, Mr Collinson. There was the administrative medical officer from the Board. He couldn't remember the others—there were two external assessors who never opened their mouths. And there was his boss, Mr William Armsworth. He had urged him to say the right thing when he was at a loss for words and began to stumble and hesitate.

There were two other candidates to be interviewed after him. He hadn't seen them, as they were given their own time to appear at the advisory appointments committee. But he knew that a very strong candidate had been seen before him—he was a senior lecturer and honorary consultant in a London Hospital, and had been on the professor's firm locally before that. But the prof, when Jim had gone to see him earlier to ask if he could use his name to support his application, had been very nice, very friendly—friendlier than he had expected, in fact. "Of course, Baxter," he had said. "It's a good job at the Royal Reid—there's no one around as senior as you. There's no one I'd support as happily as you. I don't know of anyone else applying. I hope you get it."

The professor was quite right. There was no-one else around. His own senior registrar was only in his post for one year. The senior lecturers weren't interested. Baxter was now what every senior registrar dreaded—he was time expired. He had had the dreaded letter from the secretary of the Health Authority saying "To allow you to continue to compete for consultant posts in the National Health Service your contract has been extended for a further year." He knew very well—and so did his wife and everyone else—that if he did not get a job soon he would have to emigrate or leave surgery.

As he drove back, Jim thought of the past two years. Two years ago, the Health Authority had promised they would expand the consultant staff in the Teaching Hospital, not by one, but by two new posts. It was called "consultant expansion." It was to take account of the steadily increasing load of work in those early 1960's. It was also to help solve the problem of too many staff in training chasing far too few senior posts, and having to hang around for so many years. "Getting greyer in the hair and greyer in the face" was what his kindly chief used to say of Baxter. And then, this last summer, the Regional Health Authority had finally announced that because of what they called "financial stringency," the new surgical posts would not be advertised. Instead, two new medical posts had been created, one in each of two sub-specialities the professor of medicine wanted developed. It had not been financial stringency after all. The Hospital Authority had accepted one bid and turned down the other.

Jim remembered how over those years the first flush of excitement about the posts had been replaced by doubts and rumours. Over those years, the lure of the jobs had kept him and Peter in their posts—he had applied for two in the interval, one a university one. He had no real regrets about that—the interview had gone too easily. He knew he had been given an easy ride that afternoon, because it was obvious afterwards that the winner had been picked before. That one was fair enough. The man appointed, a pugnacious Scot, had special training the department required, and was a couple of years older. He had not been too happy in that department, since his arrival. Or so Jim had been told. He had some regrets about the one in

London, but accepted the claims of the local man. Such was life in the N.H.S.

There had been another consultant post filled nearby, just before Peter Millard had left for the U.S.A. It was at a large hutted war-time hospital five or six miles from the Royal Reid, but it was regarded as a poor job, and Jim had been told by Mr Armsworth not to apply. It had gone to its own very time-expired senior registrar—he had been there for ten long years, but had been kept on because the job was a poor one and it was thought that if he left, they might have difficulty in getting a replacement.

But most of all, Jim knew there would have been another candidate to reckon with—Peter Millard. But when Peter came back from Chicago, he was not the man who had gone away a year before. He had lived on a small income with his wife and two small sons—it was said they had even gone short of food. The salary of his research post was so low. The cost of living was so high. He had arrived home in England, tired after a long hard year of research he had no inclination for, and found to his unhappy surprise that the job—on his own firm and for which he thought he'd be the strongest possible candidate—was not to be. Jim's letter had not changed his mind about coming back.

He had developed a cough while in Chicago and now feared it might be a recurrence of a mild infection of T.B. which he had had as a student. He had become depressed— totally out of character for his usual cheerful self. His wife had come back with the boys from school one afternoon to find his body swinging from a noose over a beam in the garage. Peter had hanged himself.

The funeral at the crematorium had haunted Jim ever since. Most of all he had watched Peter's widow, her chest rising and falling with emotion, come in and walk to her seat. But he had also watched, in anger, the row of black-coated, black-tied Board officers—the secretary, the regional administrative medical officer—a pillar of the local Methodist Church—the physician who had seen Peter when his cough had begun to trouble him, and who had not noticed how depressed he was—and his friends from the lower deck, the registrars and housemen. There was also Robinson, his chief, who had apparently not thought of letting him know what was happening earlier in the summer. He could surely have suggested Peter find a job in the States—and if he had had reasonable time he could have got one. Jim wondered whether they were kinder and more thoughtful in other parts of the country. Then he got angry again—those administrators, with their grave faces and their black ties, had more than a little responsibility for Peter's death. Perhaps this was why they had turned out in such force.

"How did you get on?" asked Sister at the outpatient clinic kindly.

"I don't know," he replied. "I'll just have to wait and see."

The clinic was a small one—the numbers had been reduced because the chief was at the interviews, and he never did a very big clinic on a Tuesday afternoon anyway. Jim felt oddly neutral. He would like this job at the Royal Reid very much, and it would not mean moving too far— about thirty miles. He would have to pay all the costs of a removal himself, and a short move would be cheaper than a long one. Then there was the children's schooling—their older son was now eleven, and their daughter nine. The son was at a more critical year in his school life than his young sister, but his marks had been good enough that a move into the upper school wasn't likely to upset him too much.

Letters dictated to dear Auntie Betty the unit secretary and he was off home. Because it was the senior surgeon's clinic, she always went to it at the end, to save him coming to the unit office, and did his letters there and then. Jim was acting for the chief, so she gave him the same perk. It was typically nice of her. He told her that although he thought he could have done better, he felt pleased he was being supported by the professor, as well as by his own boss.

He got home about a quarter past five, hugged Anne and was telling her about the interview over a cup of tea, when the telephone rang. It was the senior medical administrator. "I thought I'd give you a Christmas present, Jim," he said. "The committee have agreed to appoint you to the post at the Royal. It was unanimous—I'm sure you'd be pleased to hear that. Of course," he went on, returning to the way administrators always seemed to have of never making a definite statement about anything, "you must remember that this was only an advisory appointments committee. Our decision must be confirmed by the Regional Authority. But it'll be all right. Congratulations and good luck."

That was kind of him, thought Jim. He didn't really need to phone so soon—or to phone at all. Perhaps the few times they had taken each other's children to nursery school in the past years had made him friendly enough to do it. But Jim thought it was more probably because he was at heart a kind man.

Jim and Anne did not shout with excitement, or jump

with joy. They both felt a profound feeling of relief. Relief was the right word. Worry about the final rung of the ladder—so far away this morning yet so near—was over. They could look forward to a permanent home after the previous ten years of moving about. They had only been in their present house for three years—the first house they had owned. And even then they had had to borrow money to put towards the deposit from Anne's father—and had just paid it back at 2% commission. The rat race was surely over. Now he could sign himself "consultant surgeon"—he had been acting and working as a consultant surgeon for at least two years now, but had signed himself "senior registrar." Now they'd have a big income and could afford holidays. They clung to each other, saying nothing. Then tears came into Anne's eyes. Jim understood. For most of their married life she had watched him slog his way on. She had had to keep the children quiet while he was swotting. She had had to stay at home when he was away at the laboratory, doing his work for his thesis. She had seen him have to go out night after night when he was on call, and then go out early again next morning, for years and years. She had shared the success when his thesis was accepted. She had shared his hours of panic when he thought his chief was angry with him or when cases had gone wrong.

Then the phone rang again. Anne answered it. It was the second surgeon on the firm—the third of his referees. "Is that the residence of the consultant surgeon at the Royal Reid Hospital?" he asked her. Then he added his congratulations and his good wishes. "I'll go and have a scotch to celebrate," he said. "You should do the same."

Twice more the telephone rang in the Baxter home that

evening. The first call was an unexpected one, as it was from a man he really did not know. It was from the newly appointed surgeon at the hutted hospital nearby the Royal Reid, the Avondale, a year previously. He was the man, a good ten years older than Jim, who had been the senior registrar of ten long years standing. "I rang to congratulate you on your appointment to the Royal Reid," he said. "I was also up for the post, you know. I'm sure you will do well." Jim thanked him. But he was conscious of a little hardness in the rather high-pitched voice at the other end.

The last call was from the professor's assistant, who had been at the interview. His congratulations were brief but friendly.

Phone calls went out of the house as well as into it. There were calls to both sets of parents, to brothers and sisters, to friends everywhere. Anne's older brother, a general practitioner, was the most excited of all. "You'll do well there, Jim," he said. "That's marvellous news. I knew you'd get it, of course." Her young brother David said the same. The children were told—they were pleased that their daddy and mummy were so happy. "Does that mean you're a proper surgeon now, daddy?" said young Nan as she kissed him goodnight.

They sat talking excitedly the rest of the evening. The reality of Jim's success began to sink in. As they were going to bed, Anne said, "Now just watch. Two are enough."

Next day was Wednesday. When he arrived at the ward, Jim suddenly realised there had been no word from the chief. Everyone had heard the news. Sister White of the male ward was grinning all over. She had always liked Jim—which was fortunate for him, as she by no means liked everybody. Alec, the middle grade registrar and another dour Scot, said to him, "Well done. I didn't think you'd get it." "Miserable bugger," thought Jim. Still, Alec would now have a good chance of promotion into his S.R. job.

The chief arrived, having parked his Rolls in his place of highest privilege in the car park. Jim had known him now for five years—longer, in fact, because he had been taught by him as a student. But he had only got to know him well since coming back as senior registrar from his earlier travels around the U.K. At first he had been a bit afraid of him—a short thick-set man with blue eyes which could dance with fun like the sky of a bright summer day—but which could also grow cold with anger, like the sea when a storm was blowing. But soon, so soon, his fear had turned to respect, admiration, and then adoration.

Mr Armsworth was the senior surgeon in the Teaching Hospital—senior to the prof by several years. He was the best surgeon—a brilliant technical operator—a joy to watch. He was also the most successful private surgeon—hence his Rolls, his beautiful house, his holidays all over the world. Well, perhaps not all over the world—it only seemed like that. Mrs Armsworth was wonderful too—happy, smiling, and so kind. Although they were middle-aged, they were in love. Their eyes sparkled when they met. When they invited the staff to their home, they were kindness itself. But on the wards Mr William Armsworth was the boss, the chief. The sisters in the male and female wards, the porters, the hospital skilled tradesmen, all called him "the Chief." They referred to him in the third person. His number two—the younger consultant—though physically a bigger man, was in all other ways a smaller man. Mr Armsworth's ward rounds were quick affairs—his examination of patients so quick that his juniors could not understand how he could diagnose such obscure conditions so expertly with what seemed to them a minimum of physical examination. He was decisive, both in the wards and in the operating theatre. And most of all, he was a master of operative surgery. He had so many strokes to pass on that registrars from other firms crept in to watch him, much to the annoyance of their own consultants. Both consciously and unconsciously, his succession of senior registrars modelled themselves on him—quickly in and out of the wards, formal, polite, but a little aloof, and all quick operators. They could not help but be good operators if they had eyes to see and hands to copy. As far as they were concerned, there would always be only one surgical chief.

And here he was. "Come in, Jim," he said. He did not often invite his own staff into his private room—he preferred to sit in the side room with the ward sister, the registrars, and the house surgeons. "Sorry I didn't phone you, but I wanted to see you and talk to you today. I am delighted you got the job. You deserved it. You interviewed well. The Reid people liked you, and that made a difference. That man..." he went on "...from London—did himself no good. He was so cocky it was almost funny. The prof. pushed him, too. So did his lecturer—very much so—the two of them pushed him hard. Of course, he is one of the prof's boys, and he wanted another up here to extend his empire. You'll find medical politics are often like this, Jim."

Well, thought Jim, and after all his protestations about how keen he was to support him... He had never heard his chief speak in this way about senior staff before. Perhaps it was because he, too, was now promoted into that senior elite that Mr Armsworth was speaking to him like this. He had always been very discreet; it was now very evident, in what he said about seniors in the presence of his own juniors. Jim was a bit surprised, he had to admit to himself, at finding how someone he'd always respected could dissimulate—and his first assistant speak in such a friendly way on the phone when he too had apparently been just as keen on supporting someone else a couple of hours before.

Coffee was brought in by Sister White. Plus chocolate biscuits. This was a special occasion. Jim and the chief sat by themselves once again.

"Now Jim, I've grown fond of you" (he's fairly letting his hair down, thought Jim) "and I'm going to tell you a little of how your professional life is going to go (what's coming now, wondered Jim). You will find your life at the Royal Reid will go through distinct phases. First of all you'll be the new man and the doctors will refer you patients to see what you're like. Then if they like you they'll refer you some private patients. And you'll find your workload will go up. If you do as well as I expect, this will go on for a good fifteen years. But then there will be a change. You'll then be in your early fifties. Several, perhaps many, of the practitioners who referred you patients will be retiring from practice. Their successors will now be much younger than you—half a generation or more. You'll find that they relate to a younger colleague—and your referral rate will go down. When this happens—for happen it assuredly will—don't be upset or annoyed. This is the natural history of a hospital consultant's life.

"Remember, too, that you'll have a younger colleague when Mr Collinson retires from the surgical department of the Reid. He's got a few years to go—seven, if I'm not mistaken. Whoever succeeds him will be quite near you in age—and that's better than if he were ten or twelve years younger. Remember that it's more important to appoint someone you can get on with than someone who seems very clever and very advanced. That's what university departments do. And that's why (he could never conceal his dislike of academics, thought Jim) they're always fighting so much amongst themselves in university departments.

"Those two general surgeons at the Avondale I don't think you'll have much to do with. Mr Charles Wilson will be retired in about five years. He's all right. I met him a couple of times in North Africa, in the War. The other one"—here his tone changed, and he frowned ever so slightly—"the other one—D.G. Jones"—he hesitated—"do you know him?"

"No, sir," replied Jim. "I've hardly met him. He was an S.R. a very long time there, and it was only when the Platt committee report upgraded his job that it was made a consultant one—he got it."

Jim remembered how Mr Armsworth had warned him against applying for that Avondale job when it came up. "That job is not for you, Baxter," he had said. "A job at the Avondale isn't for you. If you take my advice, you'll not apply." He hadn't been altogether surprised. The Avondale was a war-time hutted hospital. Mr Wilson worked his S.R. very hard. There were no students, no university appointments for the staff. There were no private beds. There was no decent library. The empty beds no longer needed at the end of the War had been used for orthopaedics, plastic surgery, and neurosurgery. There were all those geriatric beds, too. It was a bigger hospital and a busier one, probably, than the Royal Reid. But he had done what he was told and he had given no further thought to the consultant post there.

Mr Armsworth went on. "Don't be upset when you find you're getting less work. It's always been the thing in hospital practice that you do a bit less as you get near to retiral—look at me," he laughed, "and no one gets upset at that, either."

He was in flow, now. "Do not run around trying to please everybody. There will always be some people you don't get on with, and some G.P.s who never refer you anybody. It is just the same with them. When one of your friends retires, his successor will never refer you another patient. That's the way of the world.

"Whatever you do, do not try any big stuff when you arrive first. I told you they will test you out—doctors do this more than a new man ever supposes, you know. If you try any heroic operating when you arrive you can be sure it will go wrong. And that won't help your reputation—especially for private work. So hold off to start with. No one can complain if you are careful. But they soon complain if they think you aren't.

"You should be all right with Sheridan and Bell. They're really a very good pair of physicians, even if Sheridan does drink a bit. You'll find they'll help you. You may need help, you never know. Not many people go through their professional lives without needing help some time."

Dr Sheridan was the physician on the appointments

committee who had been so fierce. He was the chief, and Dr George Bell was the next senior. Two physicians to two surgeons. It was not the same at his present hospital—nine general physicians to seven general surgeons. And it would soon be eleven physicians to seven surgeons, because the new posts were to be medical and not surgical. But that was all in the past now. There always seemed to be more consultant physicians compared to general surgeons, apart from all the specialist ones. Jim had spent the last years doing consultant's work, of course, seeing patients on medical wards, especially emergencies, but he was only a senior registrar. That was why his present post was supposed to be made into a consultant one. But it never was. And he was alive and promoted. Peter Millard was hanged and was dead.

Now there was so much to do. Auntie Betty typed his letters for him—one to the Regional Health Authority resigning from his S.R. post. Back came the reply congratulating him on his appointment and thanking him for all his services to the Health Authority in the past. It was a standard letter, he reflected, and a bit odd—because he was going to work for the very same Regional Authority in the future—he hoped for more than for five years, too. There were letters to his lawyer, to the school head, bank manager, university. There would be many more when they got the removal completed—but that was three months or more away. Finding a house would be the biggest problem, and after that, schooling. Luckily the Royal Reid was only thirty miles away, so they could see what the house agents turned up with fairly easily, and could drive over in a morning or afternoon.

Auntie Betty, as everyone called her, was Jim's fairy

godmother. She was several other people's fairy godmother, too—a marvellous person. Her husband had left her to bring up her two children on her own, and she had worked a lifetime as a medical secretary. They had had many afternoons of laughter together when they sent for the waiting list or arranged the student teaching for the next week. She could be so funny, and always in a kindly way. There was almost never any hardness and never any malice about Auntie Betty. Everyone loved her. Jim would miss her more than most.

They would miss the Macgregors, their neighbours. But perhaps not all that, suggested Anne. Ken was just that bit abrasive and wore his Socialism a bit too prominently.

One pair they would miss when they moved house to the Royal Reid would be the Mortons. Andrew Morton had just been promoted to senior lecturer on the professorial medical firm—just before Jim's consultant appointment. Andrew was five or six years older than Jim, and old enough to have been in the end of the War as a doctor in the Royal Air Force. His wife Mary had become the closest of friends to Anne, and Anne loved her for her cheerful, inconsequential nature. Nothing ever seemed to ruffle her and she had a great sense of humour. Their families had come to know each other through the usual way of sharing the carrying of their children to school—first nursery school, then primary school. While Jim had worked for his M.S., Andrew had been working for his M.D. in the next room of the research building, and they too had become the firmest of friends. Andrew had had his ups and downs in the academic world—his trip to the U.S.A. had not got him the promotion he had hoped for, but that disappointment was forgotten now he had won his senior university post.

So he was something of an older brother to Jim, who thought the world of him. On receiving nights, they had supported each other in their respective medical and surgical roles and each had grown to respect the other's judgement and hard work. They had shared those years of anxiety all senior registrars go through in the National Health Service, as they work and wait, and wait and work, for promotion to the goal of consultant status. Yes, the Baxters would miss the Mortons most of all when they moved away.

CHAPTER 3

Their move to Reidham went remarkably smoothly. The Baxters bought the first house they went for—the previous owner wanted a quick sale and there were no interlopers. It was a substantial house only a mile from Jim's new place of work. Such a prize obtained so quickly seemed a good omen to Anne and Jim.

"Excellent," said Mr Armsworth. "Your first house should be near your hospital. It'll help your private practice, too, this house." Mr Armsworth could temper his views on patient care with an unashamed eye for business. There was a small but pleasant private wing at the Royal Reid. Although there was a rather dignified old nursing home about a mile away in the town, in a quiet suburb, the hospital facilities were the better place for private practice.

Schooling, too, was re-arranged without difficulty. John and Nan, their son and daughter, found places in the local school. Jim hoped that with their mother's no-nonsense, realistic attitude they would settle in happily.

Shops were good—better in fact than where they had lived before. The smaller size of Reidham was the reason, said Anne. The best shops were farther away from their new house, but that didn't matter. "In a year or two," thought Jim, "Anne will be able to afford a car. I mean," he thought again, "I'll be able to afford a car for her."

They were able to move into their new home well before

Jim's starting date. This too was a bonus. The short distance for the removal van was another, especially since the Regional Health Authority made no contribution to removal fees or lawyer's expenses. At first the small amount of furniture from their tiny bungalow looked lost in the larger and grander rooms of the consultant surgeon's residence. They bought an inexpensive desk and three cheap chairs, an old screen, a side table for instruments, an examination couch, a filing cabinet, all for the consulting room. Mr Armsworth advised them about stationery, and they bought headed notepaper, envelopes, bills, appointment cards, and compliment slips.

The Armsworths came all the way to Reidham for a Sunday lunch and to inspect the new premises. The Baxters felt that day that the Armsworths paid them the great compliment of treating them as equals. Mr Armsworth left Jim a present of a diagnostic set and a sphygmomanometer. Mrs Armsworth said how well Anne had chosen the new curtains and carpets. If Mr Armsworth thought the consulting furniture a bit basic, he did not say so. He was always a man to speak his mind, and Jim thought his silence signified approval. The Armsworths could not have been kinder.

During their visits to Reidham they made contact with Tom and Pat Stone. Tom was a class-mate of Jim's, and a year or two older as he had done military service before starting medicine. Pat had been a staff nurse. They had been friends, but not close friends, as students. But it was nice to have someone you knew and liked nearby. The Stones invited them to their home where they met their children and their small dog. Jim asked Tom if he would take them on as patients, and he agreed.

An exciting and unexpected extra came Jim's way during this waiting period. He was phoned by the Dean of the Faculty of Medicine and asked if he would be willing to take on the new post of Clinical Tutor to the Royal Reid Group. After hearing what was involved, and that the salary was £200 a year, he happily accepted. "Dr Sheridan has made a start on this already," the Dean said. "But he finds he has not enough time to do the work as thoroughly as he would like, and he suggested your name to me."

The three months between appointment and starting date had passed quickly. Their house hunting and domestic arrangements were one side of their new life. Anne's doctor brother and his family and her younger brother visited them and shared their excitement. They had the Mortons and the Macgregors in for meals and talked happily about their new prospects and hopes. They tried two of the more expensive restaurants in Reidham, enjoying a better wine than they had been accustomed to during their years of registrar restriction. Anne told Jim with pride in her eyes, "You're a consultant now, you know."

The week before he was due to start, Jim turned to the other side of their new life, the hospital.

The retiring surgeon he had succeeded, Mr James Rollands, proved to be a kindly man. He presented Jim with his diagnostic instruments, saying he had no use for them now. On the Friday before he was due to start he took Jim to the wards and introduced him all around. He took him to the medical wards, the laboratory, to casualty, the records department, the head porter, even the telephonists. His sincerity took Jim by surprise. If this was consultant kindness, it promised a happy future. The physicians he met—Dr Sheridan, Dr Bell, and Dr Stewart the local chest physician—all seemed welcoming. Dr Richard Turner the pathologist seemed more gruff. The biochemist Dr Holmes was by contrast very quiet. They did not meet the radiology staff, though Jim didn't notice this at the time. His head was in something of a whirl.

They spent the longest time with Mr Peter Scott, the Group Secretary. Group Secretaries were always powerful men, and Mr Scott was no exception. He had been in post for several years, and knew how to get things done. Although he worked at the Avondale, the Reid was very much his headquarters. Jim found him very helpful—they had of course met before—and as well as asking what Jim wanted in particular for his hospital work, he offered to get him some items for his consulting room, which he explained to Jim he could obtain at contract prices through his contacts with suppliers at Region. He advised Jim about some new bathrooms just installed in the surgical wards, said they had caused some problems, and asked Jim to let him know how they were working when he got started the next week.

The junior house surgeon, the senior house surgeon, and the registrar in post were standard. The houseman, with a shock of unruly fair hair, seemed ordinary enough. The registrar was a quiet polite Indian with his F.R.C.S. and a good deal of experience, Mr Rollands told Jim. Jim took to him. He had a cheerful, rather chubby face, and a sense of humour.

A much more important person than all these was Sister Helen Billings, the ward sister. She was in charge of both the male and female wards of Jim's flat of the firm. She had been there for only a couple of years or so, and was unusual because she had done nursing administration for a short while after being a sister elsewhere, had disliked it, and now had come back to what she loved doing. She must, Jim thought, be about his own age. They talked politely. Jim was then taken upstairs to meet Sister Fletcher, Mr Collinson's sister. She was pleasant and welcoming and altogether more chummy than Sister Billings. Lastly they met Sister Pope, the senior theatre sister.

Mr Rollands took his successor to lunch. The senior staff dining room seemed small after the Teaching Hospital one. But now Jim was a member as of right, and did not just peep in the door. He met only one or two staff. It seemed that many went home, or were at the Avondale like the radiologists, or had sandwiches in theatre like the surgeons. They then retired to the library for coffee. By a special tradition this room was reserved for consultants over and after lunch time. The old woodwork, the books, the comfortable chairs—it was all a new world. Jim thought he would like it.

In the afternoon, Mr Rollands drove Jim to a small town some miles into the country. On the way they passed within sight of the Avondale Hospital. It was the standard hospital of its type, and had a rather dingy air about its single storey grey huts, roofs with some moss on, and big car parks. As they drove past, Mr Rollands said "That's the Avondale Hospital" in a rather flat tone. He said no more.

His object, he explained, was to introduce Jim to a practice of doctors in this small country town who were his special friends. His interests were fishing and horse-racing, he went on, and this group practice was not only made up of fishing friends, it was a particularly good one. They had begun to improve it as the result of the new general practice contract. Jim was duly introduced, shown around, given tea and home baking, and assured he would see more of both doctors and their patients.

And then, to cap this exciting day, Mr Rollands took him back to the private wing, and introduced him to Sister Hoddie, its ruler, and to a pleasant oldish lady recovering from an infection. After further introductions, he passed her over to Jim's care. Mr Rollands wished him every success and every happiness. "You'll have to earn it, though," he said, laughingly. And off he drove, into his retirement.

Jim got home to Anne positively purring. He kissed her for a long time, and when they went to bed she said amidst their pleasure, "Isn't it nice to be in bed with a consultant surgeon!"

The year of 1965 was an eventful one, but not for hospital staff. It was the year of huge activity by the General Services Committee of the B.M.A, who were negotiating a new General Practitioner's Charter with Mr Kenneth Robinson, the Minister of Health. Family doctors, very many of them working in old premises, were unhappy that they were unable to give the public the good service they knew was needed, and were overwhelmed by the demands of that same public. In many towns in England, doctors were called out at all hours by demanding patients, and often felt they were being abused.

Over the previous winter, negotiations to improve their

conditions of service had begun, and on January 1st, Mr Robinson had written to each of the 22,000 general practitioners in the United Kingdom, telling them that a working party was being set up. He also told them that prescription charges were to be abolished from the 1st of February. The family doctors asked that their status as independent contractors be continued and that they still have continuing responsibility for their patients—refusing any offer of an on and off shift system. They did not want a full-time salaried contract, as some politicians had advocated, and did not want to be paid by item of service—a payment for each and every consultation or visit they made.

In February of 1965 the average general practitioner's income was £2765—an increase awarded for that year by the Review Body, the government committee responsible for advising on the level of doctor's pay. The same Review Body asked that a further £5.2 million be added to the total money pool, to pay for the improvements asked for.

As so often in the history of the N.H.S, it was the doctors and not the Government of the day who had demanded improvements in patient care. Their Charter was published on March 13th, and asked for adequate time for consultations in their surgeries, improved premises and equipment, a working day which allowed them reasonable leisure, and the possibility of time off for postgraduate study and training. Because there was no response by the Government, undated resignations by general practitioners were signed and collected by the Medical Guild, a pressure body which discontent had fostered. A special representative meeting of doctors was held in London on March 24th, and another on June 23rd. At this meeting it was agreed that the

17,815 undated resignations should continue to be held by the Medical Guild and that negotiations should continue. The B.M.A. also asked that pay—which the Minister had so far refused to discuss—was to be related "directly and realistically" to the doctors' workload and responsibility to provide a service.

Mr Kenneth Robinson was a caring and helpful Minister. His own father had been a doctor. He wrote again, in early June, to all the country's family doctors. "Medicine is not something that can be parcelled out in standard units of medical care," he told them. But at the Annual Representative meeting of all the profession in Swansea, a motion was passed making the request that patients should pay for items of service done them by their family doctors, and this, as Dr J.C. Cameron, the Chairman of the General Services Committee of family doctors said, "put the cat among the pigeons." He knew it was a symptom of the doctors' frustration at being abused by patients, and tried to play it down before it was rejected—as was inevitable—by the Minister of Health.

By October the Minister was coming around to the doctors' viewpoint. He accepted that the "capitation system of payments" to general practitioners be modified, that separate payments be made for call-outs between midnight and 7 a.m., and that the basic practice allowance include extras for holidays (to cover cost of locums), study leave, work in unattractive areas of the country, setting up of group practices, seniority payments, and a special expense allowance. Dr Cameron's patient and sagacious diplomacy had won the day.

By the end of October, when Jim's starting date at the Royal Reid as maximum part-time surgeon, being paid nine-elevenths of the full-timer's salary but still being contracted "to give substantially the whole of his time to the National Health Service" came along, much if this medical heat had cooled. There were the usual outbursts from the more vociferous doctors and the more vociferous members of parliament. But the Minister of Health had done an unusual thing—he had taken the advice of the men and women primarily responsible for the actual running of the service. And time would show they would willingly reward him by improving their premises, practices, and services over the succeeding years.

Jim had first met Mr Charles Collinson, now the senior surgeon at the Royal, when he made his pre-interview visit. Mr Collinson was a London graduate who had moved north by choice and not by default. He was a keen fisher too, like Mr Rollands, and also a good shot. They had met several times since Jim's appointment. He had let Jim know of Mr Rollands' wish to take him around the policies himself, saying he thought it was a good idea. Jim sensed that these men had been good friends for many years. He prayed he would be as fortunate. He remembered Rollands' words on the Friday evening—"You'll have to earn it, though"—and wondered just a little if there was any hidden meaning in that remark.

CHAPTER 4

Jim began his consultant career in the out-patient department on his first Monday morning. His clinic was a small one—only twenty patients. But they were all new except for two; Mrs Porter, the long-experienced staff nurse, told him Mr Rollands had arranged this carefully. Another example of his consideration, Jim thought. His cheerful registrar, Mr Shah, saw follow-up patients in the next room and anyone referred by the casualty officer downstairs. Along the corridor was a huge clinic of skin disease patients. Farther on a neurologist from the Regional service was seeing a few specially referred patients. The W.R.V.S. ladies dispensed tea and biscuits in the waiting area. It was like the clinics Jim had done before except for one thing. When he went to the secretaries' office to dictate his letters at the end of the session, he had the thrill of knowing he was going to sign them with the words "consultant surgeon" after his name.

After lunch in the hospital staff dining room, and coffee with the other consultants in the library, Jim did his first ward round. The wards were full of everyday sorts of patients—those with duodenal ulcers, gallstones, hernias, and old men with enlarged prostate glands. It was a true general surgical ward. There were the usual emergency diagnoses—acute appendicitis, abdominal pains of other sorts, head injuries, and two road traffic accident patients. And they were all *his* patients. Mr Collinson's were upstairs. He felt like a chief. The House surgeon, Mr Shah,—and Sister Billings—had got everything arranged and set out as well as in the Teaching Hospital. The patients for the next day's list had been seen several months before by Mr Rollands, and Jim had to explain that he was the new consultant surgeon.

After the round was over and Sister had told him about one or two items of hospital policy and procedure—she was still a little formal and distant—Jim went to the office to sign his letters, walked out of the front door after pushing his name plate to the OUT position, and got into his car. As he drove home he wondered if he would ever reach the heights of Mr Armsworth. But then Mr Armsworth was a senior Teaching Hospital consultant, he a mere District Hospital one.

Next day was the excitement and anxiety of his first operating session. The senior theatre sister, Sister Pope, had already seen him and asked him what stitches and needles he preferred to use. She also gave him a form to sign, authorising the purchase of several new instruments Mr Scott had told him he could order. All new consultants could do this, Mr Scott had explained. But now here she was—and she was obviously a stickler for discipline—all ready to "take his cases"—to have ready and hand to the new surgeon his swabs, knife, retractors, artery forceps, ligatures, clamps—as he asked for them.

Jim had been told he had inherited for this regular Tuesday list the senior anaesthetist, Dr Bobby Sugden. He had already heard on the inevitable grapevine complaints that

Dr Sugden spent a good deal of time in the private wing. But when he asked further he found that he did his private cases either very early in the morning or in the evening after his N.H.S. lists were over. Having been used to assisting Mr Armsworth at these times of day when he had been an S.R., Jim found this no novelty. And when he enquired further still, he found that Dr Sugden was in fact the hardest working anaesthetist in the Royal Reid for his hospital patients.

They took to each other at once—the anaesthetist half a generation older than his thirty-seven years old new colleague. Jim saw at once that Dr Sugden was highly accomplished in his specialty and a highly polished man in every way. Dr Sugden was pleased in his turn to find that the young man was a quick and neat operator.

One case was a little frightening, however. Jim thought for a few minutes that he was going to fail to mobilise a cancer in a patient's bowel and have to concede defeat. But he persevered, thought hard of what Mr Armsworth would do in such circumstances, and finally to his great relief, all was well.

During the morning he was asked if he would be breaking for lunch at about one o'clock, when Mr Rollands used to stop, or if he wanted to go on a little longer. After consultation with Dr Sugden, he said "one o'clock."

"They'll bring along the sandwiches for one, then, sir," said Sister. "Tea or coffee?"

"The sandwiches" proved to be a large tray, covered with an embroidered cloth, and on it three china plates of roast beef, ham, and tongue sandwiches. They were neatly quartered—as in a swanky restaurant, Jim thought. There was French and English mustard, salt and pepper, napkins, and coffee cups, sugar and milk. This was a cut above even Mr Armsworth's Regional Board crockery and the wads of bread which were always on the thick side. "If there's anything else you'd like…?" said the maid. Bobby Sugden's eyes twinkled as he saw the surprise of the new boy. "Rollands and Collinson have always had a theatre tray like this," he said. "They treat the medical staff like gentlemen in this hospital!" he laughed.

After the list was finished and Jim had thanked the theatre staff, he went along the corridor to the ward for a post-op. ward round and a word of explanation and reassurance as Mr Armsworth had taught him to. He also saw one or two emergencies who had come in. Then he found himself invited to Sister Billings' office for a cup of tea.

"You've finished early, Mr Baxter."

This was a compliment. Nursing staff and anaesthetists like their surgeons to be quick.

"Yes, sister."

"We're admitting today but so far we're quiet."

"Do you ever run out of beds here?"

"Not very often, Mr Baxter. We are really very well off for beds in this hospital, compared with most. Mr Collinson would always lend a bed if need be. So did Mr Rollands."

Once again Jim realised the previous surgeons had obviously worked together well. Another plus for the surgical service in the Royal Reid.

"What about the students? How did Mr Rollands take the students? Did you pick out special patients off the waiting list?"

"No. Mr Rollands just took the students on the ward. So does Mr Collinson."

This was going to be a problem, thought Jim. Especially as the Dean of Medicine had told him he was to develop postgraduate teaching. His own room was tiny—far too small for half-a-dozen students.

"I've been given the job of postgraduate clinical tutor here, sister. What teaching facilities are there here?"

"Dr Sheridan takes students in one of the nurses' lecture rooms, Mr Baxter. But that's not often as they're always in use."

"Is there anywhere else we could use that you know of?"

"I don't know. You'd have to ask at the office. Mr Scott would know."

So on his way out Jim went upstairs to Mr Scott's office and explained his problem.

"I'd been thinking about that too," said Mr Scott. "There is a room in the nurses' school which is used as a store. It would do if it was cleared out. But we do have some plans to develop a postgraduate centre."

"We really need something soon. Could the Board of Management or the University help?" asked Jim.

"I'll arrange a meeting with Dr Sheridan and yourself and Mr Collinson, Mr Baxter," said Charles Scott. "I agree we need more accommodation and better accommodation than we've got just now. We'd have to put any proposals to the Board of Management, of course."

"Good," said Jim. He was determined to make a go of the challenge he had been given by the university.

"Never a dull moment," said Jim to Anne when he got home. "How was school today?" to the children. They had both got on fine.

It had been a good start. All surgeons are relieved to get their list day over without mishap.

The next day was the day each week when a group of final year students came for teaching. They travelled by bus and went to medicine, surgery, and to obstetrics and gynaecology—there were twenty or so in all. Half-a dozen went to each specialty. In the afternoon, after lunch, they were taken back to the Teaching Hospital.

The arrangement was unusual because the normal absolute divide between teaching and non-teaching hospitals had been broken for the Royal Reid earlier than elsewhere. A former Professor of Medicine had been very friendly with the senior physician at the Reid when he was Dean of the Faculty. He was extremely keen that students be sent to a non-teaching hospital—later called a District Hospital—as part of their final year training. The arrangement had been going for ten years now, and it not only meant that students came to the Reid, but it meant some of its senior clinical staff were given honorary lectureships on the university departments' books. This was one of the perks which gave an appointment at the Royal Reid its extra status.

Thursday was another clinic day and another emergency admitting day—Jim's were Monday, Thursday, Saturday— he was the junior. Mr Collinson's were Tuesday, Wednesday, and Friday. Sundays alternated. So this gave Jim his two days in a row. At supper Jim and Anne thought Thursday afternoons might be his day for private consultations. Anne would open the door and do the books. But this was only his first week. They'd make a firm decision later.

Friday was his next operating day. His first Friday's experience stamped itself on his memory. The anaesthetist who appeared for this session was called Maurice Garretts—dark, handsome, and Jewish. Unlike Dr Robert Sugden, ex-public school, ex-surgeon lieutenant commander, Maurice was from a poor background. His father had been a small shopkeeper. Unlike Dr Sugden, he worked not only at the Royal Reid, but also at the Avondale.

"So you are the new surgeon?"

"Yes," replied Jim.

"Pleased to meet you."

"Thank you," said Jim, offering his hand. Maurice Garretts took it guardedly.

"Well, let me tell you something—it's as well you know right from the start."

"What's that?" asked Jim, in some alarm.

"It doesn't matter what you do while you're here, or what you're like. You are Rollands' successor, and because you are Rollands' successor, the staff at the Dale will all hate you. They hate Rollands and they hate Collinson. They even secretly collected cases of Rollands' that had gone wrong a year or two back and went to the Regional Health Authority with them, to complain."

"What happened?"

"Oh, the Senior Administrative Medical Officer said he would take no action. He knew they were doing it out of spite."

"Charming," said Jim. In himself, he was suddenly aware of a dimension in hospital medicine he had never really been aware of before. He had seen the enmity of many of the academics in the Teaching Hospital towards others—the snide remark, the innuendo, the loaded question at academic meetings. But he had put this down to academic rivalry. Also, it was between a level of staff beyond the registrars—something for them to smile or even to laugh at. Now he, too, was at that higher level. He was a consultant. Yet consultants were vulnerable. That people who entered a so-called caring profession would go to this length to attack another member of it was news to him.

He told Anne about Garretts and his remarks as they had supper that evening.

"But why," she asked, "do they dislike these surgeons? They must have done something sometime."

"I don't know. But Mr Armsworth told me I'd have to go around all the staff and introduce myself. I wonder if they are all as bad as Dr Garretts says. He seemed a queer sort of man. It may just have been him."

The Royal Reid had been in Reidham in the early years of the century. In its two hundred beds it had included all the traditional specialties. It had the maternity and the children's unit. A wide frontage of good brick building, with two storeys and wards either open on the traditional Nightingale system or partly converted to the recently popular cubicle system, on each side of corridors, gave a good first impression. Each surgeon had a pair of wards. The physicians had more beds, but there were three of them, one, Dr Stewart, having some chest beds as part of the regional chest service. The other specialities had their share. As Sister Billings said, there were plenty of beds.

Inside, the woodwork was elegant in the front hall, the senior staff room and library, and in the resident house officers' private dining room. The library, as Jim had noticed on his first Friday visit, was an unusually pleasant room. Major benefactors' names were in gold script around the entrance hall, and their photographs in faded black and white were around the little-used board room. It had the atmosphere of a teaching hospital writ smaller.

In front of the main entrance the original grass lawns had long since disappeared as the ground was inexorably converted into car park; the senior staff—of whom Jim was now one—had their private slots each with the owner's name. He had fallen heir to Mr Rollands' space. And inside the door, just like the Teaching Hospital, were name boards for the senior staff on one side, the resident staff on the other, each in its slot with the brightness of the name in inverse proportion to the seniority of the staff member. Mr Collinson's name was in old dull letters, Mr Baxter's in shining new gold ones.

How different was this from the Avondale which Jim had seen so briefly. It was a war-time hospital seven or eight miles into the country. It was hutted with long corridors and wards stuck on at right angles, and covered a large area of land. It had had a thousand beds in its hey-day during and after the war, but was now reduced to five hundred. It had the new specialities of plastic surgery and geriatrics, but the biggest unit was the regional orthopaedic one of two hundred beds. It also had gynaecology, eye and ear, nose and throat surgery, as well as general medicine, general surgery, and some neurosurgery. The specialities of neuro and plastic surgery, geriatrics, and orthopaedics were not represented at the Royal. It was here that Jim now went, to introduce himself as the new colleague.

Some of the staff he had met already at the Royal as they

had beds in both hospitals. He had met the senior of the two general surgeons at his interview, though he did not realise it at the time; for the general surgical staff at the two hospitals went their separate ways—they had little in common. The Dale hospital staff took little or no emergency surgery and drew their non-emergency surgery, called elective surgery, from the country on their far side, away from the town of Reidham.

As far as medical politics were concerned, the orthopaedic service was the most powerful. This was because all its beds were in the name of the professor. The neurosurgery, plastic and geriatric services were part of the regional service as well, and so they too took patients from all over. This was unusual in geriatric medicine, but the patients and the relatives seemed to manage. Their consultants were of a generation near to Jim's own. The plastic staff were also younger, and he had met them at surgical meetings at the Teaching Hospital.

Jim civilly introduced himself to the two general surgeons Mr Wilson and Mr David Jones. It seemed Jones was referred to as "D.G.." Mr Wilson was a man of sixty who had moved from a teaching hospital post elsewhere some eleven years before after he failed to get advancement and had a younger man promoted over him. Mr Armsworth had told Jim this, in strict confidence. "D.G." had been senior even at that time. He was nearly fifty—thirteen years older than Jim. He was the man with the sharp and high-pitched voice who had made the unexpected telephone call to Jim on the evening of his appointment to the Royal Reid. He was the man who had been a senior registrar for ten years— a man known among the S.R.s at the Teaching Hospital as

47

the awful spectre of what could happen if you failed to get a consultant post. He was known to have worked hard for years—always the servant, never the master. He had never appeared at regional meetings of any sort. But he had been saved by the Platt Report—which had produced an upgrading of many registrar posts to consultant ones—otherwise he would surely be in general practice or overseas. Ironically it was Jim, during his time as chairman of the Regional Hospital Junior Staff Committee, who had argued before the Board sub-committee for the upgrading of this post, and had had his arguments accepted. Yet he had not been able to persuade them to upgrade his own S.R. post—or that of his friend Peter Millard.

It had been a source of wonder to the Hospital Junior Staff Committee when they discussed all registrar posts in the Region before making representations to the Health Authority why Jones had been allowed to stay so long. The length of time he had been in post had been unknown to them till then. He was far in the periphery. It was generally believed he had simply failed to get a senior job in spite of many attempts. But why he had not been moved on, as they were, remained a mystery. Some said he had been kept on because he was useful, a good surgeon, and because his job was perhaps not likely to attract a good successor. And now Jim was waiting to meet this man who had only been a name to him before. His eyes were just a little hard, behind their friendly, almost effusive brightness. His manner was tense, while Mr Wilson was more relaxed. But neither of them looked really friendly, as Mr Rollands had.

"We will see more of each other, I think. The Regional Health Authority have plans to alter the surgical services here and make them work more together."

Jim knew nothing of this. "What are the plans?" he asked.

"We are going to come more into the emergency services for the town and we are to get a share of student teaching. We've always been kept out of teaching, even though we've protested to the university again and again."

Mr Wilson had left the room.

"When is this to happen?" said Jim.

"The sooner the better. We've always been kept out, you see, but when the old guard are gone, we will get our due place."

The expression "our due place" seemed rather odd. But it said a lot.

If there was a certain coolness on the part of the general surgeons, it was radiant warmth compared to the reception Jim got when he presented himself at the orthopaedic staff room. This big unit had only four local members. The rest—six of them—came from other hospitals in the Region, and travelled to operate on their waiting list cases. Jim met three—all local. They were all hostile, especially Mr Fleischman, the senior one. He was called "Baxter," briefly spoken to, then shown the door.

So Dr Garretts was right. Jim had felt he should see the surgeons of the orthopaedic department because there was a big casualty department at the Reid, and he supposed there was a good deal of coming and going between the surgical units as there had been at the Teaching Hospital. It was also good manners, as Mr Armsworth had said. He drove back feeling decidedly upset. It was as complete a contrast to his last journey that way, with old Mr Rollands, just a short time before, as could be imagined. He had wanted to talk about referrals of patients and ask how the registrars liaised. He had been turned away, and the door closed on him.

When later Jim consulted Charles Collinson, the situation was explained. Until the end of the war—in fact, until the professor had arrived in the fifties—the surgeons at the Royal had been responsible for orthopaedics there, especially the emergency trauma. When broken hips had begun to be treated by putting in steel pins, he and Roger Rollands had done this with good success. And when the orthopaedic surgeons had insisted that all orthopaedics be done by their staff, he and Rollands had agreed at once, but supposed they continue to treat smaller wrist, hand, or ankle fractures, or broken collar bones, as they had done for the whole of their working lives. But the orthopaedic surgeons had next begun to find fault with cases they had treated. They had been quick to write letters—often harsh and spiteful letters, criticising their management—to the local general practitioners. They wanted total surrender of all patients with even the smallest broken bone—be it fifth finger or fifth toe. And woe betide the old surgeons of the Royal if the slightest thing went wrong with any patient seen at the Reid casualty and not sent immediately to the orthopaedic unit. A letter of criticism would reach the patient's own doctor at once. When their attempts at compromise proved unavailing, Rollands and Collinson just gave in, and patients with the most minor injuries were needlessly taken by ambulance the seven miles to the Dale. As a result, said Charles, relations between the surgical services of the hospitals were impossibly bad.

Inevitably other specialities had taken sides. The pathologists were neutral, since their service served both hospitals from their twin laboratories. But anaesthetists, who worked only in one hospital or mainly in one, became identified with that hospital, as did physicians, surgeons, even dentists. The doctors at the Dale attended their own postgraduate meetings, and the doctors at the Royal attended *their* own postgraduate meetings. There remained a large divide; the Royal Reid was the prestige hospital—its staff had university appointments. The Dale had no students, and its staff had no university appointments. The Royal had its own private wing—well patronised by those covered by medical insurance, but also by the establishment of the county around—the councillors, business people, farmers, and one or two small gentry. Even those who did not patronise the private wing would still seek admission to the public wards of the Royal. They did not go to the huts of the Dale. It had always been so. Even in orthopaedics there was the same divide—the Dale's unit took workers from heavy industry, and miners from the county, but the professor, who did private work, took his patients twenty miles away to the private wing of the Teaching Hospital, and the family doctors sent their patients there also.

Jim found it all hard to follow. As far as the general physicians and general surgeons at the Dale were concerned, they seemed very content to grumble at the good life of their opposite numbers at the Royal but made no attempt to use its private wing. And then he understood that this was because they were not on the staff and so had no access to it. At first, he could not understand the antagonism. And then, after several chats with Dr Garretts, it all began to fall into place.

There were abundant beds at the Dale. The staff on the

general side of the hospital—medicine, surgery, having between them almost 100 beds, were in the almost unique position of taking in few if any emergency patients. These all went to the smaller, establishment hospital, centrally placed within the town. They had in many ways a surprisingly easy life. They had no students to teach. None had any regional duties to perform, or were tutors to a Royal College. Having no private practice, they were not tied to the telephone in the way the part-timers were. And yet they were jealous of what the Royal Reid had. And as their jealousy was fomented in their senior staff room at lunch time, said Garretts, so they had begun to look for insults which did not really exist.

There was another, said Garretts. There was word that a single new hospital was due to be built, to replace the present two and provide a service into the next century for town and county communities. This had been discussed at Regional and local level for at least five years, he said, but no agreement had been possible. The staff at the Royal took it for granted that the new major build would be on *their* site—central, accessible to the bulk of the people, and continuing the tradition of a hundred years. But the staff of the Dale—especially the powerful orthopaedic lobby—were even more determined that the building should be on *their* site. They openly sneered at the "old men" of the Royal and at its private wing in a campaign, according to Dr Garretts yet again, to denigrate it and by contrast enhance their own claim. At the local Management Committee there was bitter conflict, members of the hospital staffs taking opposing views, but the vote of the lay chairman and town members being enough to nullify the arguments of the Dale lobby.

This failure to make political progress further enraged the Dale staff, and the anger generated at committee meetings spilled over into the two hospital camps.

But Jim Baxter, while watching rather sadly the entrenched position of those much senior to himself, was too busy and too happy doing the surgery he so much enjoyed to be much concerned. Charles Collinson, so much his senior, bore the brunt of the arguments and hostility. It was easy to see why the other side so disliked him—he was tall, distinguished-looking, carrying the confidence of his famous London Medical School with him, and aware of his long-established seniority in the city. He had operated on former Lord Mayors, he fished and shot with the county, and he found it hard to put up, at his time of life, with all this rancour and unpleasantness. Needless to say, the others regarded his very assumption of authority with resentment—they called him aloof, patronising, and autocratic. His opposite number on the medical side of the Royal, Charles Sheridan, was equally senior, and also distinguished himself in the Second World War. Dr Bobby Sugden was a natural ally. Garretts was not above stirring things when he felt like it, Jim learned. Many of the other consultants in specialties not immediately involved just smiled sadly. The divide was the age-old one of the class which saw itself deprived from their due place by the arrogance of those who represented privilege and social superiority on the one hand, and the representatives of the ruling class who could not understand what all the trouble was about on the other.

Baxter's practice and share of the work increased steadily in his early years. He worked hard, got good results, and found he was earning the respect of practitioners and patients. Most of the doctors he knew best were the senior partners in their practices. Tom Stone was a constant ally and friend. The Stones were a couple Jim could really drop in on at any time and be welcome—and they could equally drop in on Anne and Jim. Jim and Tom shared confidences with total trust. If the Baxter children were ill, Tom was like an uncle to them. Tom was in fact the junior of one of the prestige practices in the town. This helped Jim's private practice, but it was his own work that gave him his reputation.

His early house surgeons were students he had known and taught at medical school. They were pleased to work for him. Helen Billings, though always keeping a certain distance, was friendly and chatted over the life-supporting tea. His registrar of his first days left in due course to return home. Successors came and went. He enjoyed teaching the nurses in the training school. They did not rise to their feet when the lecturer came into the room with the same military precision as they had done in the Teaching Hospital. He worked very hard trying to develop the postgraduate training programme with meagre resources and against complaints from staff at the Dale—for the clinical tutor's parish covered both hospitals and the mental and infectious diseases ones too. A most helpful colleague was Bill Spiers, the local Medical Officer of Health, who was also keen on postgraduate medical teaching. On the other hand, he received two or three peevish letters from D.G. and Dr Mark Scott, the second physician at the Dale, attacking his running of the postgraduate events as a "one-man show" and demanding that they be involved. It remained difficult to entice staff at the one hospital to travel to the other for a lunch-time meeting, but he kept trying. The promised custom-built postgraduate centre seemed as far away as ever.

Mr Collinson was now approaching his retirement, and his workload had decreased as Jim's had increased. The older man showed no resentment, and though he maintained his distance from Jim like those of his professional vintage, he was a helpful and loyal colleague. Jim grew fond of him in these first years; he realised this man was now in his thirtieth year of service to the hospital and had done a huge amount of work over that period. He had served with distinction in the Navy in the Second World War. Mr Rollands had continued at the Royal. But here Rollands had done his full share of work during 1940 and 1941, the years of the air raids, and again at the Dale when wounded came back from the campaign in Normandy.

Though less flamboyant, Mr Collinson had a good deal in common with Mr Armsworth—he too could make up his mind, he seemed to need the barest minimum of questioning, examination and investigation before coming to the correct diagnosis, and he was an excellent technical surgeon. He always, like Mr Armsworth, seemed to have things under control. He was like the schoolmaster who never needed to use the cane—his presence, and the hint of what might happen if he was forced to take severe measures—were enough to make certain that he never needed to take them. Jim sensed that his ward and theatre sisters, and Miss Hoddie in the private wing, were fonder of Charles Collinson than they would ever be of him. The same he thought would be true of Mr Armsworth, now also due to retire.

Of course he was set in his ways. He was the product of his time—he had trained in the years when anaesthetics were primitive and diagnoses were made by eyes, hands, and ears and not by technological aids. He had his rules of thumb, and he had his regular quibbles about what was to him incorrect detail of treatment. Not academic, his background was of correct English and he did not let his staff—including Jim—forget this. He liked things to go right—and they usually did. But if they went wrong—or if the wards became too full of patients and he was asked by his registrar—or Jim's—for help in sorting things out—he would become disinterested and walk away. Sometimes he just did not want to know. He avoided medical strife and Jim noticed him beginning to take the easy way out by doing nothing. Because they shared wards, Jim was at hand to help, and if the registrar staff sometimes tactfully asked his advice, he learned to give this in such a way that the older man's self-esteem was never lost. Mr Armsworth, his hero, had taught him that loyalty to other members of the firm was one of the most vital attributes of a hospital consultant. Mr Armsworth's anger at disloyalty was one of his fiercest.

In these days the senior consultant was still "the chief." He took the major decisions on the firm, he had the first choice for leave dates, he took precedence in the allocation of beds—in fact, if perhaps not in the strict letter of the law. In the Royal Reid, however, this dominance was not as absolute as in the big Teaching Hospital—both Charles and Jim shared emergency nights on call, and Charles shared decision making with Jim more and more as time passed.

When he went to surgical meetings in the Teaching Hospital, which he made time to do, he was greeted by everyone—though the professor of surgery always remained a little aloof. Students parodied Jim in their final year concert and included his name as a teacher with those of the academics in their year record book.

Then one day the Mayor took suddenly ill. Jim was called to see him—not Mr Collinson and not Mr Wilson. He operated on the Mayor, who after being a little oddly confused for a day or two, made an uninterrupted recovery. The Mayor passed his praise around. The newspapers commented favourably. Jim had arrived. And the Mayor got him membership of the local business and professional club—exclusive in its small way—as reward for his successful treatment. In the next three months his increase in referrals accelerated, and his private practice increased further.

He graduated to a smarter car. Anne got hers, too.

But better by far than being able to afford a bigger car and newer furniture for his consulting room was the letter he received on a day in the Spring of 1970 on behalf of the Royal College of Surgeons. It was from Mr Frank Nicholson, who was regional adviser in surgery, nominating him as a College tutor for his part of the region, for a period of three years, renewable to six. The President Rodney Smith and his Council were asking him if he would become one of the College tutors for the Region. The years ahead looked golden. It was all too good to be true.

CHAPTER 5

One Sunday evening Anne and Jim were sitting in their home talking about summer holidays. Their children were now 17 and 15 and had thoughts of going off with their own friends. Their son looked set to get into university and their daughter wanted to become a nurse like her mother. The telephone rang—for Jim. It was Andrew Morton.

The two families had seen less of each other since Jim's move to the Reid six years before. But the wives had kept up their friendship and the menfolk met at postgraduate meetings in the Teaching Hospital. The Mortons came to visit at weekends and more than once Andrew had said he had thoughts of moving out of his university job into the National Health Service. Jim and Anne had always felt he was too settled and too successful in his clinical research and teaching to be serious. But tonight Andrew was very serious.

"Hullo, Jim. How are you?"

"Fine, Andrew. How's that new research paper of yours you were talking about?"

"It's all right. But that's not what I want to speak to you about."

"What, do you want to come through?"

"Yes. I've decided to apply for Charles Sheridan's job."

"Are you serious?"

"Of course I'm serious. You know me."

"Yes, I know you. Half the time you're not serious."

"This time I am. I want a move out of the department here. I'm not going to get a professor's post anywhere. I've always fancied a job at the Royal Reid."

"What about Mary?"

"Mary's keen to come. The family are all right—they're both at university—you know—if it had been a year earlier it would have been a problem. But this comes at a good time. It couldn't be better."

"Well," said Jim, "It'd be great if you and Mary were here. Anne would be delighted—so would I. You know that. Do you have any idea of the field?" he asked, a little hesitantly. For Andrew was now in his 40's—and his age must be against him.

"The prof. says he doesn't think I'm too old—I know what you're thinking, Jim," laughed Andrew.

"Does he have any idea of who else would be after it?"

"No. He says the local senior registrars, of course. But he says he doesn't know of anyone strong from outside who had been making enquiries."

Dr Sheridan was due to retire in three months. He had been telling everyone how he wished he could go on, but 65 was the retiral age and his 65th birthday was in three months' time. He was an active, energetic man, who didn't look his years. He was a good physician, too, as Jim had found on his many visits to the medical wards. It was largely due to the friendship of Sheridan's predecessor with the previous professor of medicine that the Reid had broken the normal great divide between the Teaching Hospital and the rest and had won students to teach and university appointments for its staff. Dr Sheridan had carried it on.

Jim had got to know both physicians well as he had become the surgeon to see and operate on their medical patients with a surgical complaint. They all got on well. It would be a pity if things changed.

Jim had got Andrew down a couple of times to take part in postgraduate meetings—once to speak, once to chair a group discussion in his special interest of blood diseases. Dr Bell, Jim knew, thought a great deal of him, both as a specialist and because of his open, friendly, cheerful manner. George Bell had in fact mentioned to Jim over lunch one day not so very long before what a good man Andrew Morton was. But Jim never thought Andrew would want to apply to move away from his lecturer's job, and had done no more than agree.

"Have you spoken to George Bell, Andrew?"

"No. But I did come to see Dr Sheridan."

"Sneaky bugger," said Jim. "You kept that quiet from us."

"I'll have you know," said Andrew—who could draw himself up and be rather formal if he was slightly annoyed— "that you are the next person I've spoken to down there. Apart from the prof. and Sheridan, no-one else knows. I'm never sneaky." He was laughing again, over the phone.

"Well, if it's any help, George Bell said some time back that he thought you were a good man."

"I hope you agreed."

"Of course I agreed. I did. I told him. But I didn't think you would ever think of moving here."

"Well, I'm putting in a formal application the minute the job's advertised."

"Great, Andrew. I'll do what I can to help."

"Tactful now."

"I'll be tactful. You know me."

"I do. That's why I said be tactful. Could Anne speak to Mary?"

Anne was put on the phone. The two chattered happily. Anne was enormously fond of Mary. Often she said to Jim how nice it would be if Mary was nearer and they could drop in on each other or go out for coffee the way they used to.

By now Jim knew George Bell well enough to speak to him in confidence. George Bell had calmed him many times after some Dale anger had upset him. Jim asked Andrew to let him know when his application had gone in, and then he went straight to see Dr Bell.

He knew he had to be careful. Dr Bell was an almost disarmingly honest man. So much so that he might even be put off by canvassing.

"You'll miss Charles."

"Yes. He will be missed."

Jim suddenly realised that George Bell, for all his honesty, did not ring entirely true as he spoke.

Sheridan had tended to drink a little more than was good for him, and this weakness had meant that George Bell had sometimes—though not very often, it had to be said—to cover up for his colleague. He could also be quite sharp at times—Jim still remembered his interview when after some of Sheridan's questions he thought he was done for. So perhaps Bell was not too unhappy that his older colleague was leaving. In a flash it occurred to Jim that Andrew had the very qualities George Bell might be looking for in a younger colleague—affability, honesty, kindliness—and sobriety. Andrew—and Mary too—had always had these in

abundance. It was their openness that was so attractive—
they had a simple engaging way with them that people liked.
Andrew had a certain sharpness of temper too. But he kept
that well under control. Mary was so sunny and sweet one
could never imagine her doing a hurtful thing to anybody.

"I will miss him too. It's a pity he hasn't many interests
outside his work. Do you know if they mean to stay here?"

"No. I know they've thoughts of going south to be nearer
their family."

"What do you think, George? When a hospital doctor
retires, about staying or moving away?"

"It doesn't do to move away, I don't think, if you've
plenty of local friends. We don't get many retired people
here, but then this isn't a part of the country people want
to retire to. Charles is from down south—so is his wife. So
it might suit them all right. They're both given over to those
grandchildren of theirs, too."

He paused. "When you get to retiral age, Jim, things look
different. I've ten years to go and I wonder what I'll want to
do. Charles was saying just yesterday that he realises now at
65 that he really has slowed up since he was 55. You
wouldn't think it to see him around the place, but I've
noticed he drives his car slower and he hasn't been so
particular about the wards this last month or two. He's been
a bit anxious, though—he doesn't in his heart want to retire.
He knows he hasn't any interests outside his work. His wife
plays bridge—but he doesn't."

"He's always been a good physician—a general
physician," said Jim. "But I suppose if he had any special
interest, it was anaemias and that."

"That's true," said George Bell. "That's a thought. We've

no-one here with any expertise, as they keep calling it nowadays, in that line since Turner left."

Richard Turner was one of the pathologists. He had a special in blood diseases—haematology—and gave a good opinion. He was good at coming on to the wards, too, and discussing cases. Only a year ago he had left to go to Scotland, pulled and pushed by his Scots wife. He had been replaced by yet another Charles—Charles Pollock, who had done a spell abroad and had been appointed at the age of 43—the same age as Jim was now. He was very much a general pathologist, meaning he had no special interest but knew a bit about everything, probably because he had had to cover a wide range of work in his overseas post. When he had been abroad, he had done a good deal of organising and administrating, and his views were already in demand on the Regional laboratory committees.

Jim took the cue. The way the conversation was going had given him the perfect chance to introduce his friend Andrew Morton. "If you want a haematologist here, what about Andrew Morton?"

"Andrew Morton? *He* wouldn't want to come here. He's well set in his academic job."

"I don't know. He isn't a tough enough chap to go for a Chair—a professor's post—at least, I don't think so. He could be persuaded to come to an N.H.S. job, perhaps."

"I think he is very good. He is such a likeable man. But he's too old, I think."

"Not necessarily. Look at Charles Pollock. He moved here all right and he's over 40. And *he* has no special interest."

"That's true. There's no one in the path. department with

any interest in haematology. We could with someone like Andrew Morton. But I think he's a bit old."

"Well, George, you know we know the Mortons well. They were neighbours when we were senior registrars. We'd—I'd get on well with him. I think he's very good and I think he'd fit in very well here.'

Jim then played another card.

"And I think James Stewart would get on with him better than he'd get on with a younger man."

That was true. James Stewart, the chest physician who was not really part of the medical firm, but had, rather unusually, a number of chest beds at the Reid, was exactly the sort of person who might not take to a bright young pusher but would happily accept a quieter colleague nearer his own age. Jim remembered Mr Armsworth's advice: "Choose a colleague you can get along with, Jim, not someone who's frightfully clever." But he didn't quote him.

Said George Bell: "I know you and Anne know the Mortons and it would make good sense if he came here. We get on well together, Jim. Another physician whom you liked—and who liked you—would give us a good team. For years, all being well. Yes, you and the Mortons are life-long friends—would be life-long friends—it's a thought. I'll speak to James Stewart. And I'll have a word at the university."

Off went Jim. This had been a promising start to his campaign to get their friends to rejoin them as neighbours.

But there was a long way to go. A number of smart, handsome, personable senior registrars came up to view the hospital, talk to the staff, make themselves known. One of them, an elegant Londoner, also professed an interest in blood diseases. Jim left Anne to relay a judicious amount of news to Mary. George Bell, honest and thoughtfully kind as ever, sent the candidates to see Jim, because as he told them, Mr Baxter was the surgeon his medical firm would use as long as he was in post.

Andrew came through as just another candidate and talked for a long time to Bell and then to Stewart. He kept out of Jim's way, but Mary came through once or twice to talk to Anne at the house and she seemed very keen to move. Andrew, she confided to Anne, was a bit tired of writing papers and had got the idea into his head that he wanted a pleasant job with a bit of private practice. This was exactly what the Reid would give him.

Jim did as much spadework to help his friend as he thought he safely could. By now he knew several of the local general practitioners well—they were getting older but still had a good deal of pull with local people who mattered and one in particular was as it happened friendly with two of the Hospital Board at Region. He was careful not to say a word to Garretts. He did not say anything to Charles Collinson either.

At 6 o'clock in the evening of the great day Andrew rang. He was cock-a-whoop. "I've swung it!" he said. Jim and Anne saw that he was genuinely delighted to have been appointed. As ever, Anne chatted happily to Mary.

"Grand, Andrew," said Jim. "I tried to help a bit." He retained a respect for his five year older friend and always liked to appear good in his eyes.

"Help?" returned Andrew. "Did the trick for me, Jim. We'll never forget your help."

Happy expectation was the way Anne and Jim's mood could be described. They both liked and respected the

Mortons. And Jim could not but hope that now they would share a lifetime of friendship together: Anne even more so. He was now all too aware of the resentment and dislike from D.G. Jones, in spite of his affability. He was very aware of the antipathy of those other members of the Dale staff. This realisation was strengthened by Garretts, who regaled him regularly with tales of how the Dale staff disliked the superiority of the Reid's establishment and how their lunch table dissected eagerly the characters of the Reid medical staff. Although Jim was aware of Garretts' enjoyment in stirring the pot, he had found by his own experience that there was always truth in what he said. In fact, he was a source of information about everybody and everything. Jim always wondered what Garretts said about *him* behind his back.

One evening Jim called the senior orthopaedic surgeon from Avondale to see a patient. This man treated all the Reid staff with coldness. He had always called Jim "Baxter" since their first meeting in a hostile and condescending manner. Charles Collinson had a thick file of letters Mr Bill Fleischman had written to local general practitioners containing attacks on the Royal Reid—referring always to some slip or failure one of the juniors had made in the Reid casualty department which had then made an appearance at the Dale orthopaedic department. How it never seemed to occur to Fleischman that he was putting himself at risk by writing the way he did was a mystery to both Charles Collinson and Jim. His animosity spoiled his case.

Recently it was Jim who had suffered, because a registrar had consulted him about a casualty patient whose small injury had been treated at the Royal when according to the strict letter of the law it should have been referred at once, to have the same sort of bandage applied, to the Dale. A furious letter to the patient's doctor had followed, found later in the notes accidentally by Jim.

The patient Jim was asking to be seen was one whom Fleischman had seen at his outpatient clinic and dismissed her as having nothing very much to complain about. As she had had a breast operation in the past, Jim was asked to see her. The new scan test he had arranged at the Teaching Hospital had shown cancer in her spine, only a month after her orthopaedic appointment. Jim showed him the patient, then the notes, and the bone scans. He then showed him the letter he had written about the casualty case. Fleischman laughed off the letter in an embarrassed way and walked out with a face like the proverbial thunder. Later Jim reflected that it was perhaps a dirty trick. But Fleischman never to his knowledge wrote against him again.

But now that the Mortons were on the scene, the Baxters felt they would be a strong support in their hospital world as well as good friends. Anne in particular enjoyed going around with Mary looking at houses. Jim advised Andrew on his private practice requirements. Jim remained a regular visitor on the medical wards for consultation, coffee, and chat. George Bell was delighted with his new colleague; he too looked forward to Andrew's help and support. For in 1971, the question of the new hospital and where it was to be built had arisen yet again and the Dale staff were still lobbying strongly to have it on their site.

Although the new general practitioner contract had put so much right for the family doctors, the government plans for reorganisation of the N.H.S. did not fill hospital staff with equal hopefull expectation. A first white paper had been published in July 1968, and its main proposal was the formation of a single administration authority. Standing committees of the new authority were to cover all three parts of the N.H.S.—family doctoring, hospital doctoring, and public health doctoring. A significant change in the composition of the proposed Area Health Authority was that the professional members were not to be allowed to represent special interests and were not to be in a majority. Though the doctors did not know it at the time, this was going to be the beginning of their decline in influence.

The first green paper was modified in 1969 by Richard Crossman, the Minister of Health. This introduced a second tier of control, a Regional Health Council, which was rejected by hospital staff as not being strong enough to be effective.

1970 had seen the consultant gynaecologists' report on abortion. 97% had voted against abortion on demand. But this report, issued on 30th May, was totally overshadowed by the delay imposed on the Report of the Review Body on the pay of doctors and dentists by Mr Harold Wilson, the Prime Minister. He had given the imminence of the general election as the excuse for not paying the doctors and dentists what had been awarded, but doctors did not believe him. They believed that his reticence was because of his refusal to accept the recommendations. The Royal Commission on Doctors' and Dentists' Remuneration of 1960 had advised that an annual Pay Review Body be set up, and had also insisted that the government of the day should give its decision quickly on each year's pay award. This was not being done for 1970.

The B.M.A. threatened, in response to Mr Wilson's

statement, to refuse to co-operate with government and to give up certification under the National Health Insurance Acts.

Over the month of June, just before the election, events boiled over. A leader in the B.M.J. of June 13th declared that "Independence was at stake." This followed the resignation *in toto* of the whole Review Body—not just Lord Kindersley its chairman—after the Wilson government had asked on June 5th for a second opinion. Mr Wilson asked the National Board for Prices and Incomes to review the Review Body. The original Review Body had proposed increases of 30% in the pay of consultants and an increase in the size and number of their distinction awards—for outstanding contributions to their work. Proportionate improvements had been proposed for general practitioners. The government made things worse by saying they would implement the award in full to hospital junior staff but only 15% "on account" to consultants, senior hospital medical officers, and general practitioners. Public sympathy, in spite of considerable media manipulation by the government, was for the doctors. The "doctors' pay" issue played a large part in the somewhat unexpected Tory victory.

On June 27th, Sir Keith Joseph was appointed Secretary for Social Services. A month later the second Green Paper, now burnished by Conservative enthusiasm, was brought forward again. The later-to-be discovered as ominous statement that the post of Regional Medical Officer was "to be primarily a managerial one" was made at this time. And since the boundaries of the new Local Authorities proposed by the Redcliffe-Maud Report—the start of the destruction of the old County Councils which the Heath government would in time carry through—were to be co-terminous with those of the new Area Health Authorities, it looked to the doctors as if the old large Regional Boards were to transform into some 90 small ones. On the credit side, the new Review Body of September allowed newly appointed consultants the full 30% salary increase. Others—like Jim— were to get an extra 5%, making 20% in all.

Jim's enhanced status as tutor for the Royal College of Surgeons brought him more and more into contact with staff in the Teaching Hospital and surgical trainees throughout the whole region. When he went to see D.G. Jones about one of his registrars, he was conscious more and more of the man's resentment towards him, and comforted himself in the knowledge that their surgical firms were never likely to be less than ten miles apart. But now, by 1971, old Mr Charles Wilson was due to retire—like Dr Sheridan, he was a pre- and post-World War Two generation and was reaching his 65th birthday. His post would be coming up for renewal next. (So would Mr Armsworth's, thought Jim. He had decided to move to Devon, he had announced, when he retired. A move back to the Teaching Hospital? Jim and Anne discussed the possibility, and in fact Mr Armsworth did as well, saying he would help. But things were too good at the Reid. Why move?)

Because he was College Tutor, Jim found himself a more regular member of appointment committees than he would otherwise have been. He was involved with the various registrar training schemes which were now being established in a less haphazard way than in the past. Though the registrar and senior registrar ranks were still too big for the number of consultant posts available, the realisation was being forced upon the hospital members of the medical profession that these ranks would have to be reduced in size and progress through them made easier. For while in the 1960's it was easy for a registrar with his fellowship or one of the memberships to emigrate to Canada, the U.S.A., or Australia if he could not get an S.R. post or a consultant one, it was now becoming clear that these countries were filling up with their own graduates. In the 1960's a suitably qualified registrar could still go to the U.S.A.—perhaps not "on spec," but certainly with the promise of an entry visa and a job. Those going to Canada especially had their fares paid for them. Now it was getting much more difficult. But it was still possible to move sideways into general practice, for those who wanted to stay at home, and one or two transferred from general surgery into a less crowded specialty.

Who would succeed Mr Wilson at the Dale? George Bell seemed quite concerned, and confided his anxiety to Jim.

"We need somebody there who's not going to get like the rest of them," said George.

"I suppose you're right," said Jim, "but it shouldn't really affect us."

"Except," said George, "that a pleasant and sensible man there will be a help to the whole district. Mr Wilson has kept pretty well neutral in all the troubles we've had. We need someone like him."

"It's not really for us to say. I don't suppose any of us will be on the committee. The Dale people won't really want us on."

"But they don't have the final say in nominating the committee. That's the Regional Authority's prerogative."

Andrew Morton was non-committal. He was too busy

getting on with his private practice, where he was making steady progress. Jim sent him his private patients if he wanted a medical opinion, and Andrew was pleased with this help. Jim also encouraged Tom Stone and his other general practitioner friends to refer patients to Andrew.

Mary had gone around with Anne looking at houses, and when the Mortons had got one they both had a great time together choosing curtains and carpets. Andrew had asked Jim's help to introduce his brother to the local golf club when he came to visit, and Jim had obliged with pleasure. But as far as the Dale surgical appointment was concerned, Andrew just wasn't interested.

What was interesting Andrew, however, was who was to succeed Dr Bechell the senior physician at the Avondale. For Dr Bechell, too, was due to retire in 1971—a bit later than Mr Wilson. Jim had spoken to one of the medical senior registrars at the Teaching Hospital about the job, but his chief had put him off, just as Mr Armsworth had put off Jim. "Not there," he had said. "Not the place for you."

There was a spate of new appointments everywhere. Jim was called to Region to a consultant appointment at the Teaching Hospital—the first time this had happened. Peripheral staff were not usually invited. The status gap, hallowed by tradition, remained. While it was now becoming usual for a consultant from a peripheral hospital to attend an appointment committee for a Teaching Hospital senior registrar, this was because it was now an obligation for such an appointee to rotate out to a district hospital for one year of his four year contract. The same did not apply to consultant posts, even where, as so often in England, regional services in new major specialties were as often as not placed in district hospitals, around the prestige Board of Governors hospitals and not in those hospitals themselves. Avondale was just one of those. Yet its status remained "non-teaching," with the lower-deck connotation that term implied.

Jim arrived for the meeting in his good suit and suitable tie. He remembered the joke "Cavemen went to meetings fingering their clubs. Englishmen went to meetings fingering their club ties."

Three candidates were on the short leet. As the chairman went over the information about the candidates, it became clear to Jim that of the three, one had "done it all" and seemed most suitable; the second was a bit behind, and the third probably nowhere. As the interviews proceeded—the references being read before each candidate appeared—the number one man came over to Jim as not only capable and experienced, but unusually pleasant. It was equally clear that Robinson, the senior Teaching Hospital consultant, was backing the number two.

Jim was somewhat peripheral in this committee. He could be entirely neutral about the final decision. After all had been and gone, the discussion started. Number one was warmly praised.

"Yes," said Robinson, "he's so good and so nice that it wouldn't be long before he will make big inroads into the private work here."

On the road home Jim laughed to himself at this masterstroke. Consultant after consultant began to have second thoughts. "Well you know…" "…perhaps…" "…he might not really fit in…" until at last number two, Robinson's man, was somehow found to be better. He was offered the job. "I wonder what went on at *my* appointment," said Jim to himself, thoughtfully. "What a set of hypocrites we are."

No time later, and the new surgical appointment at the Dale was advertised. Charles Collinson and Jim discussed it.

"I wonder who they'll get?" asked Jim.

"We always ask that question. But it's about time one of our own S.R.s got promoted here in this Region."

"It's not advertised as any sort of special interest," said Jim. "A good number of the new jobs—even the Teaching Hospital ones—seem to be special interest ones now. But at the Dale they don't require anyone with a special interest."

"The trouble with the Dale," said Charles Collinson, not for the first time, "is that everyone knows it is an E.M.S. hospital being run down and that puts people off for a start. No need to remind ourselves of what that's led to. And then, the orthopaedic, neurosurgery—and the plastic units—are all regional centres so they get more money put into them than the general surgical. All *it* really does is serve those big units if they've a general surgical problem and do the bread-and-butter stuff they get referred from the other side of the county."

"Then there's the talk of this new build. It's not the only one in the pipeline. I don't really know anybody who has the inner ear of the Health Authority at Region. But I wouldn't be surprised if they start to run the Dale down now."

Charles Collinson was right. A new neurosurgical centre was being planned for the Region in the Teaching Hospital extension. One of the other big city hospitals was being cleared for a purpose-built, regional plastics department. The visiting orthopaedic surgeons—including the professor—and he, too, was due to retire in the next couple of years—were doing less and less at the Dale and more and more twenty miles away in their big town beds. All the evidence was there—Avondale Hospital, in its rather isolated surroundings, was steadily on course to be run down before closure. It had never had much of a status, but it had always had a big workload. Now even that was going to go. They did not need the inner eye of the Board officers to read the signs.

Jim was not very bothered. He was now established and he thought secure. He would follow Charles Collinson as surgeon in charge and have his own unit with a younger colleague of his own. When the successor to the Royal Reid was built—and Jim and all the Reid staff knew that it would be on *their* site and not at the Dale's—they'd probably be nearing retiral themselves.

For that was the way it was in hospital building in the British Health Service. Hospitals took years to be planned, and then it seemed years to have government approval for the cost and the choice of contractor. Many more years had to pass while the building went on. A Teaching hospital in London and one in Scotland—major projects—were years behind their completion dates. In Scotland, litigation was proceeding between architect and contractors and the health authorities, so miserably slow had building been, and so greatly had costs escalated. No, the local hospital was not going to be above ground till the end of the century.

Charles Collinson did however make plain to Jim that he, and not himself, should get on the appointment committee for the new Dale job.

"You'll be working with the new man. You want to be in on his appointment."

"I don't think I'll be working with him."

"Even if you aren't, we are the nearest hospital. We share the emergencies now. You *will* find yourself working with him, Jim. Remember, I'll be retiring myself next year."

All was arranged. Jim and Anne planned to take their holiday—in Italy—the week after the appointment date. Again it was September—"things in this place always seem to happen in September or October"—said Jim to Anne.

They were looking forward to this holiday. They had wanted to go to Florence and Rome for several years. This year they were going to be there and back before their son started university. They were taking both the children with them.

There were to be four on the short leet—two senior registrars from the Teaching Hospital, one from the north east, and a senior lecturer from London. His College tutor's post meant Jim knew the local candidates well. One of them would be very good. He would press for him. He went to see Jones to help make up the short leet, and found him very friendly and very chatty. He had been in touch with the university, he said.

"When this new man is appointed, we are to get a few students attached—final year students."

"That's good," said Jim. "How long will you have them for?"

"It's all part of this expansion they're having. They're putting students out to a lot of hospitals. Of course," he went on, "you've had students for years." Jones had gone on about students since the first time they had met. It had always been a source of Dale envy. Jim changed the subject.

"Is there anything more about the neuros and the plastic

people getting their new places built?" Jim knew there was, but he wondered what Jones thought about it.

"It's the beginning of the end for this place. This hospital has done so much over the years since the war. But if we are the site for the new hospital..." He spoke with that sharpness, that higher pitch of the voice, that Jim had come to know and to recognise.

"We have a good case. We're getting a new physician—two in another three or four years when Scott goes—and we'll have an active new surgeon. The radiologists are very pro this place. So is Pollock the new pathologist—he likes coming over here, even though his main lab is with you."

He did not mention the orthopaedic bloc. They were still the strongest protagonists of the Dale site. Their attacks on "that old cottage hospital" or the "other hospital" had been somewhat muted in the recent past. Perhaps this was since Jim's episode of Fleischman or perhaps because of the professor's reduced commitment; his interests were now largely elsewhere.

But Jim did not get to the Dale consultant appointment meeting. The date was put back a week to suit people at headquarters and the interviews were held when the Baxter family were strolling over the Ponte Vecchio. Charles attended in Jim's place. Both external assessors, one a professor from across the Pennines, were very critical of what they called the inward-looking Regional Board policy of "just appointing their own people." This was untrue, but this professor was a strong personality and the man appointed was the Londoner.

Allan Berrill was the new appointee. A well-built strong man of 36, he had spectacles and a brown moustache to match his mid-brown hair. He had a pleasantly cultured voice and was known to be an excellent pianist. He had played cricket for his Cambridge College during his pre-clinical undergraduate career before moving to his London Teaching Hospital. There he had developed, during his higher surgical training, an interest in cancer, in the new specialty called oncology. On paper he had an impressive *curriculum vitae*, with undergraduate prizes at both college and medical school, and a spell in Florida where he had worked in the H. Lee Moffit Cancer Center and Research Institute at Tampa. There he had written an excellent thesis for his M.S. He had a striking range of papers written both while he was a registrar and in his lecturer's post. Against this, background information suggested that he had had rather too many interviews for one with that excellent c.v., and he had not been retained by his own medical school. Had he had a less impressive record, he could have been diagnosed as a good, middle-of-the-road senior registrar, who was destined for district general hospital status—like Jim, in fact. But he seemed a formidable addition to the Dale staff—in every way having more strings to his bow than David Jones.

CHAPTER 6

One day Charles and Jim were talking about the ever-changing population of hospitals.

"The ones who come and go fastest," said Charles, "are the patients."

"Yes," said Jim, "the guests."

"The next fastest must be the nurses going through training," said Charles. "Relatively few join the permanent staff. Most of them seem to leave soon when they get married, or do more training, or move elsewhere. The junior staff—the house doctors, the senior house doctors, the registrars—even the senior registrars—are birds of passage. I remember when I was in training and there was an amusing assistant matron who used to say to the sisters when they complained about a resident or a registrar, 'just a bird of passage, sister, just a bird of passage'."

"I suppose that's right," said Jim. "I've never been anywhere long enough to realise that. The trainees in physiotherapy and X-ray and in the labs—they pass through too in only three or four years."

"Yes," went on Charles, "there's a big gap between all of them and the permanent staff. The porters, engineers, hospital tradesmen, the cooks—and of course the secretaries—they stay for twenty years or so. And the nursing sisters, the matrons, the staff midwives—and ourselves and the medical assistants—we put in about a quarter of a century, unless we're carried off sooner. In the large majority of district hospitals senior medical staff are unlikely to move elsewhere. Policy demands that posts when they come up for replacement are filled from the senior registrar ranks, to keep promotion going for the younger members of the profession. A few move to consultant posts elsewhere. The ones that move to Teaching Hospitals you could count on the fingers of one hand."

"And then," said Jim, "they're forgotten in six months. I always remember we had a retired ear nose and throat surgeon who left after thirty years on the staff. He fell in a faint in a shop nearby six months after he retired, and banged his head. He was brought by the ambulance to casualty. He sat sadly on a bench and no-one took any notice of him. The nurse at casualty and the secretary who booked him in were both new. One of the assistant matrons happened to be passing and she was aghast to see one of the most respected and influential members of the Teaching staff sitting there and… well… just sitting there."

"Six months is about right," replied Charles. "But I think senior nursing staff are remembered a bit longer—perhaps as long as two years."

Now the Royal Reid, and its neighbour whom it was now doing more business with, the Avondale, were together going through one of those periodic mass retirals, when four, five, six staff all depart over a period of six months or a year. Somehow the very senior nursing staff never seem to have the same mass departures. But of course there are many fewer of them.

So here were Dr Charles Sheridan, Mr Charles Wilson, and soon Dr Bechell all retiring over this year. They had similar backgrounds, similar lengths of career at their hospitals, and all seen the same astonishing changes in medicine. They had all known the days before antibiotics. The surgeons had seen not only enormous changes in surgery, but even bigger changes in anaesthetics. They had all seen the beginning of the National Health Service, and its consolidation especially since the general practitioners' charter of five years earlier.

A few months before the introduction of that same National Health Service on 5th July, 1948, the doctors of the day voted in an 84% poll against the contract proposed for them by 40,814 votes to 4,734. Mr Aneurin Bevan, the Minister of Health of the day, offered an Amending Act promising that the doctors would not become salaried civil servants as they had feared. 40,062 doctors answered another ballot. This time 25,842 voted against the Act—still a majority, but small enough to make the mass of doctors agree to accept Mr Bevan's offer.

Hospital staff were different. They were full-time employees of the State. But a large number were free to do private practice—on condition that they gave virtually the whole of their time to N.H.S. work. Their working week was divided into "sessions" of three and a half hours' work. Mornings and afternoons and Saturdays every week made the full-time commitment 11 sessions. But if a consultant decided to do private work, he was paid nine- elevenths of the full-time consultant's salary. The difference he made up in his private fees—and whatever extra he was able to make from other sources. The "full-time" staff were prohibited from doing any private work. And because the "part-timers" were paid in a year only nine-elevenths of the full-timers' salary, they were regarded for pension purposes as having put in less time than those working the full eleven-elevenths. So in 11 years, they had only earned 9 years of pension. But they were allowed to put money by—from their own private earnings—towards private pensions of their own.

In the event, senior hospital staff worked very much longer than their "sessions." Lists especially in district hospitals could regularly go on from 9 till 5. Emergency on-call for these consultants added another workload, as did committee work and time for administration. Someone like Jim Baxter, with a successful private practice, saw patients on two afternoons each week—for two hours each afternoon, on average. His private operating, with Bobby Sugden anaesthetising, he did at 8 o'clock in the morning or 7 o'clock in the evening. While he could fit in his early work in the hospital's private wing, some of his evening work he did at the town nursing home.

On-call depended on the number of doctors on the rota. For his first two or three years, he had been wakened on alternate nights. Then in 1968 the Health Authority had directed the Dale surgeons to share emergency work with the Royal Reid, so that instead of two two-man teams working for practical purposes independently, there was a four-man team with each consultant admitting emergencies once every four days. This was to everyone's advantage, except for the number of patients who had to be taken the extra miles to the Dale for their admission and treatment. Everyone agreed the new arrangement was an improvement. Otherwise, the Dale and Reid units remained entirely separate.

On went the daily and weekly round of outpatients, ward rounds, operating, student teaching every Wednesday morning, more outpatients, more operating, on call one day in four and one weekend in four. Jim's job as College tutor took up a good deal of time, but he enjoyed every moment of it. The stimulus of talking to enthusiastic young men who as the years went by got younger compared to himself he found in itself refreshing. A spin-off was that he had a good share of the home-grown variety as his registrars. Not always so—many of those from abroad were very good— careful, hard-working, good with their hands, as they trained in surgery before going back to their own countries. Jim would have dearly liked a senior registrar. But there seemed no prospect of this—though the medical firm in the Royal had one for part of each year, the Teaching surgical firms refused to part with theirs. Garretts, saying it was the same in anaesthetics, told Jim it was because they were too useful to their bosses—helping them to keep in their beds on receiving nights and to break off their operating lists early, so that they could see more private patients.

One of the pleasantest things over these years, as far as the Baxters were concerned, was the friendliness of the Royal Reid staff. They were invited out by all the physicians after they arrived, by the Collinsons, by the gynaecologists, by Peter Scott the Group Secretary and his wife. They visited the Mortons regularly, but they were old friends. Bobby Sugden invited them out regularly too; Maurice Garretts never did. In turn, the Baxters invited all of them back to their own home. They were not going to be close friends with all of them, but to have failed to return hospitality would have been the height of rudeness. Best of all were the Semples; as often, someone you knew and liked at medical school became a friend for life.

The Royal Reid had a regular annual dinner for its staff, and a Christmas lunch. These were good affairs, especially those at Christmas. Each Christmas Day the consultants dressed up as cooks and carved the turkey for the patients and ward staff. Each Christmas Day the sisters vied with one another to produce the best ward eats—baking, fruit, biscuits and sweets, sherry for everyone not on call and for those on call too. Matron went everywhere and so did Peter Scott. The residents had their own dinners apart from the official one, and young staff like Jim were invited to these and as a *noblesse oblige* gesture gave a contribution in wine. Children—and even grandchildren of staff—were made welcome. Married nursing staff as well as medical brought their children in. Members of the Board of Management Committee came along, and one year even the local Member of Parliament made an appearance.

Nurses' prizegivings were also happy affairs. The older medical staff at the Royal Reid attended these diligently— saying, quite rightly, that they could do no less than support the nursing profession—their colleagues in caring. George Bell and his wife in particular never missed one, and Jim and Anne were annual attenders also. The Bells and the Baxters became firm friends. And the first Christmas after the Mortons arrived, all three families went together to the social events.   The time came for Charles Wilson to have his retiral presentation. At the Dale these were held in the medical staff dining room, which suited best. It was big enough to take everyone who wanted to come and small enough still to look comfortably filled if the numbers were not so very large. The usual lines were followed—the presents on display bought with the money collected, the tea and cakes, the eulogy speech and the reply, the presentation of the bunch of flowers to the spouse. The retiring consultant would leave for the last time—and be seen in the next few weeks looking cheerful but as often as not telling everyone how much he missed his work and his patients. These were happy years in the National Health Service.

Jim and Charles went over to the Dale for the presentation. They both liked Mr Wilson, and even if they had not, it was the courteous thing to do. He had not been so very long there, having moved from a previous Teaching Hospital job when he was about 50, and this move had been forced on him following a serious enough disagreement to make him decide to move. David Jones had in fact been a senior registrar when Wilson was appointed. Perhaps because of his Teaching Hospital background he had worked Jones very hard. But he had made up for this when Jones' post had been made into the second consultant one. Perhaps also because of his background, he did not have the chip on his shoulder towards the Royal so many of the Dale staff seemed to have.

Dr Bechell was different. He was very much an Avondale man. In fact, he had gone there as a sub-consultant, called a senior hospital medical officer, at the end of World War Two, and had been promoted consultant physician when the elderly physician who had been there throughout the war retired a little later. He had never been kindly disposed to the Royal or its staff, both because he was a less successful physician and because he had seen the campaign to have the new hospital on the Dale site fail as it was inevitably going to. A stout man who always looked unhappy, he had had a particular antipathy to Dr Sheridan over the years.

The standard procedure to appoint Dr Bechell's successor took place. The advertisement went out in the *British Medical Journal* and the *Lancet*. Interested seniors— one was from overseas for Betchell's job—appeared on the scene, walked around the unit, asked polite questions, put in their multiple applications to the Regional Authority. The post was advertised as a general physician's one, without any comment about special interest. As always, the post would be, "whole-time or maximum part-time at the decision of the successful candidate."

Andrew Morton sat up and took more notice for this appointment. He was senior enough in his former university background to know the potential field. As ever, locals from along the road were showing interest. Andrew worked hard to get himself on the appointment committee, making full use of his contacts at the university to do so. But he failed. "It's never so true—not what you know but who you know," he confided in Jim.

But Andrew was cautiously pleased with the man chosen. A midlander, he was of medium height with long fair hair and a pair of rather sharp blue eyes. His reputation from his own centre was undoubtedly a good one—the references full of praise for his "unusual determination, attention to detail, and a special ability to express himself clearly and succinctly." He had obviously impressed his present chief, because his reference expressed an enthusiasm which rang true. So often references for senior registrars applying for consultant posts only stressed the person's standard virtues, and followed a pattern you could anticipate as soon as you had read the first sentences. Sometimes you were deceived—a glowing account with a row of virtues could indicate that the employing hospital were just a little anxious to get *this* senior registrar off their hands. Equally a candidate with less flowery letters of support could appear at interview as a sound and sensible person. It was also important for the appointment committees to know the personalities of the seniors writing those references—a few were known as regularly unfair to the seniors who had worked so hard for them. Then there were a very few who would telephone to give a spiteful criticism of another chief's candidate—but they tended to be known and their malicious interventions ignored. The new physician at the Dale was called William Dick.

Jim was excited about the prospect of a new surgical colleague. He happily acknowledged Mr Collinson's contribution in the past. Several times he had been most grateful for his advice. Charles had carried the heavy end of the arguments with the Dale, but in the recent past had left them more and more to Jim. For a number of years now he had aged, his back stooped a bit more, his hair greyer, his skin looser over his collar when he bent his neck. He admitted frankly being out of date, and made no bones about his tiredness if he was called out at night. Unlike his medical opposite number Sheridan, he had grown tired.

For surgeons have the disadvantage compared with physicians, as they age, that they remain the last line of defence. Dr Sheridan could leave the management of seriously ill patients to his registrar, but Mr Collinson had the technical experience and skill his junior just did not have. And if a junior ran into trouble, it was not enough to give instructions over the phone. The surgeon had to come in and physically sort it all out. Perhaps this was why physicians could run down more gracefully than surgeons and not be noticed by their peers. But although everyone in the theatre and the wards knew that Mr Collinson was doing less operating than he used to, seeing fewer patients, and spending a shorter time teaching the students, no-one criticised him for it or sneered at him behind his back. One of the happiest things about the Reid was the kindness of all the staff towards one another.

Moving among various surgical firms in the Region brought Jim into contact with changes in surgical thinking in a way that would not have not have happened otherwise. He became aware of the start of a conscious effort for a consultant to develop a "special interest"—to concentrate on some sub-division of surgery and try to become more skilled at it. He himself had been trained as a general surgeon, and this meant especially an abdominal surgeon, but also one who operated on breasts, thyroid glands, prostate glands, and kidneys as well as stomachs and gall bladders, varicose veins and piles. And there were also the road accidents.

The most important abdominal operations, apart from cancer ones, were for duodenal ulcers and gallstones. As a senior registrar, Jim had assisted Mr Armsworth at countless operations for duodenal ulcers, removing a large portion of the patient's stomach, as this seemed the best way of getting a lasting cure. He had done very many himself. In the eight years he had been a consultant surgeon his work had not changed, and he still undertook a wide range of surgery. In this he was typical of the District Hospital surgeons then in practice. But Jim hadn't failed to notice the increasing trend towards specialisation, and the effects it was having on registrar training. He had begun to notice, too, that patients were beginning to ask about specialist procedures and new operations they had read about, and that a few were beginning to ask their general practitioners for referral to a "specialist." He began to wonder whether he should think about developing a specialty of some sort himself.

Back at the Dale there was another change, this time an unexpected and sad one. Dr Scott, the second physician to Dr Bechell, had developed a lung cancer and had retired early on medical grounds. A bright Irishman, Patrick Joseph Healy, replaced him and became William Dick's junior colleague. He promised well—George Bell, Andrew Morton and Jim, all liked him.

CHAPTER 7

For some reason it didn't occur as strange to Jim that as Charles Collinson's retirement date came nearer, there was no word from the Regional Health Authority about the appointment of a successor. But by early 1975 it was becoming not unusual for an Authority to delay the appointment of a consultant as a device for saving money—six months of delay meant six months of consultant salary saved; locums paid at the basic rate cost much less than the retired man's maximum. And then, about four months before his retiral date on his sixty-fifth birthday, the Regional Medical Officer wrote Jim telling him that it had been decided not to appoint a successor to Mr Collinson. He said further that he was coming to the Royal Reid on a date a week away to discuss the proposed arrangements. He "hoped the date would be suitable." It was Jim's operating day, so it wasn't. The letter ended with the usual handwritten "kind regards."

This Regional Medical Officer was an unknown quantity because he was a new appointment and a new man. The government of the day had decided upon new administrative arrangements for the Health Service which were hailed by them as the most important since 1948. The aim of the Heath government of 1970—which was also pushing a local government reorganisation altering county boundaries, changing the names of some counties, and even destroying altogether the County of Rutland—was to introduce what was called "management" into the Health Service—and the plans were radical.

The greatest single change was the amalgamation of hospital and general practitioner services. Till now, Regional Hospital Authorities had dealt with the hospital service, and the Senior Administrative Medical Officer, the SAMO, was their senior medical administrator. Family doctors had been organised by Local Medical Committees, with their own clerk who attended to all the arrangements for paying practice expenses, collecting special fees, and generally doing all the paperwork they needed in relation to their practices and their management. Now the whole was to be administered by a Health Authority. The Public Health Service, formerly the province of local civic authorities for day-to-day running, appointments and allocation of resources, was to be done away with and replaced by what was to be called community medicine. Its doctors would now also come under the new overlord, the Regional Medical Officer, the RMO. He, in fact, would be the direct boss of this new breed of animal, the community physicians. They would no longer be answerable to the City or County Medical Officer of Health; that distinguished, century-old title would disappear. Bill Speirs' job would go.

In National Health Service Hospitals, there were to be sweeping changes. For a start, the post of Matron would disappear. The Salmon Report on the future of nursing had decreed that there was to be a hierarchy of nursing officers, numbered on an ascending scale. Boards of Management or Governors would disappear and be replaced by hospital district authorities, answerable to the new Regional Health

Authority in a more direct way than in the past. The Matron would be replaced by a District Nursing Officer, and she would be under command of the Regional Nursing Officer—another new animal. But the district officer would no longer live on the job, go around the wards daily, know everything that was happening, and run the nursing side of the hospital. She would live in an administrative headquarters, together with the District Medical Officer. The group secretary was to be replaced by the District Administrator. So Peter Scott's job would also go. But as the new District Administrator he would have new power and live in the district office, as would the district treasurer. These, with their clerks and secretaries, would make up the "District Administrative Group."

Within a hospital or group of hospitals—in fact throughout the whole United Kingdom hospital service— the well-tried system was to be destroyed. Ward sisters would now have to deal with what the new regulations called "line management." All cleaners would no longer work under the ward sister or unit, but be allocated by the domestic staff supervisor. All hospital tradesmen would now have line management, with a district and a regional engineer, district and regional carpenter, electrician, laundrywoman, and on and on. These services would report no longer to Peter Scott's secretary, who presently ran the hospital, knew where everything was, came from and went to, but to their senior up or down their own line. Hospital records were not exempt—the two ladies who ran these were to be replaced by five. Even Teaching Hospitals were to be changed.

All this put Professor Parkinson's First Law into effect.

Work at once expanded to fill the time required for its completion. The changes were a first-class means of creating employment, because all line managers at once required clerks, secretaries, rooms, typewriters, stationary, holidays to take management courses, and, of course, deputies. Hospital records previously run by two walking computers were now run by the district records officer, her deputy district records officer, with three secretaries and desk space. The ward sister could no longer ring the carpenter to replace a worn curtain and broken curtain rail. She had to send a written request to the supplies manager and the carpentry manager, who authorised, on other appropriate forms, issue of a new curtain and repair of the broken curtain rail.

The hospital doctors were to be reorganised, but along somewhat contrary lines. The chief of the firm was to lose his permanent authority. Consultant staff were to be organised into divisions. These divisions would include all the surgeons, all the physicians, all the obstetricians, laboratory doctors, and so on, each group specialty in their own division. The old line management of chief, sub-chief, would be replaced by a conglomerate of equals—for all consultants were now to be equal as members of the division. The appointment of chairman would rotate. Because of this, the politicians stated, old animosities against seniors would go, and be replaced by consensus decisions, arrived at after free and fair discussion. Being supported by all, these decisions would be good ones and lead to greater efficiency and higher morale. There was "no other way."

The new Regional Medical Officer—the RMO—for the

Region, was very much more powerful than the old Senior Administrative Medical Officer. Not only had his office control over hospital staff, it had control over general practitioners through the new mechanism for Health Board Committees—before, these had been Hospital Board Committees—to oversee prescribing costs, disciplinary measures, complaints, and inspection of premises, but it now directly controlled community medical services and the as yet unknown quantity of community specialists and community physicians. These last would in fact become the RMO's staff. Power was now to be centralised in the Health Authority, and that inevitably meant power to allocate finance.

The new Regional Medical Officer was a tall, rather stout and poor-postured individual who had been a failed registrar in medicine and then gravitated into administration. Dark-haired and now slightly balding, he had large brown eyes and a rather full mouth. He had already shown himself something of a bully and Andrew Morton, who was the secretary of the Regional Consultants and Specialists' Committee, had told Jim how he had been telephoned by him after a meeting to demand, with menaces, that a minute be modified to place his remarks in a light more favourable to himself than the minute had indicated.

So Jim went along to see Bill Spiers in his new office. Bill had been translated into the job of District Medical Officer or DMO. "What's this about Charles' job not being advertised?" he asked. Bill looked out of the window.

"The Regional Authority (how often the words "the Regional Authority" would cause anguish over the next years) think there are far too many surgical beds here. And they don't think there's work for four consultant surgeons between here and the Dale. So they're going to amalgamate the beds into one unit."

"You mean combine us with the Dale?" asked Jim.

"That's right," answered Bill.

"But how will that work? I can't do all the work here myself."

"You won't have to. The idea is that you'll share it with Alan Berrill and D.G. Jones."

"But there won't be room for us all to work here. Charles mayn't have used his beds all that, but three won't fit into two ward units. In any case, they've half as many more beds there as we have here."

Spiers looked out of the window again. "The plan is for the surgical unit to be split on a functional basis. All emergency work will be done here. All list work—all cold surgery—the waiting list work—will be done at the Dale."

"But that can't work. You can't expect the wards here to admit every day. At the moment it's one in four. You remember what it was like when I came here first—in old Rollands' day. It was alternate days then. But each pair of wards got a rest on alternate days."

Spiers looked blandly at him. In a moment, Jim realised that this was not the Bill Spiers he had known up till now—the cheerful, helpful Medical Officer of Health. This was Bill Spiers, the newly-designated District Medical Officer. He had become a different person.

"Dr Hubbard the new RMO is keen on the idea. He has plans for all the services here. He can see no reason why it shouldn't work."

"But Dr Hubbard…" began Jim. Spiers interrupted him.

"It won't just mean D.G. and Berrill coming here. *You* will have to go over to the Dale to do all your elective surgery."

"But why should I do that?" demanded Jim in alarm. "I'm not appointed to work at the Dale. My contract is to work here, at the Royal. And it's ten miles away."

"I'm sorry, Jim," said Bill Spiers. "You know the new hospital site is to be decided on soon. The RMO thinks a rearrangement of services would rationalise the work here and give the new Health Authority a better chance to assess where it is to be."

Jim was annoyed now. "You know very well we've often discussed this. You've always said yourself the new hospital will have to be built here."

"Yes, and I think it will. So this will be a chance to run down the Dale a bit."

Jim couldn't see that moving the elective surgery to the Dale would run it down. It seemed to him it would do the reverse. The idea seemed senseless. The wards, the theatres, the clinics at the Dale were old and extremely basic. The bulk of the population lived around the Royal. The university had consistently refused to send students to the Dale just because it was farther away and its teaching facilities were non-existent. Well, perhaps not non-existent, but certainly not like the Royal's. The new postgraduate centre was being built at the Royal and would be commissioned soon.

"But this idea of doing only emergencies here. What about cases that need second operations?" he asked Spiers.

"Well of course," replied Spiers, "D.G. and Berrill will

have lists here just like you. They will be operating here just like you will be operating there."

Jim Baxter retreated in confusion. He made a last complaint:

"Why didn't they tell me about any of this? Why spring it on me just like this?"

Spiers looked out of the window again. "But they did tell you."

"When?" Spiers pushed a button for his new DMO's secretary.

"Bring in the file on the reorganisation of surgery. The one we had out yesterday."

Back it came. And there was a letter to Dr William Spiers at District Headquarters, dated six months earlier. It must have come in about the same time District Headquarters had opened. It said that changes in the surgical services in the areas served by the Royal Reid and the Avondale hospitals were being considered by the Policy and Resources Committee of the Health Authority, which might involve staff reductions and/or reorganisations. There were copies to all the four surgeons, including Mr James Baxter, M.S., F.R.C.S. Nothing definite, and no details, but as ever the careful administrators had covered themselves by a letter on file which they could refer to later. Jim had seen his copy, but had not thought it of any importance. He remembered there was a huge pile of correspondence when the new Health Authority was set up, which both he and Charles had laughed at. Now he had forgotten ever receiving it, and yet there was the original and his name among the recipients.

No sooner was he home than he accosted Anne.

"Do you know what they're going to do?"

"What are who going to do?"

"This new man called Hubbard wants to change the surgery here. He wants me to go and do cases at the Dale. David Jones and Alan Berrill are to come to the Royal. I'll have to share wards with them. They're not going to replace old Charles."

Anne, percipient as ever, saw the implications at once. They talked back and forwards, going over the ground as people do.

"It may not happen. It's just a suggestion. You'll have to wait and see what this man says at your meeting next week," said Anne.

Jim couldn't wait. He went over the ground again, thinking aloud the various possibilities. Then he had a thought. He would telephone George Bell and see what he said. Significantly, he did not think of approaching Andrew Morton.

"Yes, Jim," said George in that wonderfully quiet reassuring voice of his. His voice rose on the word "yes," fell on the word "Jim." Jim poured out his story. "I know," said George quietly. "But they've already proposed this for the medical side. I've written to say I will not have anything to do with it."

The meeting was in Bill Spiers' room. Jim did not take to the new Regional Medical Officer. He had a rather whiny voice and he had a way of lowering his head as he spoke so that you could not really see his eyes and what he was thinking. But he was clearly an able opponent, if not an obvious friend.

"The Regional Health Authority," he began, "has come

to the conclusion in its new Policy and Resources Sub-Committee, that the hospital services in this district of the Region require development. It is their view that the developments they have in mind will necessitate a reduction in both staff and beds, and with this in mind they have decided not to replace Mr Charles Collinson on his retiral in four months' time. You were advised of this in the earlier part of the year." He cleared his throat and looked around the four others present: Spiers, Baxter, Jones and Berrill.

"Because of Mr Collinson's retirement, beds will become available for development here in the Royal," he went on. What a clever phrase, thought Jim—"available for development."

"I consider it now likely that the new hospital, so long planned for this district, will be built at the site of the present Royal Reid. That will not of course be a final decision, and will also be dependent on funds becoming available. But it now seems sufficiently likely that I think you can take it as constituting a basis for planning.

"With this in mind, I am going to put into effect some preliminary changes. There are not enough surgical beds here at the Royal for all the surgery of the district to be done here. But as this hospital provides most of the acute services, has casualty and X-ray and laboratory services, has the children's ward and the maternity, I consider it should be obvious to anyone that acute services continue to be provided here. It is for this reason that all emergency surgery, by three consultant surgeons, will be done here following Mr Collinson's retiral.

"There are at present many more surgical beds at the Avondale Hospital and they are under-used. They can be used for elective surgery, and will be available to you, Mr Baxter, as well as to Mr Jones and Mr Berrill, as they are at present."

Jim could see the angry eye of D.G. Jones he had come to know well over the years, and recognise. Dr Hubbard certainly did not know that angry eye—certainly not yet.

"But there will have to be elective lists at the Royal as well," Jones said. "You can't do emergency surgery and nothing else. Many cases come in as emergencies—like someone who has a catheter passed for retention of urine and then needs a prostate operation later. Or someone with a bowel obstruction from cancer who needs that removed after the obstruction is relieved. So we will have to have elective operating lists here."

Jim found himself agreeing. "What Mr Jones says is quite right," he put in. "There could well be very many patients who are just like those. It wouldn't work just to have all emergencies here and all waiting list operations at the Avondale Hospital."

Dr Hubbard frowned. He obviously was not a man who tolerated disagreement with his own views. "I can't see that there would be any difficulty," he said.

Mr Jones spoke. "There could be problems with the wards being on call all the time for emergencies—problems for the nursing staff. And how would the beds be allocated? The present wards at the Royal are satisfactory for two surgeons, but difficult for three—just by the way they are built."

This was true. The arrangement of a male and a female ward at opposite sides of a central corridor, on two flats, had been the way wards had been arranged for a medical or surgical firm for a century at least and was designed for two surgeons, not three. Each pair of wards had its consultant's room—and so there were only two of these as well.

Jones then made another point. "It will be difficult to fit in lists for three," he said. "How do they work at present?"

Dr Spiers intervened, for he saw that Dr Hubbard's face was hardening into a look of anger, to assure the RMO that the local surgeons would study the proposals and would work out the best way of achieving the Authority's aim. Again, Jim saw a new Bill Spiers here. Spiers had always been his own man, aware that his service was to the community, the staff, and to the local Board of Management. Today he was nervous, continually glancing in the direction of Dr Hubbard, clearly keen to please him.

As the conversation continued, Jim saw Jones' eye soften, and a look almost of anticipation appear instead of its former hot resentment. He had been surprised at the proposals—had Jim been close to him, he would almost certainly have discussed them on the telephone with him before this meeting. It had not occurred to him, because they were not close friends. Nor had it in any way occurred to Jim to speak to Jones. Now, David Jones was quickly latching on to the prospect of working at the Royal—of doing routine work there—lists, and...

"Will it not be sensible for all three of us to do outpatient clinics at the Royal as well as lists?" he enquired. "If we are to have routine operating lists, then it will be essential to do clinics as well, won't it? There's Mr Collinson's clinic day and Alan Berrill could get another, I'm sure. I'd take Mr Collinson's clinic day. It suits my week."

"What about clinics at the Dale, then?" asked Bill Spiers. "Your main clinics are there just now, David, and you've patients who come from the town well beyond, on the other side. You'd have to keep some clinics at the Dale."

"Of course I'd keep my clinics, where I've worked for twenty years," said David Jones. "My patients would expect it. But I'd expect them to get much smaller, because the bulk of my new referrals will be coming to the Royal. Jim," he added with a friendly smile, "would have to do a clinic at the Dale, to make us all the same."

"I would not do a clinic at the Dale," replied Jim. "I already do two at the Royal. All my sessions are full. And I don't really want to operate at the Dale—I can get through my work at the Royal on my present two days and still have beds to spare. My sessions are at the Royal."

"And mine are at the Dale. My loyalty is to the Dale. I want to keep lists there as well. But I'd have to have a list at the Royal to clear off emergency cases who need second operations—or anything else done once they are in."

"It is the view of the Regional Authority," said Dr Hubbard, "that the arrangement whereby emergency operations only need to be carried out at the Royal Reid is entirely satisfactory. For this, the majority of elective, waiting list procedures would in consequence be carried out at Avondale. This will allow us to reduce the number of beds designated as surgical in both hospitals."

Jim could not see the logic of this new administrator, no matter how often or how confidently he stated the view of the Health Authority. If the Authority wished to run down Avondale prior to a new build at the Royal, and wanted beds saved at the Royal as well, then why not continue the present system where the two Dale surgeons receive emergencies into their own wards as they did now, allow him to receive emergencies on the third days, and carry on his lists from his own wards as *he* was doing? He said so. What he forgot was that there would now be an empty flat.

Jones' eyes became hot and angry again. "There's no reason why Alan and I shouldn't come to the Royal," he said. "And there's no reason why, if we are coming, you shouldn't go over to work in my—our wards. The Dale is a very good hospital, you know, even though *you* may not think so."

"I never thought the Dale wasn't a very good hospital," replied Jim. "But my contract is to work at the Royal and if I can do my work there, I can't see why I have to go elsewhere. In any case, I don't see this idea working, Dr Hubbard. All that will happen is that the nursing staff here will find that being on emergency call *every* day gets too much for them."

"But they won't have to be on call every day. They can alternate."

"No they can't. There are two units of male and female beds, but there'll now be three surgeons admitting and not two. So they'll find they are on every day. If you think how many emergencies come in when we're on take here, you'll see that is right." Jim was right. Because the Royal was the major hospital, and was in the city centre, it always had a steady load of emergency surgery.

Dr Hubbard was looking thoughtful. He would certainly know of the attitudes between the Royal and the Dale. What he couldn't know till now was the personalities of the surgeons concerned. Now he could see—Baxter feeling alarmed at his position at the Royal being threatened, Jones showing an eagerness to get into the Royal in spite of his professed loyalty to the Dale and his criticism of the idea about concentrating emergencies. Berrill he supposed would follow Jones' line—he was a good twenty years younger anyway. "The Regional Authority," he said, "want the new arrangements put into effect as soon as Mr Collinson retires. That will be at the end of February. I've already spoken to Dr Spiers and Mr Scott about the arrangements as they will affect the nursing staff, and they will liaise with Miss Shields." (Miss Shields, thought Jim— the new District Nursing Officer—another unknown quantity.) He got up, thanked everyone for attending, and left the room. He was going to be a cut-and-dried man, the surgeons agreed when they were alone. They also agreed the idea was not going to be popular with the nursing staff at the Royal. But here their agreement ended.

Rumour travels fast, not least in hospitals. Jim's anaesthetists' comments were predictable, as were those of the ward sisters. Sugden saw the move as the start of the run-down of the Dale, because he said the next few years would see a quicker turn-around of hospital patients, and it would not be long before fewer beds were needed. Jim questioned this; his older colleague would be proved right and he wrong. Garretts was as ever forthright and critical. "Jones is desperate to come here. It's been his life's ambition. He knows he couldn't get in by merit, so he knows this is a chance to get in on the back of a reorg. But he will go about professing his loyalty to the Dale, because that's what he's been doing for the last twenty years, and he can't stop now. Or it would look funny. Berrill's about as bad. He wants to get in by the back door too. *And* he wants to take over the private stuff."

Mr Collinson had Jim into his office for a coffee on the morning of his retiral presentation. He said, as he smoked his fourth cigarette, "David Jones has always been jealous of you, and always hated you, because you beat him fair and square for the plum job here eight years ago. And now that I'm away, he will squeeze you, and squeeze you, and if he can he'll squeeze you out. You are in for a bad time. We've been many years apart in age, but this difference has got less and less as we've both got older. I've been pleased that you've done well and I know that people respect and like you in the community. But things won't ever be the same again. I think you'll come through, but you're in for a bad time. You'll look back on your years with me as your golden years."

Jim sat and looked at Charles. Now grey haired and with his moustache white, he looked old for his sixty-five years. Or Jim thought so. He was still too young to know that in a very short time he too would be at retiral age, grey-haired, having fewer patients referred, seeing younger colleagues overtake him. And tired. Collinson looked a tired man. But he had never spoken to Jim in such a dramatic way before. Never. They had talked about patients, fishing and golf and gardening, medical politics—especially over the past few months. They had shared decisions and had protested to the administration in joint letters when something important came up. But this warning was something new. Jim was alarmed, and talked about it at length to Anne that evening. He telephoned Anne's doctor brother, and Tom Semple.

He also discussed the problem with Andrew and George Bell. Andrew listened but said nothing beyond telling Jim that the medical firm was being threatened with the same proposal, that he and George Bell work in the Dale. He could not see the point of the proposals either. There was not the same sort of workload in medicine compared to surgery—medical admissions were for practical purposes all emergencies, and there was no waiting list as there always was in surgery. So the idea of having one hospital for emergencies and one for elective work just did not arise.

George was very much more forthcoming. He told Jim: "The Dale staff—the two new physicians there—seem to have got the ear of this new RMO man—Dr Dick has been to see him several times—and want to have beds in my wards. So to keep the numbers up, we—Andrew and I— would be expected to go and work there. The idea is nonsensical. I told them in the divisional meeting that it would only happen over my dead body."

It was with some trepidation that Jim and his ward staff awaited the new arrangements. Not only did they mean the arrival of two new consultant surgeons on the premises, but they meant the arrival of new registrars. And what was to happen about the house surgeons? They were newly appointed. Their position had not been thought of by the clever administrative minds, who as time went on seemed less certain about what should or should not happen. They produced all of a sudden an idea that the empty surgical ward at the Royal should be filled with orthopaedic patients, but quickly retreated when the powerful orthopaedic lobby, led by the professor, turned it down flat. Jim when asked said he had no objection. The orthopaedic surgeons saw no increased status in moving to the Royal, which in any event they looked down on.

What did become clear was that the running was being made by Jones with the support of his junior colleague

Berrill. They were supported at every turn by Bill Spiers. Peter Scott kept his distance; he did nothing. Dick and Healy were also working hard. Jim found to his annoyance that his newly appointed house surgeon, a burly rugby player, had been approached by Jones without his knowledge and told he was to move to the Dale in three months. He also approached the new houseman on Mr Collinson's wards, telling her she would have to move in the same way, and swap with the Dale houseman. She agreed, but Jim's refused, after telling him about it. He told D.G. bluntly that his contract was as house surgeon to Mr Baxter, and that he was not prepared to change. Jones also appeared on the surgical wards and criticised the nursing staff, to the fury of Sister Billings. When Jim went to complain to Dr Spiers, he found him unhelpful. He made a significant remark: "Don't be obstructive. This has to go through. Dr Hubbard says so." About this time it was announced that community medical specialists were to be eligible for merit awards, and the unkind thought crossed his mind that perhaps Bill Spiers' new-found insistence on agreeing with the new boss was not wholly disinterested.

It took a surprisingly long time for the changes to be set up. The date for the first emergencies to come to the Royal Reid on days previously covered by the Dale was put back from mid-February till the 1st of April. And so for six weeks Jim continued at the Royal as he had been doing for eight years—his two lists a week, his teaching, his twice-weekly visits to the medical wards in consultation with George Bell and Andrew Morton, and no interference from anyone. Or so he supposed. This breathing space was punctuated by a demand to appear in Dr Spiers' office, "to formalise certain details about the changes." He went to see Dr Bell just before, and told him of his fears—that he was not just being obliged to work a system he saw no advantage in, but that he felt he was about to be treated unfairly and with hostility. "I'll come into Spiers' office with you, Jim," said George in his quiet way. "The way things are going upsets me. I don't like what they are proposing for the medical firm either."

Spiers was furious. George Bell sat calmly beside Jim and supported his attempts to defend himself against the attack that he was standing in the way of "the Regional Medical Officer's master plan." When George quietly asked Spiers, "What master plan?," the interview came to an end. He said to Jim outside: "There are wheels within wheels here, Jim. I've never known Bill Spiers carry on like this." From that day, Spiers scowled at George Bell every time they passed.

The impending changes were a source of excitement everywhere, especially in the hottest bed of hospital gossip and character assassination, the theatre staff-room. A new senior sister, rated Number 7 on the new Salmon scale, appeared unannounced from the Dale with details of the instruments and sutures Mr Jones and Mr Berrill used, which was reasonable, but with details of how procedures on the surgical side of the Royal Reid were to be improved, which was not. The surgical ward sisters asked every day what was happening. There was now no matron to tell them, and Miss Shields was conspicuous by her absence. Andrew Morton tried to cheer Jim up, and Mary got Anne in for coffee to talk it all over. What was so upsetting was not the changes, but the atmosphere of hostility the Dale surgeons brought with them whenever they appeared.

Jim and David Jones now came into open conflict. Jones

told Jim that he had arranged theatre time for him at the Dale to do a list there every week. Jim agreed under protest, but when he kept his lists very small, he was attacked by Jones and told he was insulting the Avondale Hospital. Jim's next encounter was on the telephone when after an acrimonious discussion, Jones all too plainly told him how he was to do things from now on. He angrily told D.G. not to try to take him over, and put down the receiver. He would, he insisted, continue to do the bulk of his work at the Royal. That was where his sessions were; that was his contract.

By now it was May. And now an overwhelming disaster occurred. George Bell went of on holiday to the north to fish. He usually went later, but this year his son-in-law had got a beat for a couple of weeks a little earlier, as a surprise. While walking down the river side to push the boat out on the first evening of his holiday, he died of a massive coronary thrombosis.

George Bell had been a greatly loved physician for nearly thirty years—since his appointment soon after the end of World War Two. His integrity was known far and wide. He had never done any private practice. He was dedicated to the N.H.S. and worked long and hard. It was the knowledge that he would work with George Bell that partly made Andrew Morton so anxious to come to the Royal Reid, to give up his senior lecturer's post in a prestigious academic medical department. But to Jim and to everyone else he was if not a father figure, then certainly an older brother figure, who always saw both sides of an argument fairly and who disliked petty intrigue and antagonism. He invited all the registrars—especially the overseas ones, to his home, and Jim and Anne had several times had supper or afternoon tea with him and his kind, delightful wife Susan. Their family were all the greatest of fun, too. His youngest son was just qualified in medicine in London. And not only did the staff of the Royal respect him, so did most of those of the Dale.

Jim and Andrew were desolate. Jim especially had felt secure, while George was about, that their troubles would be sorted out. And now he was gone from the scene. They would no longer see his tall figure in the corridors, hear his kindly voice. The evening of the funeral Anne said, "We'll certainly miss George. Dear George."

Now D.G. was completing his take-over. Jim found himself asked if he wanted to keep his room on the ward— the room he had had by right for eight years, as he and Berrill would require rooms and there were only two. In pique he said he would move elsewhere. Paula, his secretary, was appalled at his foolishness, and told him so.

Jones and Berrill moved in. But then Jim became attacked on all sides, for Dr Dick was very clearly supporting the Dale surgeons at every opportunity, and one day the husband of a friend of Anne's took him aside and said, "You are being accused of every sort of crime in the town by Mr Jones. You're supposed to be trying to keep the Dale staff out of the Royal."

Next he was told by Jones, who now appeared with a large black folder sporting the words in grand red dymo letters 'DAVID G. JONES, F.R.C.S, CONSULTANT SURGEON, ROYAL REID HOSPITAL', that he was taking over the running of the casualty department and the appointment of casualty officers. In private, he attacked Jim, while in public he was civil. Jim even found himself about to be moved out of the theatre where he had always done his operating to one of the smaller theatres. Allan Berrill was also hostile to him. Both Dick and Healy joined in.

And then, one evening, Anne confessed to him, almost in tears, that she had been dropped by Andrew Morton's wife, Mary. For years they had been the closest of friends, dropping on each other, and in earlier years sharing the upbringing of their children. Their meetings for coffee had stopped. No further invitations from Mary; Anne's invitations somehow at an unsuitable time or date. Anne was deeply upset. She had always said how she loved Mary, and felt her her best friend.

The snub was especially hard, they both thought. When Andrew had told Jim and Anne of his hope of getting the consultant's post at the Royal, they were both delighted. Jim had worked hard but tactfully in Andrew's support before the appointment committee met. Dr Bell had asked Jim about Andrew—always totally fair, he had said there were other good candidates. Jim's obvious sincerity in support of his friend of senior registrar days had come across. When Andrew was appointed, he had telephoned Anne and Jim: "I've landed the job." Mary had come on the line, bubbling over with enthusiasm and telling Anne how delighted she was that they would be neighbours.

When Andrew had arrived first and been very keen to join the local golf club, Jim had canvassed support for him as well as proposing him. When, before he became a member and had friends or relatives visiting and had asked Jim if he would introduce them, Jim had happily agreed. When Andrew was put up, again by Jim, for the local professional and business club, Jim had willingly taken him to lunch and introduced him all round.

But perhaps there had been an inkling. As soon as George Bell died, Dr Spiers moved fast. Within days he had announced that no successor to Dr Bell would be appointed, on orders of Dr Hubbard, and the two Dale physicians, Dr Dick and Dr Healy, would be moving into the Royal. Most of the beds at the Dale for medicine were to be closed, but some would be left. Dr Morton had agreed without argument. He had confided to Susan, George's widow, that he had no choice, because he was outvoted by the two newcomers. These two were pushing themselves forward more and more—especially Dr Dick, who spoke strongly and persuasively in committee. Like the surgeons they were openly eager to move to what they saw as a more prestigious appointment in a more prestigious hospital. "They're right, of course," laughed Bobby Sugden. Andrew did not put up the defence that Jim had. He was prepared to swim with the tide. He certainly knew the unpopularity Jim had brought on himself by refusing to do the bulk of his elective work at the Dale. And he knew that even so senior a figure as George Bell was under attack for his stand against the changes. Andrew knew the faster turnover of patients Jim achieved, and the fact that he had since Charles Collinson's retiral as many new patients referred as the other two put together, only made him even more unpopular in Dale surgical eyes. Perhaps he felt unwilling to be associated with Jim because of that unpopularity—the very reverse of George Bell's attitude of strong support in the month before his sudden death.

For Dr Spiers had been putting it about that "Dr Bell was obstructing the new Regional Health Authority policy" and was by innuendo and open criticism attacking him.

Dick and Healy were openly and vociferously antagonistic, saying everywhere "There will be no progress here until a certain senior physician is removed from the scene."

The two young men were in post at the Reid by the end of June. Said Andrew Morton to Jim in the corridor between the medical and surgical sides of the hospital: "Well, Dick and Healy are here now. Thank you for all the help you have given us in the past."

It may have been said without ulterior motive. But it may have been that Andrew, too, had thrown his lot in with the newcomers and saw Jim as a loser. And so, human nature being what it is, he had been prepared to drop his friend of fifteen years. Perhaps he was right. But there was no need for Mary to drop Anne. She would be hurt for the rest of her life.

CHAPTER 8

The next two years were increasingly miserable for Jim and Anne. Jim found himself pushed to the side in the hospital where he had so recently been happy and contented and feeling that he was making a central contribution. He had been looking forward to taking more of a share in the planning of the new hospital when it came along, after the retiral of Charles Collinson. The Baxters had both looked forward to the friendship of the Mortons, Mary as Anne's best friend, Andrew as Jim's medical colleague. But this had all disappeared. No more did Jim visit the medical wards for happy cups of coffee and regular consultations. No more was it the easiest thing in the world to phone his medical friends to discuss a patient. No more did he feel secure in his wards as he had felt over the previous years.

He went along with the directive to carry out some of his routine operating at the Dale, going there once a week, on Wednesday mornings. This had been his former morning for student teaching, but with the arrival of the Dale surgeons—now newly appointed to the honorary staff of the university—the teaching at the Royal had been rearranged. D.G. Jones had his great wish satisfied—to have students. He had them at the Reid, not the Dale.

The Dale theatres—twin theatres with flat roofs as in the style of the wartime emergency hospitals—were well run. The senior sister was a Yorkshirewoman called Pickering, who had a larger staff than Jim's old friend Sister Pope. Her staff of two sisters and two staff nurses was less than that of Sister Pickering. They made a tough bunch, Jim soon found, though the oldest, who was in fact just Sister Pickering's 30 odd years, was a pleasant Sister Samira. The others were a stout Sister Ferrie and a thin Sister Turner. They were both rather sharp and complaining, and like Sister Pickering, openly anti-Royal Reid. They were almost a caricature pair— both tall but one fat and one thin. Sister Ferrie at least had the capacity to be cheerful if she was having a good day, but Sister Turner was regularly glum and even sullen. Sister Pickering ran them a good deal more harshly than ever did Sister Pope run all her Reid staff. Jim could not escape being aware of what was being said about him but was carefully polite and always ready to accommodate to the way the Dale did things. He comforted himself that he only saw them once a week at the most.

Jim also found D.G. and Berrill an interesting pair; Jones busy and so conscious of his new self-created status as the Senior Surgeon at the Royal Reid Hospital, Berrill very busy too and very confident of his ability to take over all the surgery in the area within a short time. Garretts relished telling Jim stories of how Berrill bit off more than he could chew and ran into trouble. Jim had long ago learned to take Garretts' stories with a pinch of salt, but another of his anaesthetist friends confirmed at least some of his tales.

The Baxters invited the Berrills to their home shortly after the amalgamation was completed. Jim and Anne were both aware of the hostility they had brought with them from the Avondale, but were genuinely hopeful that they could establish if not a warm friendship with them, at least a good working relationship.

The evening began a little stiffly, but after some good wine Allan Berrill became more relaxed and talkative. Jim asked him about his research.

"I did a year in a good centre in the States," he said, "in Florida." As he talked about his work on cancer he spoke freely and confidently. But he always kept his voice tense.

"Did you do any clinical work?" asked Jim.

"Yes, I was lucky. I did an extra three months after I'd finished my research. I worked in Chicago on a special cancer unit. My prof fixed it for me. I also did some transplant surgery. I enjoyed Chicago. It's a fine city—not like the reputation it has here."

"Which centre were you attached to?" asked Anne.

"Northwestern University Medical School."

Jim and Anne looked at each other. Northwestern was where Peter Millard had been. But Allan Berrill, unlike Peter, had come back to England with a thesis of great merit. He had won a gold medal for it from his medical school.

"Did you enjoy your work when you were there?" Berrill looked pleased with himself:

"I was working in first-class centres."

"Did you enjoy your year there?"

"It was excellent. It was wonderful to get access to such a good research lab. The ones over here are all rubbish compared to that one." Jim thought back, inevitably, to Peter.

"Did you have any job lined up when you got back?" Berrill stiffened. His mouth became drawn.

"There were jobs coming up. But none in particular. Sir James, my chief, was always away and I had to do all his work. Except his private stuff, of course. I got to help with that. He was no help as far as jobs were concerned. Neither were any of the rest of them." His eyes flashed with resentment.

Jim wondered about this. He had seen the application, of course—and how could he have missed the fact that Berrill had worked in the same hospital as Peter Millard? But as he had not been able—so unfortunately as it had turned out, he had often thought—to be at the interviews when Berrill was appointed, he did not know what had been in the references. These were as customary read out at the appointments committee meeting and then supposedly destroyed.

A brandy with his coffee and Berrill had more to say. As well as having little good to report about Sir James, he warmed to his criticism of other members of his famous Teaching Hospital staff. They had been unhelpful. He had done two important pieces of research he had been given to do, and no notice had been taken of the results. He had failed to get the support he knew was his due. Nor had he any reverence in his remarks about the local Professor of Surgery either.

Anne managed to change the subject to families and schools. After the conversation returned to the rather neutral exchanges it had started with, the Berrills left with the customary expressions of thanks and praise for the excellence and originality of the meal. The evening had been interesting and instructive to the Baxters. Perhaps it had been to the Berrills too.

Percipient as always, Anne said to Jim as they were loading the dishwasher:

"He's a disappointed man. I think he feels deep down—

or maybe not all that deep down—that he ought to have got a job on his Teaching Hospital. I wonder if he feels he's too big for a small place like this."

"I remember he had a great list of prizes as an undergraduate," said Jim. "Medals and all that. He was a lecturer for a time on their professorial unit, too. But he seems to have got stuck."

"So do a lot of people."

"Yes. We were lucky to get this."

The Berrills did not return the Baxters' invitation. The Baxters were never to see the inside of the Berrill home. But Jim continued to try. While cricket and lately squash were Alan Berrill's own games, he professed an interest in golf, so Jim invited him to the local club. But in spite of his efforts, he could make no headway. Berrill was always distant. "I hope this bad time blows over," said Anne several times.

A few months after his arrival at the Reid, Alan Berrill went part-time, circulating all the general practitioners with the information that he would now be available for private consultations. He never mentioned this to Jim. But he did do one or two cases at the private wing of the Reid. Jim said to him one day:

"Allan, if you're doing private work, do you have any instruments?"

"No."

"Well," said Jim, "if you'd like to do cases in the nursing home, I have my set there. You can certainly borrow them if you wish."

"That's most generous of you."

By contrast, D.G. Jones did not even trouble to be civil towards Jim. He scowled at him whenever they met. He made arrangements with Dr Spiers and then informed Jim by curt letter. He insisted on taking over all the administration of the unit, even the appointment of house surgeons, in spite of Jim's protest, and was as hostile as he could be when Jim had to be away on his College Tutor's business. Most of all, he was desperately anxious to be seen to be the surgeon working the longest hours, doing the biggest lists (as he was a tediously slow operator, he had no difficulty in achieving this), ordering the unit's activities. The atmosphere was charged with unpleasantness. He was supported by Dr Dick, who was openly contemptuous of Jim and critical of Andrew Morton behind his back.

And yet there was an almost amusing contrast between Jim's ostracised position in the hospital and his status outside. He still found himself the surgeon the people who mattered consulted. His private income did not reduce. And after a year, Berrill reverted to a full-time contract again, because he had had so few referrals. His failure became, Jim soon realised, yet another cause of bitter resentment.

Jim's isolation increased when Dr Sugden died. Bobby had continued to anaesthetise for him in the nursing home, though he was no longer able to work at the hospital private wing. He had had a heart attack some years back, but it seemed to have been very mild and he was off work for almost no time at all. But his sudden death while working in his garden was another big shock for Jim. Coronary artery disease was the ever-present threat to men in their sixties and George Bell's and now Bobby's death had removed his two best medical friends in the district. Bobby though away from the Health Service had been a support and someone he could have a moan to—and Bobby was aware of his troubles.

Yet another support collapsed when Tom Spence, whom Jim and Anne had got to know so well and confide in, surprised everyone by going off with a widow in the town—not a patient, which was fortunate. Anne and Jim were once again astonished. Sudden death had removed two of their good friends, and in quick succession, but this was something equally unexpected. They had been aware of some irritation between Tom and his wife from time to time, but the break when it came was a bombshell. In almost no time Tom had left his practice and gone off with his new wife to the South, to a totally unlikely job in Community Medicine. It seemed to Jim that his whole world was collapsing.

Because of the geography of the wards in the Reid, the three surgeons now had patients in all four of them. This had soon led to difficulties for the nursing staff. Three different consultants inevitably had their different ways of doing things, and for Sister Billings in particular the appearance of two newcomers was unwelcome. She had got used over years to the way Mr Baxter did things. Because the former Dale surgeons spent more of their time at the Reid in their new role as consultants on the staff there, the nurses found themselves doing ward rounds in endless succession. But it was not just the fact that there were more consultants on the staff—multiple consultants on a unit was nothing unusual in hospital medicine—it was their attitude. Mr Jones in particular angered Sister Billings, as she told Jim as they were having tea in her office.

"He's always picking fault. He tells me how much better they do everything at the Avondale. He takes *hours* going around, Mr Baxter. He's always wanting to inspect the wounds, and he won't take my word for anything. Mr Berrill's not much better. But he's not so slow."

Sister Billings, like Jim, was indignant at the obvious take-over, and yet she remained extremely fair, making sure that all three surgeons had their due beds available. To get his cases turned over, she and Jim began to send his own patients home earlier than they had done in the past, arranging more and more for the general practitioners to take the stitches out. When he began to do this at the Dale, Jones turned on him furiously:

"You are just sending these patients home to drop the bed occupancy here. You are just trying to bring Avondale to its knees."

This was so ridiculous that Jim just ignored the accusation. He became alarmed, however, when he heard that Jones had complained to Dr Spiers and Dr Hubbard. But fortunately they did nothing. He became alarmed again when he did receive a letter from the Health Authority, this time from the regional personnel officer, a new appointee in a new post:

"It has been brought to my notice that you were absent from duty on the 22nd of August. The office here had no notification of this absence. In future I will be obliged if you will complete the regulation leave request and have it signed by Mr D.G. Jones, the head of your department, for his approval."

Jim went home angrier than usual. He showed Anne the letter.

"This is D.G. again. He's just trying to humiliate me. I'm dammed if I'm going to go cap in hand to him."

"Where were you that day? Oh, yes, you'd a registrar review meeting."

"These are my tutor's meetings. They don't count as leave. I wasn't away anywhere I shouldn't have been. Even if I had, it's no business of Jones. He must have written out of spite." He threw the letter down.

"Jim, you'll really *have* to try and not get so worked up over D.G. Jones. You've not been fit to live with for months now."

"But love, he just goes out of his way to be unpleasant. He was on about holidays, the other day, to Berrill and me that he should have precedence because he is senior."

"Well, he is senior to you."

"He's not. You know that *I* was appointed to the Royal Reid and *I* did all the arranging there. If he'd even been prepared to discuss things with me, it wouldn't have been quite so bad. But he just goes and does things like writing this letter. There was no need for that."

"You don't know he wrote the letter."

"Well, who else would? Spiers wouldn't. In any case, he's always snooping at what I do. Garretts tells me he sneaks into the surgeon's room in theatre to look at the case sheets of my patients."

Since Bobby Sugden had retired, Maurice Garretts had become the senior anaesthetist. He had continued to relate to Jim the aims of the Dale staff, Jones in particular, but the others also.

"Jones has been desperate for years. Now he's achieved his ambition. He always spoke quietly and pointedly."

"He still can't make up his mind when to stop running this place down. He's run it down for years while all the time he was desperate to get here. His poor wife Vera must have had a hell of a time. Now he's here he's out to rub your nose in the dust."

These contributions did nothing to improve relations. Jim regularly wondered whether Garretts might say the same sort of thing in reverse to Jones.

"Dick is a crafty fellow. He's got the Dale chip. He was worked on by Jones when he arrived. He and Healy give Morton a pretty thin time too, you know." Jim *had* heard. Andrew still occasionally confided in him, but their previous cheerful intimacy was a thing of the past.

"Berrill's a great friend of Pollock's, did you know? They're always popping off in the afternoons to play squash. Berrill's teaching him to play."

Maurice Garretts was consistent in one respect, thought Jim. He was careful never to get too close to any other member of the staff. He did his work, did it well, then off he went. He kept out of medical politics, though since becoming head of the division of anaesthetics he had shown himself capable if called upon to chair a meeting. For years under the shadow of the bigger figure of Sugden, he was now a man of increased stature.

"I always think that Dr Garretts is a bit of a stirrer," said Anne. "You should take what he says with a big pinch of salt."

"I'm fed up, Anne. I'm going to try and get away from here. I'm going to look for a job somewhere else."

Anne said nothing for a moment. Then:

"Well, if you feel as bad as all that, I suppose you must."

"Let's have a drink."

"All right."

A short year ago, Anne would have gone to have coffee with Mary Morton to tell her all about it and get some sympathy. But now that friendship, too, had gone, and not as far as she could see from Anne's fault. They both felt their isolation would never end.

As they were having supper, Anne said:

"Why not go to see the Macgregors sometime? We haven't seen them for ages."

"That's a good idea. I'll ring them up."

"You'll have to get David Jones' permission," said Anne, smiling. Jim grinned. He hadn't lost his sense of humour.

It was a free weekend and so the Baxters felt they could safely be away for a whole Sunday without comment. They had gone off once before to see Anne's general practitioner brother, when Jones was on call, and had had to rush back because one of Jim's patients had become unwell and Jones, although he was on call, had refused to see him. He had told the staff: "Get Mr Baxter." They found their former neighbours well and looking no different. Ken asked how things were in the N.H.S. With Labour back in power once more, he said, they did not seem any better. Anne and Jim decided he must be less of a socialist now than he used to be.

"I do not think it matters which Party is in government," said Ken, sucking his teeth in his same old way. Jim had no doubt:

"These new changes are doing no good," he said. "We were supposed to get a new hospital built when I arrived at Reidham, and that's ten years ago now."

"Consistency is the characteristic of the second-class mind," was Ken's retort. "But what about all that argy-bargy you used to have with the other hospital you used to complain about? What was it called? Some temporary place, you said."

"The Avondale. Well, though there's no definite word, it looks now as if the new place is to be built on our site.

They're supposed to be running the Avondale down, but the latest plan is doing just the opposite."

"Well, that's not quite true," said Anne. "They've reduced the medical beds, and you don't need so many surgical ones. You're sending patients home earlier now."

"They came along with a notion that we should split the work between emergencies all in one hospital and waiting list operations all in the other. It's daft. All it means is that our surgical wards in the Royal have to take in emergencies every day. The nurses are fed up. So am I."

Ken Macgregor sucked his teeth. "But don't all hospitals admit emergency patients every day? What's wrong with admitting emergency patients every day?"

"Because of the way hospitals are organized," replied Jim. "Some wards admit some days each week and other wards admit other days. This gives you the means of organizing your work so you can plan to get patients in for operations on a day you know your wards won't be filled up with emergencies. Most hospital firms only admit emergencies three days a week. If emergencies come in every day, you can't be sure that you will ever have free beds for your waiting list cases. Some days we get ten or twelve emergency admissions."

"But I remember you said when you went to Reidham first, Jim," said Ken, "that you said you were well off for beds."

"Yes, compared to many places in England. But we were never what you'd call flush for beds.

"The real trouble now," he went on, "is that I've been forced to share my wards with the surgeons from this other hospital. That would always be difficult, because we used to have two male and two female wards—designed for two surgeons, not three. I'd looked forward when Mr Collinson retired to getting a friendly new colleague whom I could have worked the rest of my life with. Instead I've got to share with two who're—to put it mildly—distinctly unfriendly."

He explained what had happened and of his being taken over by an older man who had always disliked him.

"But why don't you go and work in the other hospital?" persisted Ken.

"Because I was appointed to the Reid and it's a far nicer hospital. Nearly all the patients I get referred come from the town. The bulk of the patients the other hospital used to get came from the country and the towns in the other direction. While *they* still come to the Dale, *mine* don't want to go there. They want to go to the Royal. It's near their homes. They can see no good reason why they should have to travel ten miles when there's a perfectly good hospital next door to where they live.

"The other silly thing is that you just can't split surgery up in this way. If someone comes in with an acute illness, they very often need a second operation once whatever brought them in has been dealt with. It's silly for general surgery. They just haven't thought it through. And they've amalgamated the medical units too. Do you remember Andrew Morton?"

"Yes, I remember him."

"Well, Andrew has also been forced to go ten miles to this hutted hospital just like I have. Just the other day they said this is to make a pair of medical wards available for re-development. I can't imagine what they will try to put in them. They are just unbelievable, these administrators.

126

There's talk of new building, but it's just talk. There's a rumour that they are going to stop surgery at this Dale Hospital. There was a rumour that the orthopods were going to be moved to the Royal Reid. They wouldn't come—they've run a campaign against the Royal ever since I went there. And before."

"Well, that's your friend Mr Heath's government did that. Still, I'm sorry you're unhappy. Do you do a lot of private work?"

"Well, yes, I suppose I do a good amount."

"You do," said Anne. "That's what makes the others so mad."

"You know very well what I think of private practice. The Health Service was never meant to let people jump the queue by paying. The government are going to stop it, I hope, this time round."

Jim always found Ken's arguments against private practice difficult to counter. He gave his standard reasons.

"Nearly all the people I see and operate on in private are insured. Many of them are insured by their firm. If they want to insure themselves against illness, why shouldn't they? It's not different from insuring against anything else."

"You know very well it is. There is a service in this country which is part of our welfare state and it's supposed to provide care for everybody who needs it. If you worked your system better, there wouldn't be the delays there are.

"You doctors are a miserable lot," he went on. "As far as I can see, in the Royal Reid and this other place you're no better than you were when you were here—you're jealous of one another and you're more concerned with your status than your patients. Why can't you let these two come and work with you, if it is going to make the system better?"

"But it is *not* going to make the system better," said Jim, getting annoyed. "I know hospital doctors don't always get on. But we always got on so well at the Reid Hospital. It's these others who are being as nasty as they can. It's such a change. You know how I used to tell you what a happy place it was."

"That's true," Ken conceded. "But these other two you speak about. If they have been asked to share work with you, what's wrong with that? Why not just let them?"

"The trouble is," said Anne, "there are old grievances the Avondale staff have had against the Royal Reid where Jim works. They were there long before he arrived. The Dale staff were always jealous of the other hospital. So are the nurses at the Dale. I've discovered that, being a nurse myself."

"What about these orthopaedic surgeons you used to go on about, Jim?" asked Ken. "Are they being asked to move as well? You said there was some rumour about that."

"Well, Fleischman, the senior one, is due to retire soon," said Jim, "and so is the professor. They are building a bigger new orthopaedic block at the Teaching Hospital. So when Fleischman goes the rest of them may be a bit less unpleasant. As Anne said, they've had a feud with the Reid surgeons well before my time, and I've seen some of the most scurrilous letters about us. Charles showed me his file of them when he retired. They run down the X-ray people at the Reid too, which is a bit daft as the same radiologists work at both hospitals."

"But the radiographers don't," put in Anne. "And the copy of the letter from Fleischman to that G.P. you showed me was criticising the radiographers, not the radiologists who reported on them."

"As far as sharing the work with the Dale surgeons is concerned," said Jim, "I don't mind sharing duties with them and having them in the Reid so much. It's that they have come on to *my* old wards, have been very rude and unpleasant, and have taken over all the things I used to do without a by-your-leave.

"And not only that. I genuinely do see no reason for this change in the system, to put all the emergencies in one hospital. We are promised a new District Hospital—have been for ages. Why they can't just let things be till they begin the new place—people don't want to travel that distance. People ought to be treated as near their homes as possible."

"You're right there, Jim. But I'll tell you what it looks like to me. It's personalities, but it's more than that. You lot are unlucky. But *you* are the member of the privileged class. The others want to bring you down. It's just an example of the class struggle."

"Maybe," replied Jim, "but the fact is that the class struggle, as you call it, has made a thorough job of making me the underdog. But these others—and there is one of the new medicals as well—a fellow called Dick—want to be bigger dictators than *I'd* ever even start to be."

Ken Macgregor was unimpressed. "And there's something else," he went on. "You doctors have ruled the roost for so long in the N.H.S. that it's about time central government took you in hand. They are going to have to make your N.H.S. more efficient, because it's certainly not that just now while you are running it. Look how long ordinary people have to wait for operations. If you won't improve the service, the government will have to bring in someone who will. But these two do sound an unpleasant pair. I think they would have been the way they are no matter what you had done."

"You know," said Anne as they were driving home, "we seem to go over the same ground, year in and year out. When you were all senior registrars you used to complain about all the work you had to do and about how hard it would be to get a job. Now you've got a good one, you're still all complaining, only now it's about more things. We seem to have heard nothing but the Dale and the Royal and how they don't get on for years and years."

Anne was finding it difficult to put up with Jim's new-found misery. She was frustrated to find that what had looked like a happy, secure future for the rest of their lives had been thrown into turmoil and hatred—yes, hatred wasn't too strong a word for it. She kept her thoughts very much to herself, but was increasingly upset by the change in her husband. The moans and groans of the senior registrar state she knew would come to an end. But now, ten years older, she wondered what the future would hold— luckily their children were doing all right in their careers of medicine and nursing—but what of themselves?

Troubles didn't come singly or even doubly for the Baxters. There was a succession of them. Anne's younger brother by six years—"the boy" as she called him—was now diagnosed as having multiple sclerosis. He had had a succession of odd symptoms, but the diagnosis of this sad disease was now confirmed. David—she was closer to her younger brother than to her older—was a clever biochemist and worked for Beecham's in Welwyn Garden City. Because he was on his own, she rang him regularly and kept a sisterly eye on him. She cried all over Jim when she got the news.

Next day Jim told Allan Berrill about Anne's brother David.

"Oh really?" he said.

CHAPTER 9

The 1970's were continuing. The districts with all their increased administrative staff became established. The old Boards of Management had gone, and the District Managers—Medical, Administrative, and Nursing, had district medical committees to "advise them." Peter Scott worked away in his office and was no longer the ally he had once been. Bill Spiers became more and more the servant of Dr Hubbard. Miss Shields was never seen on the wards— the disappearance of the post of Matron was the great loss the critics had predicted. But the proponents of the new system of government for the N.H.S. insisted that everything was for the best, and became skilled at outpointing doctors or nurses who complained and wished for a return to the former arrangements.

But the excitement of the changes the Conservative Government had brought in were as nothing compared to the excitement after the fall of the Heath Government, swept away by the miners' strike and the three-day week. Early 1974 saw the return of a Labour Government with Mr Harold Wilson as Prime Minister. By the autumn a second General Election had seen his government returned with a bigger majority.

From 1974, expenditure in the N.H.S. had become a national issue. In May, a working party under the chairmanship of Dr David Owen was set up to investigate possible new contracts for consultants. In October the Royal Colleges and Faculties took the unprecedented step of sending a joint statement to the government asking for a careful scrutiny of the funding of the National Health Service, in view of the threat of inflation and the realisation by the doctors that from now resources would have to be rationed. For the first time the possibility of cuts in the traditional number of high-cost beds was raised. The idea of trading off some conditions against others whose cure would benefit the community and reduce costs appeared at this time too. Letters were exchanged between the B.M.A. and Lord Halsbury, the chairman of the Review Body on Doctors' and Dentists' pay—he was regarded by the professions as *not* impartial.

The General Election of 10th October gave the Labour Party a comfortable majority. In the Queen's Speech on the opening of the new parliament, her Government proposed changes in private practice in the N.H.S. Pay beds were to be progressively eliminated from N.H.S. hospitals—the government was committed to phasing them out, said Mrs Barbara Castle, the Minister of Health.

"This'll fairly please Ken," laughed Anne.

Fierce medical politics continued for nine months. Back and forward went the exchanges. The B.M.A. attacked the proposals. Mrs Castle said she would exclude private patients form the N.H.S. Hospitals. The B.M.A. said she was doing this to appease her militant union supporters. It claimed that the private beds issue "was a smokescreen to hide the government's refusal to face the financial realities." The B.M.A. became a Trade Union. Mrs Castle, after denying that the government was abolishing private practice, but only separating it from the N.H.S., then proposed a whole-time salaried service. New contracts, she and Dr Owen announced, would contain a "complete commitment allowance"; old part-time contracts, such as Jim had, could continue with the right to use N.H.S. private beds until such time as they were phased out. But such consultants would not be allowed the new distinction awards.

The profession's hostility made Dr Owen think again and Mrs Castle too made some concessions. The Government accepted that all consultants should take the opportunity to sign a 10-session contract—more than Jim's 9-session one—but still allowing the right to do private work. On 20th December Mrs Castle ended the Owen Working Party peremptorily. In the New Year the B.M.A. called consultants to "work to contract."

Mrs Castle now acknowledged that her objective was indeed a whole-time State Service. The General Practitioners then threatened mass resignations if the Review Body's recommendations on pay were not met. Hospital Junior Staff were offered a new contract with what was called "Units of Medical Time," to cover their extra hours of work for various extra duties. It was all very hectic.

On and on it went. In February of 1975, Dr David Owen said that medical care would have to be rationed. Talks with the doctors broke down, and Mr Harold Wilson refused to meet the profession. In April, the Doctors' and Dentists' Pay Review Body under its new chairman Sir Ernest Woodroofe awarded a 30% pay increase. In May, Mrs Castle said the government would now proceed to phase out pay beds—then only 1% of all beds in the N.H.S.—and that they would license private nursing homes more strictly. And in

August, a "Consultative Document on Separation of Private Practice from National Health Service Hospitals" appeared. In the country at large, it was only too clear that financial restraint was the order of the day.

But the government's aims were not realised. There was so much medical opposition that on the 20th of October, a Royal Commission was set up. In the November, the British Medical Association organised sanctions to get the pay beds dispute referred to the Royal Commission.

In February of 1976, the B.M.A. ballot of 13,000 consultants resulted in a vote of 73% against separation of private beds, 30% for resignation from the N.H.S., but 63% favouring acceptance of much less aggressive government legislation suggested by Lord Goodman, a Labour Peer.

The Health Services Bill, to separate private practice from N.H.S. practice, was published on the 12th of April, 1976— 4 days after the replacement of Mrs Castle as Secretary of State by Mr David Ennals. Medical political activity at national level subsided. In due course 1977 arrived.

Back in Reidham in 1977, the master plan of the Health Authority did not seem to be proceeding with the authority so confidently announced by Dr Hubbard in early 1975. Everyone agreed the surgical arrangements were nonsense. Even Jones and Berrill were less happy. The Reid nursing staff were constant in their complaints at being on call for emergencies every day. The physicians, on the other hand, were obliged to do more and more work in the empty beds at the Dale, so that their two double wards at the Reid became underused. The plan of "redevelopment of a pair of medical wards" at the Reid remained a rumour. That was until Dr Hubbard called another meeting, this time of the physicians, and told them that the redevelopment was to prepare for all general surgery to be moved to the Reid. An idea had once again been floated that emergency orthopaedics might be moved into this renovated pair of wards. But the orthopaedic department, supported by the newly appointed professor at Region, once more refused to have anything to do with this. Jim Baxter, when asked, had again offered no disagreement, because in his view there should be an emergency orthopaedic service available within the town centre. Jones and Berrill had been against the move. The orthopaedic proposal was shelved. The united and powerful orthopaedic unit, with their professorial support, were more than a match for Dr Hubbard. He had retreated in anger from their meeting.

The Reidham physicians were an easier target. Dr Andrew Morton made no complaint—by now he was just one of three with William Dick and Patrick Healy—but he had not blotted his copy-book like Jim by being "obstructive!" The RMO's proposal was accepted, and the medicals would do the bulk of their work at the Avondale. There were then in time to be three pairs of general surgical wards at the Royal, and all surgery was to be done there and not at the Dale. The medical arrangement would continue until "new building began" and a statement was promised "soon." Jim saw some relief for himself; Jones protested, saying that the Avondale was being "sacrificed"; Berrill went about saying he was the pig in the middle.

But there was one at least nominal ratification required before the new plan could go ahead. This was by a new advisory body set up by the Grand New Order of 1974—the Regional Medical Advisory Committee.

This was a statuary body. Its role was to give advice to the Regional Health Authority. But it was only one of a whole series of advisory bodies—there was a Regional Dental Advisory Committee, a Regional Nursing Advisory Committee, a Regional Pharmaceutical Advisory Committee—and many more. The Health Board were under no obligation to pay any attention to the views sent them by any of these. Older doctors saw the system as a further means of weakening the voice of the medical profession in the N.H.S.

In their constitutions, these advisory committees were allowed to decide for themselves, subject always to the final say of the Health Authority, the details of their structure— the numbers of various sub-groups—for general practitioners and academic staff were included in the committee—the numbers of representatives, term of office, and so on. By 1978 the Regional Medical Committee had already run for 4 years, and were into their second term of appointees. Those ambitious for medical political power sought a seat on the Regional Committee; those most ambitious of all tried to twist the tail of the honorary secretary to let them extend their tenure beyond the laid down three years; Dr William Dick was gravely hurt when the secretary of the day refused to bend the rules for him. Jones was however quite happy to let Berrill take over from him, he told Jim.

As ever with doctors, dissension and in-fighting diminished the effectiveness of the medical advice, and when it became all too clear that the Regional Authority were as likely to ignore the advice as accept it, a certain cynicism appeared. Much discussion centred around developments in the Teaching Hospital group, where university politics and rivalries added a further dimension of disagreement. But with good chairmanship and hard work on the part of the secretary in the preparation of evidence, meetings could reach a high standard of debate and result in sound well-ordered and well-argued letters passing to the Board.

Some Medical Advisory Committees won the right of their Chairman to attend Health Authority meetings, others did not. The RMO, of course, attended Medical Advisory Committees as of right, and Dr Hubbard being much more skilful at political persuasion than the clinicians, and much better informed in fact or by implication, he could usually bring the meeting around to his way of thinking.

Their own Regional Committee's most important decision as far as the Royal and the Dale were concerned was to agree to the Authority's proposal that the new District General Hospital was to be on the Royal site. This would effectively stop any further money going into the Dale, and the inevitable consequences would follow. David Jones, still on the Advisory Committee, protested hotly. To Jim his protest seemed hard to understand. He had now established himself in the Royal, his life's ambition. Why should he now want to challenge that hospital's rebuilding? Like so many of his complaints, this one seemed irrational. But he grew more and more agitated, and spoke with increasing anger at the small district advisory committee meetings whenever the subject was raised.

One Thursday about a month later Jim heard during his afternoon list that D.G. Jones had been admitted with a myocardial infarct. It was Dr Dick who was asked to see him—they were now very firm friends. Next morning, at his outpatients, Jim was telephoned by Bill Spiers. They had hardly spoken for months, exchanging only a nod or good morning if they passed in the corridor. Jones had taken upon himself all the decision making for the surgical unit, always emphasising his age and seniority if he did happen to inform Jim of his action before making it. At meetings he and Spiers had attacked Jim constantly, angrily dismissing any suggestion he made, always calling him "obstructive."

This was a different Spiers. The voice was no longer angry and accusing towards the renegade surgeon and former friend. "David Jones has just died," he said. "Would it be all right for me to come and see you?"

"Of course," replied Jim. It was 11 o'clock in the morning—coffee time. So he ordered some from the Red Cross tea bar—its coffee was always better than the hospital variety, and he always drank it. He ordered an extra cup, and a couple of biscuits.

In came Bill Spiers. "David Jones' death alters things," he said. "We will be able to stop all operating at the Dale, because we can use another thirty beds here—the other ward block in fact—and we couldn't do that till now. Jones wanted the Dale to go on and wanted it to fall down at his feet. We can use some of the beds the medicals are using. But there are plenty of medical beds at the Dale, so we can have more medical patients there." He said this in a tone which suggested that while certain surgeons were difficult about where their patients went, the physicians weren't. "How stupid," Jim thought to himself. "Now there will be hardly any medical beds left at the Royal. They'll have to send more emergencies to the Dale, yet they're putting all the surgery here." But he said nothing. After a pause he said, "It's been a bad time. I'm sorry about David. We were really both to blame."

What he did not say, though he felt it keenly, was that Spiers had been as responsible as anyone for the ill-feeling. Had he been a strong character like George Bell, he would certainly have brought Jim and David Jones together, even banging their heads, to get them to resolve their obvious clash of interest. But Spiers had proved a weak, weak man. Susan Bell had said as much, when George died, before the whole sorry business started. How right she was. All Spiers had done was in fact to make things worse. He was desperate to have the Authority's plan work. When it did not, he blamed everything on the unfortunate Jim Baxter. He was labelled, and would be for ever, as the arrogant individual who tried to prevent the Dale surgeons from their deserved place on the staff of the Royal. Spiers was a good stirrer, and stir he did. What Jones did to destroy Jim's name in the town locally, Spiers did to damn him when up at the Regional Headquarters. So Dr Hubbard also labelled him a dangerous man, standing in the way of their plans. In turn, the Health Authority members took note.

But what on earth *were* their final plans? More than once Jim had tackled Bill Spiers on this very question, but had eventually given up, as no satisfactory explanation was ever given. The surgical sortie had produced nothing but bitterness and not done anything to improve patient care. The local doctors were confused about where to send patients. To reduce the number of medical wards at the Royal seemed pointless as well, especially when emergencies had to be sent away to the Avondale—the very reverse of the surgical arrangement. The story always was "this is in preparation for the new hospital, so it has to work." And there was the veiled threat that if the locals did not comply, the new hospital would be delayed or not built at all.

They talked for a short time. Spiers was so conciliatory now it was almost funny. It was "Jim," and "Jim, what do *you* think about...?" But as they talked, his eyes softened. He said, "You'll have to get back to your clinic. I'm glad this is over, too. Because I admit that though you caused us a lot of annoyance, you were more sinned against than sinning."

That evening Jim and Anne talked about what had happened. Though they both felt relieved that the bitterness of the past several years must surely disappear now, they felt sorry for David Jones' widow and her family. D.G. had a sister in the town, a schoolteacher, who was unmarried. Jim telephoned her—he knew her enough to do this, and felt he must. "You know that David and I have had disagreements," he said. "But please tell Vera his wife that I phoned you to say that I'm genuinely sorry."

Hospital life is rife with dislikes and jealousies, as well as the greatest kindnesses and happy co-operation. As Anne said several times to Jim, when he was complaining about the latest angry letter from Jones, or his latest pin-prick, "You people who become doctors are supposed to go into Medicine because you're wanting to help your neighbours. But as far as I can see you're the very reverse of kind. Why on earth do you go for each other the way you do?"

As so often Anne—with her nursing connections—was right. She had seen her husband becoming more unlikeable over the past three years, his hair turning grey all of a sudden, his sleep disturbed, his temper shortened, his shoulders constantly rising with tension. She knew he had been attacked by someone deeply jealous of him. But she also knew that he could have been much more co-operative. What she did not know, till she found out later through tactful friends, was how calculated the campaign against him had been. It was the age-old story of the successful man creating one or two enemies, who then sought for their own reasons to bring him down and destroy him. It had happened in Ancient Rome, in the Middle Ages, in the competing businessmen of the Industrial Revolution in England and the Capitalist system in America. They were all full of intrigues and struggles for power leading to death and destruction, material success and failure.

Jim was only too aware of the pettiness of hospital doctors from his registrar days. He knew that some of the chiefs at his Teaching Hospital were at daggers drawn. He knew that professors spitefully decried their rivals. But this was all second hand when one was a registrar, unless the whole staff of a firm was enlisted against the staff of another, like the Montagues and Capulets. But now in his years as a consultant he had experienced it personally. Because of his status as a Royal College tutor he tended to be included in appointment committees for registrars and senior registrars in the Region. Here he watched with sadness two heads of firms fight against each other at interviews—the one more senior and more successful but less quick-witted being wrong-footed by the younger, sharper, jealous rival. He had watched the behaviour of defeated academics when the new professor was appointed. He had watched the dishonesty of the medical administration—assurances to registrars being set aside without a qualm, and the inevitable campaign against individuals who would not "co-operate." One ear nose and throat surgeon in the Region had run a successful one-man unit though still part of the larger regional service. His unit was closed by "rationalisation," although it had an excellent clinical record. The extra inconvenience for patients who had to move fifteen miles away to have their E.N.T. service was pooh-poohed by the Authority and its officers, and the surgeon was attacked and deliberately denigrated not only by them, but by other surgeons in the specialty, because of the single-minded resistance he put up to try and save his small unit. He remembered what Mr Armsworth had said to him those years ago. It was all too true.

Anne was right. Hospital doctors seldom love one another. And it might have been Jim who had had the coronary.

CHAPTER 10

Jim hoped that things would become easier now that Jones was no longer there to crib and confine him, and squeeze him out just as Charles Collinson had foretold those four years before. But he now found that Allan Berrill, who had uneasily watched the two men, one ten and the other twenty years older than him at loggerheads, proved to have been much more on Jones' side than Jim had expected. He had remained aloof, and had rebuffed Jim's attempts at social contact. Now he let it be known that he considered Jim an enemy. "He may be your friend," he would say to a friend of Jim's, "but he's not mine." As far as he was concerned, Jim was the figure, the establishment figure, who had sought to keep them out of the establishment hospital. Jim was also the man whose private practice had continued while his, Berrill's, had failed ignominiously within a year. There was no way that Jim would ever have told him of the private attacks Jones had made on him when he and Jones were alone together. And of course he could not have ever asked Berrill what Jones and he talked about when *they* were on their own. He was proud enough and sensible enough to keep silent. What Jones had made the public see was himself, the oldest surgeon in the district, striving to make a good service and help the Regional Authority but being baulked by the selfishness of the younger one who did all the private work, Mr James Baxter. The public did not know, Jim thought grimly, that the older man's campaign was to humiliate and defeat by stealth someone who in the past had defeated him by open competition. David Jones had made this perfectly plain to Jim—but privately.

Hospital staff knew, of course. Garretts loved to tell Jim: "Jones is out to rub your nose in the dust"—with relish.

No successor to Jones was appointed. Instead a locum was offered, and this was filled by an Indian surgeon. He was a stoutish and round-faced Bengali, who worked well and conscientiously for the year of his time at the Royal. He was a slow and rather ponderous operator. Berrill regarded him with disfavour, but was glad of his help when he wanted to get away to play squash. Jim and Anne befriended him, invited him to their home, and helped him as well as they could. He was a single man and as lonely as locums so often are. The year that went by was the busiest of Jim's since he had arrived. He saw as many new referrals as the other two put together.

Berrill's attitude saddened Jim. Jim respected and liked Allan because he saw his ability and conscientiousness, and tried his best to show friendship towards him. Berrill had an interest in prostate and bladder operations—urology—and Jim referred him cases. He helped to canvass support for his membership of the local golf club. He asked after his young family, and their progress at school. Never at any time did Berrill ask after Jim and Anne's family.

Jim often thought wryly how chance had decreed that he was not present at the interview when Berrill was appointed. It had been the change of date by the Health Authority and the family holiday they couldn't change. Jones had gone, of course. But another strong candidate that day had been a local senior registrar whom Jim knew well—a cheerful, friendly younger man—they both liked each other from their first meeting. Edward Jack had been senior registrar in the unit where the tragic Peter Millard once was. How different life would have been had Edward Jack been appointed to the Dale that day! Jack had got a good job in Leeds soon after. He and Jim continued to keep in touch.

As Spiers had foretold, the surgical service at the Dale was now to be closed. Jim wondered whether this would have come about if Jones had remained alive. It could have been that, just as the amalgamation of the medical services followed at once after George Bell's sudden death, the removal of Jones from the scene had been the signal for the major change on the surgical side of the hospital. But what, Anne asked Jim once, did he think would have happened had David Jones been alive and been faced with closure? Jim put the query to Maurice Garretts. "It would have killed him even earlier," he answered charitably.

The use of medical beds for surgical patients had been the plan of the hour. And then, within a month of Jones' death, and after the locum had been appointed, it was suddenly announced that the Region had made money available to upgrade the maternity and gynaecology department on the Royal Reid site. As a result of the rebuild, gynaecology would go into the new building. So the gynaecology wards in the main hospital would become available for another use, and this would be for surgical patients. Of course! This was why there was a locum surgeon.

Jim by now was no longer surprised at anything. The notion of using medical wards for surgical, and forcing the physicians to use other medical accommodation at the Dale, had always seemed nonsense to him, just as the very first surgical arrangement of Dr Hubbard had seemed nonsense four years earlier. And now, so soon after Jones' death, the new build made possible a much more sensible arrangement. The Area Headquarters proclaimed the building of the new maternity as a great advance, with press releases to all the newspapers. The fact that a pair of medical wards designated for surgical use were now being returned to medical use was headlined as another great victory. "Perhaps they were right," said Anne to Jim. "Perhaps they really *did* get money for the new maternity and gynaecology out of the blue. You've got to agree that the old gynae. wards are much better than the medical ones would have been— for a start, they're far nearer your own surgical wards!" Jim did agree. However it had come about, the new plan was much better.

The new build in the maternity block went on with remarkable speed. What had to be set in place immediately was the reorganisation of the theatre block to accommodate three more lists a week while there were still gynaecology patients requiring operation. A solution was to convert the outpatient theatre for general use, and this was soon done, since Charles Collinson and Jim had insisted on its being kept in good order in the pre- amalgamation days.

The three theatres inevitably became busier, with three general surgeons working, and two gynaecology lists. Berrill spent more of his time at the Dale so Jim saw less of him. He and Pollock, the pathologist, were becoming friendly and Allan was teaching Charles Pollock to play squash. Jim and Charles were also friendly colleagues; Jim enjoyed his help, especially with private work, but used him more than the others if he wanted to discuss a difficult case. Although Pollock spent more time at the Dale than at the Royal, he always seemed to Jim to be someone prepared to see both sides of the problems which worried them all. Jim respected his opinion more and more as the years passed, and felt that his regard was returned.

The build was complete. As the Dale theatres were now to be closed, the theatre staff moved from the Dale to the Reid. Sister Pope and her juniors, Sisters Oliver and Purland, were at the Reid. Sister Pope was designated "Nursing Officer in Charge." But Sister Pickering and her team of Samira, Ferrie and Turner outnumbered the home side, and it was not very long before Sister Pickering began to make it all too plain that she intended to take over charge of the theatre nursing just as the late Mr D.G. Jones had it plain that he intended to take over charge of the surgical unit. Sister Purland left very soon after Jones' death. Both he and Berrill had taken a dislike to her, claiming that she was slow and inefficient—"totally useless" was Berrill's expression, which he habitually used to describe anyone he did not value highly. They had repeatedly gone to the senior nursing staff to complain about her inability to give them promptly the instruments they wanted, or the needles and sutures, and in theatre made sneering remarks at her expense. In spite of Sister Pope's efforts of support, Sister Purland became so miserable that just before Jones had his coronary, she put in her resignation. Even when he died, she did not withdraw it; she knew the sharpness of Berrill's tongue. She had had enough.

So Sister Pope found herself in charge of a whole new nursing team who took their lead from the strong Yorkshire personality of Sister Pickering. Sister Pickering, like Jones, ran her campaign well. Civil to Sister Pope to her face, she began to drop hints that the older woman was not really up to her job—past her best—perhaps all right for the former surgical service at the small Royal Reid Hospital, but just too limited in training and attitude to take on new responsibility. Sister Pope like Jim was not intimidated, though like him she was progressively more unhappy. She responded by keeping her dignity, doing her work as carefully as she had always done, and refusing to be cornered by the others. They were not all unpleasant. Sister Samira was friendly and nice. The other two—almost like a music hall double act, Jim used to laugh to himself—they were as he expected them to be. They were good at their jobs—there was no doubt of that— and they did not become any more friendly. They were entirely in Sister Pickering's power. Mr Ali, the locum, had a shrewd quiet sense of humour.

"If Sister Pickering says jump to them," he said to Jim, "they all jump. She can make them play any tune she wants. If she wants them to be nice, I think she tells them. If she wants them to be not nice, I think she tells them."

During this year Jim thought he would try to develop his interest in gastro-intestinal surgery, the surgery of the upper bowel and gall-bladder. He had seen for some years now the trend in the Teaching Hospital towards special interests. There were already surgeons specialising in orthopaedic surgery, neurosurgery, and cardiac surgery, and local patients were beginning to ask about the "specialist operation" for more and more surgical conditions. Berrill was keen to learn new operations for his interest in "old men's trouble"— urology, and Jim encouraged him to go ahead.

"If we don't make new techniques available here we'll just lose patients," he told Allan. "They'll just go to the specialists in the Teaching Hospital."

For while all the surgeons in the Royal and the Avondale did a bit of everything, this was no longer acceptable if they did not use modern methods. Increased specialism was coming along in all fields. The physicians had already accepted specialist clinics for outpatients—in neurology, rheumatic diseases, and blood diseases. These were done not by locals, but by specialists from the centre. The children's department had the same changes going on. On one of the now infrequent chats Andrew Morton had with Jim, he confided: "I'm old-fashioned now. I'm what they call a general physician. I don't specialise in anything."

Andrew was becoming less confident, Jim noticed. He was the best physician locally and blood diseases remained his special interest—there was no need for a smart youngster to come from the centre to advise on those. But now that Dr Scott's chest beds had been closed and he was working only at the chest hospital and in the community—making extra medical beds empty in addition to the gynaecology ones—Andrew seemed more solitary and more vulnerable; he too had a pair of active ambitious younger colleagues regularly out-voting him in decision making. Jim decided he would not go out of date—*he* would learn the new ways of diagnosing disease of the stomach, duodenum, and gall-bladder. The duodenal ulcer era was over—new drugs cured ulcers nowadays, and the hundreds of ulcer operations Mr Armsworth used to do and was so good at were a treatment of the past. But operations for gallstones and their complications were now the commonest operations in

England, and instead of using X-rays to show up the inside of the intestine, telescopes were now used. It was said that instead of doing a difficult cutting operation for gallstones, it was going to be possible to pull the stones out by a basket passed along a flexible telescope. The telescope was called an endoscope and could be passed through a patient's mouth. It was also going to be possible to snare out disease from a patient's lower bowel by way of a flexible telescope passed from the other end.

Jim was pleased that no difficulties were put in his way when he asked for money to buy one of the new flexible endoscopes. And when Allan Berrill wanted to learn to use the telescope too, Jim put no difficulties in his way either. Although another branch of surgery was becoming Allan's interest, experience had taught Jim that it was easier just to give in to Allan's requests than to express any query whatever. He did not worry, for he still had the bulk of the hospital referrals as well as all the private practice. He encouraged Allan to go to London to learn how to use endoscopes for his bladder and prostate work. Alan was ten years younger; by the time he was Jim's age, all operations on that part of the body could well be done through a telescope.

The year passed. The divisional system launched with such confidence only a few years before was no longer used regularly,—lip-service was paid to it, but the various interests—general, eye surgery, ear nose and throat surgery, orthopaedic surgery, and all the medical specialties, went their own way to the District Medical Officer's desk with their bids for money for new equipment. The Salmon nursing system too failed to live up to its promises, and the system of numbers for more senior nurses was replaced by names. But the District Nursing Officer continued to function from her desk at District Headquarters. Sometimes she appeared on the wards. The Community Health Councils became too political to be as useful as they might have been; relations between them and the health professionals became needlessly strained.

The appointment of Jones' successor was set in train. The advert appeared in the *British Medical Journal* and the *Lancet*, for a post of "consultant surgeon in general surgery at the Royal Reid Hospital, Burshire, England. The successful applicant, etc." At this time there was slightly less pressure for consultant posts than there had been ten years before. Because the hospital was known to be a good one, with the now confirmed prospect of new District General Hospital on the site within the next five years (or so the advertisement rashly stated), there was a good field of applicants. The short list of three was drawn up by Jim and Allan. Jim noticed with interest that two of the candidates had graduated the same year he had been appointed a consultant.

They had to travel the twenty-five odd miles to the Regional Health Authority Headquarters where interviews for consultants took place. Jim drove, taking Allan for lunch to one of the local good hotels, and talking civilly. He had not been able to overcome the younger man's hostility and admitted to himself that he was perhaps not trying too hard now. But they looked forward to a new colleague coming to make up their firm, and both hoped for someone good.

The interviews followed the usual lines. The Health

Authority member, the chairman, was a retired lady solicitor. She was pleasant and put everybody at their ease. There were Jim and Allan Berrill. There were two consultants from the Teaching Hospital. There was Dr Spiers. And there was a representative from the Health Authority Officers as they were always called nowadays— an administrative doctor, with a neat millboard under his arm. It reminded Jim of D.G. Jones' A4 size block note board with "Mr David G. Jones FRCS, Consultant Surgeon, Royal Reid Hospital" on it in big block capitals. But that was now well past, and how much easier life had been. Attacks—not just on Jim but on his nursing staff— were a thing of the past. The atmosphere had changed for the better over the year, he reflected.

At this interview there were no axes to grind. Jim and Allan Berrill were on the same side. Berrill was undoubtedly a very intelligent man, with a good presence and strong personality. His advice was good. He worked hard for his own patients on the firm. Jim was the same. When they worked together—and how Jim wished and wished they could do so more happily—they were a good combination. The usual questions were asked. "What special interests do you have?" "What research have you done?" "I see you did a spell at so-and-so...." "Why do you want to come here?" "What do you think you could contribute?" "Have you been around the hospital?" "Do you know about the new building?" "What interests do you have outside medicine?"

The administrative officer said his usual piece. The chairman asked each of the three candidates if he had any questions to ask them, reminded him that this was only an advisory committee, that any decision would have to ratified by the Regional Authority, and ended by saying that there would probably be a decision made after the meeting, if they cared to wait.

Jim rather liked the dark-haired quiet candidate from Glasgow, who offered an interest in gastro-enterology—the same interest as his own. The second candidate did not interview well. The brightest was the third—a slim young man with dark hair and unusually sharp grey-blue eyes to go with it. His interest was vascular surgery, which was just what was needed at Reidham. But although this decided his appointment, he had a good all-round training so that he could safely cover the emergency roster. For he was already a senior lecturer in surgery in London, and everyone knew that these people were often over-specialised—very much into their firm's branch of surgery, but not widely enough experienced to be safe in a District General Hospital where a wider range of diseases had to be tackled.

As well as having a skill which the new trend in specialism required, he had been at the same Medical School as Allan Berrill. But unlike Berrill, he was from the north of England. This was his reason for wanting to move away from his present job, he said, almost too eagerly. Berrill liked him but showed no particular enthusiasm. He was appointed on a majority vote; Jim supported him because he seemed the best candidate and because he thought he would suit Alan. He had graduated the same year as Jim was appointed.

And so Mr David Burdon, M.S., F.R.C.S., was appointed consultant surgeon to the Royal Reid Hospital, the successor to the late Mr D.G. Jones. Because he was succeeding Mr Jones, he was to have two out-patient sessions at the Avondale Hospital.

Jim ran Allan back in his car.

"He seems a nice man. Do you remember him as a student?"

"No. He was three years behind my year and he wouldn't have been on the wards in my time."

"Although he was on the vascular unit his main research interest seems to have been on wound healing."

"It would have to be, on that unit, wouldn't it?" said Berrill.

"I wonder why he wants to come up here," he went on. "The prof there is due to retire soon and he may want to get out. He won't have any future. *That's* probably the reason he really wants to come to this place." So often Allan let slip his contempt for the provincial hospitals. Anne was quite right, Jim thought, in her diagnosis that Allan Berrill was a disappointed man. His bitterness came through every now and then.

The year was 1979 and there was a change of government. Mr James Callaghan's government had been replaced by one led by Mrs Margaret Thatcher, the first woman Prime Minister England had had. Her clear aim was to reverse much of the rolling socialist legislation successive governments had accepted, and cause everyone to learn to stand on their feet and make their own way by their own efforts. Doctors waited to see how the new policies would affect them and the Health Service.

The usual three months went by while the new appointee worked his notice at his London Teaching Hospital. During this time, two events occurred to cheer Jim up. Dr Spiers retired and his replacement was a man whom Jim had known at medical school, a pleasant and quiet Dr Simon

155

Durrant. Dr Durrant had been two years ahead as a student, done his National Service and had emigrated to Canada, to do Public Health work. He had then gone to Africa, where he had worked in a mission hospital in Rhodesia. The events of recent years there had made him decide to come back home, and after doing odd jobs in the new community health set- up, he had applied for and got the District Medical Officer's vacant post. While the District Administrator remained the boss, in this district the medical officer handled the medical staff problems. So Jim was glad to see him; the isolation of the past unhappy five years could be over. Simon Durrant could be a new start; he had no sides to take and was not tainted with the goods and bads of either hospital. Spiers was glad to be leaving. In spite of all his change of tune when the 1974 reorganisation came along, he was always a man of personality and authority. But his initial enthusiasm for the job had gone, as he found himself just one of the community medicine specialists sitting at the feet of Dr Hubbard, several years his junior, and having to be at his beck and call to carry out policy of the Health Authority.

The other happy event in the Baxter family was the marriage of their son. He was now doing a general practice rotation, and his wife was a nice girl he had met as a student. She had done an Arts degree, but had not gone on to anything further. Her parents were friendly and kind, and altogether Jane and her family were just the sort of new relatives you would hope for. Mrs Bell, Mrs Sugden, and Mr and Mrs Collinson—and the Mortons—were there, as well as family friends. Anne's family came and everyone was pleased at how well her brother David was keeping.

Mr Ali left a week before Mr David Burdon arrived. Anne and Jim invited him to their home just before he left and they had a pleasant evening. He was going home to India, he said, to see his mother. Mr Ali was the first locum consultant Jim had known since coming to the Reid. He had formerly shared with Mr Collinson. But this had had to change now there were three of them and not two pairs. For the past year since Jones' death, he had been a kindly and quiet colleague, very much the Indian gentleman. always polite and formal. He was not a fast operator, and not a quick- thinking diagnostician. But he had served them all well. Jim occasionally wondered if Allan Berrill had ever invited Tarit Ali to his house.

"You have been very kind to me, Mr Baxter," he said. "May I please use your name when I come back and am looking for other assignments in Great Britain?"

"Of course. I'll be glad to help you if I can."

He left, leaving a replica Taj Mahal for Jim and a carved soap dish for Anne. He looked genuinely sad at leaving.

David Burdon looked taller when he arrived then he had looked when he was interviewed. He had also a rather sharp expression in his eyes which had somehow not been evident before. He smiled to everyone when arrived, said how pleased he was to have got a job in this wonderful hospital, and settled in easily and without fuss. His wife was called Jenny and was a teacher. They had a girl and a boy the same ages as the Baxters' had been when they arrived. They had bought their house in a new housing development, nearer the Dale than the Royal Reid.

Everyone looked forwards to the troubles of the past— which of course everyone knew about—being forgotten.

Anne offered Jenny help—advice on shops, where to get hold of all the succession of small things you always needed when you moved to a new house. Jim took David to the golf club—for he professed to be a golfer—and introduced him all round. Soon they invited the Burdons along to a dinner party, including two pairs of friends they knew to be cheerful and welcoming, and whom they knew would introduce them farther on. They were very pleasant and friendly, and David seemed sincerity itself.

"What do think of them?" asked Jim when the guests had left.

"He seems nice," said Anne. "Oh, Jim, I hope he gets on well and we can be friends."

"So do I." The recollections of the troubles of those past years did not need to be said out loud.

The Baxters still remembered the friendly welcome they had had—Jim from Mr Rollands, both from the Collinsons, Sheridens, Sugdens, and especially the Bells—even Mr Scott the Group Secretary had invited them along and made them welcome in his home. All invitations were returned soon, and friendships continued from the contributions of both sides. This had stopped with the arrival of the Dale staff; it was now more years than they cared to recall since they had invited the Berrills to their home.

Six weeks passed. David Burdon was proving a very hard-working addition to the surgical unit—particular at his out-patient clinics, doing long lists, eager to please all round.

One morning early Sister Billings said to Jim in the conspiratorial tone she employed if she had a significant piece of information to impart:

"Do you know, Mr Baxter, that new Mr Burdon's secretary has given in her notice?"

"No, I didn't. But she just started here a couple of months ago. What's happened? Has she another job?"

"She had some sort of argument with him a week ago and had another one yesterday. She went to the office and resigned."

"That's sad. What on earth happened?"

"He was too critical of her work, she said. It was Miss Thompson who told me."

Miss Thompson was the "Surgical Nursing Officer" to the surgical unit. She had come from the Dale, was sharp but efficient, and was a great confidant of Mr Allan Berrill's secretary Marjorie who had also come from the Dale. Berrill's and Burdon's secretaries shared the same office. Jim's—Paula— was on her own. So this was why he had heard nothing about it. He wasn't altogether surprised. The secretaries were very thick. But it was obviously a news flash. Sister Billings was not normally a close friend of Miss Thompson.

Jim told Anne at lunch time. He had confirmed the news by then from Paula.

"Do you know? This new man Burdon's secretary's resigned last night. Sister Billings told me first thing today."

"Imagine her resigning. Sister Billings was full of it this morning. Paula told me it's true. She says the girl was in tears."

"Don't say he's... he seems a pleasant man. Perhaps it was her."

"It was because he was too critical of her work, Paula said."

"Well, she got on all right with Tarit Ali. But Tarit wouldn't say boo to a goose. Perhaps he let her get away with work that David Burdon didn't."

"I don't know. But it's created a real stir amongst the secretaries."

"I bet it has. There's never been a resignation like that since you've been here."

"No. We had one woman leave because she said the work was too hard. She'd come from admin to do a clinical secretarial job."

The Baxters invited the Burdons once again to a dinner party. This time they invited another two couples whom they knew were friendly and helpful. This time Jenny Burdon spoke about the difficulties she was having trying to get their new garden started, and Anne offered her some cuttings and plants. Jim did the same over the next couple of weeks. The offer was ignored. Then he gave up. Their real efforts to befriend and help their new colleague were not reciprocated. No invitation to visit the Burdons arrived.

By now the surgical firm was arranged along the same lines as it had been at the beginning of the decade, except that there were now six surgical wards and not four. The extra beds had been the former gynaecology ones. The new gynaecology wards were part of the new maternity block, the first part of the new District General Hospital to be completed. The old ones re-opened just at the time David Burdon arrived, so he moved into nice newly painted and done-up wards. It was good administrative timing. But while Jim and Allan were in the original surgical block, David was some distance away. So he was by geography on his own. But his bed numbers, his outpatient sessions, his operating time, were the same as those of his senior colleagues.

Because of the way their week was arranged, one doing his outpatients while a second was in theatre while the third was away at an outside clinic, they tended to see less of one another than if they had shared wards.

By now too all the surgical beds at the Dale had been closed. There was no need for them. The medical beds were also greatly reduced—a few were left, but the majority were geriatric. This meant that the medical consultants were all at the Reid—ex-Dale staff who had made the move not by appointment but by transfer. Andrew Morton felt he was the remaining true Royal Reid appointee. Jim was the remaining opposite number in surgery.

The medical consultants maintained their outpatients at the Dale as well as at the Royal. Sadly they retained also their Dale attitude to the older hospital. This was especially true of William Dick, who had looked after David Jones in his final illness. He had come to the Dale with a great reputation as a senior registrar in his Teaching Hospital, but in the eight years he had worked locally he had not enhanced his reputation. He was as average consultant, lacking any sparkle. He had in fact a certain grimness about him, and his eyes were blue and hard. He retained his antipathy to the Royal staff, and constantly criticised Jim and Andrew Morton, though he had never had anything to do with Jim, and Andrew, much his senior, was a much better physician.

His younger colleague was everything he was not— cheerful, witty, and flamboyant. He had been a first-class sportsman as a student, and as a young doctor had enjoyed nothing more than an evening with the lads over a pint of beer and a piano. Now he was a consultant he had taken to wearing formal suits and silk ties. Had he been on the staff of a London Teaching Hospital he would surely have worn a flower in his button-hole. Patrick Joseph Healy too had been at the Dale. But his shoulder was unmarked. His initial antagonism, present when Dr Bell was alive, had gone.

Jim felt better now, in spite of the fact that he had held out the hand of friendship to David Burdon and been spurned. His work continued at a high level, and his private consultations never went down in number. All seemed set fair, and though he still had trouble getting a smile out of Berrill, their relations had improved. He was genuinely keen to get on with colleagues, but his four years in the wilderness had taken their toll. He felt out of things and shunned hospital activities which he had enjoyed in his earlier years. He had done ten years as surgical tutor now, and though this would come to an end soon—he had been lucky his time had been extended—he had never ceased to enjoy this part of his life.

As usual, medical politics had played a part in the 1979 General Election. At the Annual Representative Meeting of the British Medical Association in June Sir James Cameron, who had been one of the most statesmanlike leaders of the medical profession in the recent past—he had been largely responsible for the general practitioners' charter of the 1960's—made a powerful speech.

"The great question mark of our age," he said, "is what is to be done with the ailing giant of the National Health Service? It absorbs billions of pounds annually and yet inspires little confidence in those who best know its intimate workings. We have had a spate of reports in recent years telling us what is wrong with the N.H.S. but little has been done to tackle its fundamental problems. It suffers from chronic underfinancing; it suffers from an overblown administration; and it suffers from all the ills that flow from bad personnel management, and, in particular, poor industrial relations.

"Most people including trade unionists," he went on, "were sick of seeing the N.H.S. treated like the factory floor. The end point of the N.H.S. was not a piece of coal or a motor car: it was a patient and often a sick and anxious patient." The Conservatives had promised to end the anarchy of the recent "winter of discontent"—"we want to see whether performance matches promises."

"There are those," he concluded, "who believe that in some magical way a change of administration will miraculously put right all that is wrong in the N.H.S. I do not believe that the Secretary of State or Minister of State will take such a blindly optimistic view."

CHAPTER 11

The Thatcher government set about its policies with a will. Management was the flavour of the day, and competition was to be introduced into parts of society where state provision had been unchallenged, including the National Health Service. The consultant contract, already modified to give previous part-timers a tenth session above their previous nine, was now going to be modified further to allow all consultants to undertake private practice. The immediate result of this was Jim was no longer the only surgeon legally allowed to do it in the district; the others could too now, even though they were on a whole-time contract. But they were not allowed to earn more than one-tenth of their gross salary from private practice. If they did, they would find themselves in trouble with the Inland Revenue—the Income Tax authorities.

Within the unit, the administrative responsibility was now to be rotated. Dr Hubbard himself came from Board Headquarters to confirm the arrangements. Mr Baxter was to be surgeon-in-charge for three years, followed by Mr Berrill and he in turn by Mr Burdon. But since the three of them had virtually independent units, each had a degree of independence they would not have had if they were all sharing. Jim at once suggested they each pick their own house surgeon at the yearly appointments; he still remembered with anger the arrogance of Jones when he insisted that he alone was to choose and allocate them. And as far as the hospital casualty was concerned, they would share the organization of this as it became their turn to be in administrative charge. They would each have their own waiting list and run it themselves. They would share the nurse teaching and the student teaching. Jim was determined not to be seen as doing anything other than being fair and sharing responsibilities and workload.

More and more he turned in on himself and stayed in his own wards. Sister Billings was now a staunch ally of fourteen years' standing and had changed from being slightly aloof to becoming a loyal friend. She had maintained, too, the fairness which she had shown from the very first moment the Dale surgeons arrived. She kept her place with marvellous patience towards the new theatre gang. Jim did not look forward to the day when she would have to retire. She began to worry Jim with pieces of information he knew were trustworthy and therefore distinctly disturbing.

"That Mr Burdon is a very rude man, Mr Baxter."

"Oh," said Jim, genuinely surprised. "How's he rude?"

"He was very rude to me."

"What about?"

"Well, you know we always take in patients even though they're somebody else's patient before?"

Of course Jim knew this. He had tried to keep the system of the Teaching Hospital, where "return patients" who had just been discharged from a hospital unit and were returned soon as emergencies, went back to their original ward and not the emergency ward of the day. This meant the staff knew them and they knew the staff, and there was no delay in their further treatment, but Jones and Berrill had refused to agree when they arrived on the scene, and Jim was overruled.

"Yes."

"One of his came in here and he came in to see her. He was very rude to me."

"What about?"

"He said the nursing was no good. He shouted, Mr Baxter. I've reported him to the office." This had all happened the previous evening.

"Was the patient transferred? What was wrong?" Jim asked.

"She was in his ward with bleeding piles. She was sent home. She bled again, and was sent back in."

"Was she bad?"

"No, she wasn't."

It didn't sound so desperately bad.

A week later, over their cup of tea in her office, Sister Billings complained again. Jim did nothing, hoping the storm would blow over. It seemed to. He still hoped that a better era had arrived, but this episode was disturbing.

There was no doubt that David Burdon's appointment had strengthened the surgical service in the district. Best of all was that he could undertake surgery for diseases of the arteries, and for the most serious complications such as rupture of an aortic aneurysm, which both Jim and Alan were untrained in. They had had to refer all their serious vascular disease away; now they did not have to. Mr Burdon was beginning however to work the wards more harshly than anyone had done in the past. He brought patients in at the shortest notice, and sent them out sooner than Jim thought was safe. But whereas both Baxter and Berrill limited what they did, Burdon seemed unable to recognise that he should not. He kept trying his hand at anything. One evening he and Berrill had a furious argument about a bladder case which Berrill thought Burdon should have referred to him. Jim told Anne about it:

"Allan and David had a terrible set-to this evening."

"Did you hear them?" asked Anne.

"No, Sister Pickering told me about it. She said David had shouted at her as well as at Allan Berrill."

"Well, at least *you've* never had anything like that. Even with D.G.," laughed Anne.

"No, that's true. But I hope they don't fall out. I'm never sure how well they get on. Berrill's been critical of David Burdon once or twice in the past few days."

"According to you he's critical about everybody."

"I've never heard him critical about David Burdon before. They were at the same medical school. They never seem to me to be very close. But then I don't know either of them well enough to tell."

"In fact," said Anne, "now you mention it, Allan Berrill's never saying anything about David Burdon suggests to me that they probably get on well. Allan Berrill criticises everyone as a rule, doesn't he?"

(A few weeks before, a new gynaecologist had been appointed. It turned out that he had been in Allan's year at university.

"What's he like?" asked Jim.

"One of the stupidest and one of the most unpleasant members of the year," replied Allan.)

"He certainly criticises me."

"You're just paranoid."

"Whatever, I hope to goodness we don't start getting the sort of trouble we had before."

Anne spoke seriously. "So do I, love. We've had this too often."

Came the end of 1980 and the first year of the new Thatcher policies. One of the early changes had been the new 10-session contract for hospital consultants, agreed by the Central Committee for Hospital Medical Services of the B.M.A. with Mr Patrick Jenkins, the Secretary of State for Social Services the previous summer. A year on, it had proved popular. Jim was on the 10, the others on the full-time 11 session contract, but allowed to do private work. Berrill had done some private work over the year, but Burdon almost none. Jim carried on as before. But he was now beginning to notice that his hospital referrals were going down, just as Mr Armsworth had told him would happen those years ago.

Things did seem to be settling. There had been a good deal of annoyance about a thing called the Resource Allocation Working Party Formula in the largest cities, where the older and more famous hospitals, especially in the capital, had found themselves having their funding reduced to give more to their less well- endowed neighbours. But this did not affect the Reid or the Avondale; they were not in that sort of bracket of affluence. In fact, planning was at last actively proceeding for the new hospital, with buying of ground, mock-ups, committees of consultation, and all on the Reid site. The war was over; most of the old combatants were dead.

There was one excitement, and it was a major one, at the end of 1980.

"Mr Baxter," said Paula when Jim came to do his outpatient letters, "Mr Berrill's up for a job in London!"

This was a total surprise.

"When did you hear?"

"Just this morning."

"Go on. Who told you? How did you find out?"

"Nancy happened to see a note on Marjorie's desk."

Nancy was David Burdon's new secretary. She was his third since he arrived. Marjorie was Berrill's—older than the others, who had come with him from the Dale. Normally a sharp, very secretive woman. It must have been a major lapse on her part.

"Well, he's certainly kept it quiet. But then he would." Paula knew enough, though not everything, about relations between the surgeons, and about what went on. Jim and she had very welcome trust between them. So he could make a remark like that.

Paula smiled. "If you were applying for a job, you wouldn't tell Mr Berrill. I don't know where it is, but it's in the North-West Thames Board Region."

"He must think he's got a good chance. He's been here too long, though, I think. He's too old."

"All the letter said," said Paula, "was an acknowledgement of his application."

Jim could hardly wait to tell Anne. As soon as he got through the door, he called to her:

"Allan Berrill's applied for a job in London!"

Jim talked excitedly. It might mean he would be leaving. He would be happier in a Teaching Hospital. They might at last get someone they could enjoy working with. Perhaps Edward Jack...

Anne brought him down to earth:

"We don't even know it's a Teaching Hospital, remember. He seemed to have blotted his copybook in the Teaching Hospital he came from. With an academic record like his, why didn't they want to keep him?"

"I suppose that's right. It can't be one of the main Teaching Hospitals. It must be a non-teaching one. North-West Thames covers a big area."

"But he's always hinted..."

"Yes. He's often as good as said he reckons he's too good for this place. The thing is, he's not too good for this place."

"Well," said Anne, "*you* certainly won't hear anything from Allan Berrill. I wonder who he might have told, though."

There were two people Allan could have confided in. One was Dr Dick. But Jim would get nowhere if he spoke to William Dick. The other was Charles Pollock, the pathologist. He was friendly with Berrill, and Jim knew him well enough to make a discreet enquiry—he was a better bet.

He saw Charles often enough in his department. He restrained his impatience for a couple of days, then looked in to ask about a specimen. There was Charles Pollock, smoking his pipe. It was interesting, thought Jim, how many pathologists smoked pipes, even these non-smoking days. It must be a left-over from the days when they all smoked over the post-mortems. Post-mortems too weren't so commonly done nowadays either.

"Good morning, Jim. Have a seat." He was as pleasant as ever.

"Just give me a moment to finish looking at this slide. How are you?"

"Fine. I wanted to ask you about Mrs Stevens' bowel carcinoma. You said it was very active. How active was it really? I've to see her relatives this afternoon."

Pollock got one of the technicians to fetch the slides and they looked at the microscope sections together. Jim respected and liked Charles Pollock more and more. He was very helpful and gave the best opinion locally. Perhaps because of the microscopic work he had done for his Master of Surgery Degree Jim had never lost his interest, and Pollock obviously appreciated this. They discussed the outlook for the patient.

"Allan Berrill was saying the other day he had had an interesting case where you'd diagnosed a simple tumour when everyone thought it was a malignant one."

"Yes. It was a bit of a rarity."

"Allan seems settled here now. He's pleased to have his own wards. I think he's settled, anyway."

Charles Pollock was older, about the same age as Jim. So Jim found him easy to talk to about the younger staff.

He looked a little sharply at Jim.

"I'm not sure that he is as settled as you might think."

The tone of voice, and the words, made an impression on Jim. There was a hint of antagonism—just a hint, in the tone. The words told Jim that Charles Pollock knew about Berrill's bid to leave for another job.

A couple of weeks later, Allan was waiting outside theatre when Jim came out between cases. This usually meant he wanted something, just as when Jim looked in on him, it meant *he* wanted something.

"Oh, Jim, you're not away at the end of the month, are you?"

"No."

"There's a urology thing I'd very much like to go to. It's at the Institute in Shaftesbury Avenue."

"Yes, Allan. What's it on?"

"It's a special seminar on prostate cancer. It's about these new anti-androgen drugs."

Jim always agreed if either of the others asked about leave. He had been happy to let them take the summer months when the school holidays were on, remembering back to the days when Mr Armsworth used to say: "I can go any time, Baxter, but you've the children's holidays to consider." This didn't stop him taking Easter, but he had always been good about his registrars' summer holidays. Now he was the one whose family was grown up.

"You can take it as study leave, Allan. Put in a slip, and I'll send it in to the office." But he thought it a little surprising that this seminar seemed to have come up at such short notice.

"Thank, you. I'll do that."

Jim and Anne had scanned the *British Medical Journal* for the previous weeks to see what the job Berrill was after might be. There had been in fact one in his Teaching Hospital, but with sessions in one of the associated hospitals, and it was only of 9 sessions in all. These jobs came along in London from time to time. The work was done in the subsidiary hospital and the carrot was the session or three in the big-name one. But there was another one in a district hospital—it could as easily have been that one.

The Department of Health and Social Security was rumoured to be contemplating a further review of N.H.S. structure and management. One weekend the Baxters went through to see their friends the Macgregors, and Ken quizzed them on the proposals which were in the press.

"This looks like reorganisation by stealth," said Ken, sucking his teeth as usual.

"It can't be as bad as 1974," replied Jim. "That one was tortuous and the amount of paper that flowed out of Whitehall was unbelievable."

"They're going to do away with Area Health Authorities and have 200 District Health Authorities. Don't they have that number already?"

"Well, I think it'll be quite good," said Jim. "It won't really affect us here, because we'll stay a district. But they are going to reduce the number of staff in the office. We'll only have a District Administrator, District medical and nurse, a new thing called a District Treasurer, and in the Reid we'll have what they call a unit administrator and a director of nursing. And there's to be a senior member of the medical staff to advise."

"How are you going to arrange the units?" asked Ken. "Are they by bricks and mortar, or based on their function?"

"I don't know," admitted Jim. "It hasn't really been finalised. Most of it's rumour."

"I must admit," said Ken, "I'm impressed with Mrs Thatcher. All that trouble we had with the International Monetary Fund's dented my faith in planned economy. And when the undertakers wouldn't bury the dead, well, it didn't exactly shine the trade union image."

Jim and Anne were amazed. For Ken, this was revolutionary stuff.

He talked as he always did, giving carefully thought-out opinions. He expressed the view that health care was getting so expensive that someday decisions would have to be taken about priorities. He considered that divisions of groupings of hospital staff giving consensus advice had been a failure, and he was distressed, he said, that the liberal hopes of the 1960's had resulted in so much socially undesirable behaviour. He was pleased that things seemed to be better after the troubles at the Reid and agreed with Anne's diagnosis about their colleague Berrill. A visit to Ken was always stimulating.

Allan Berrill came back from his seminar to London.
"Was it good?" asked Jim.
"Not bad, not bad," was all he said in reply.

Came the summer of 1981 and the new Reorganisation was all public. The administrators had got their feet firmly under the table and as usual the medicals were left behind. The ideal of a senior clinician to serve on the unit or district management team was spoiled by the realisation that the half day a week suggested was obviously too little. Who could spare that amount of time—more than a whole day a week?

But governments always have their way. The N.H.S. reorganisation was duly set up by 1st April 1982, just as they had said it would. Simon Durrant kept his post as District Medical Officer. It was more or less an automatic change, although another D.M.O. in the Region lost his job. Mr Scott had been gone for some time as District Administrator; his successor, a nonentity, had stayed for only a year, and the post had not been filled "pending reorganisation." Everyone was waiting to see who the new man would be.

Jim thought Mr Raymond Langton's face was familiar when he saw him. A short, thin-faced man, with round prominent eyes and a moustache, and a nervous manner, Jim remembered seeing him as a schoolboy who had just joined the clerical staff at the Teaching Hospital when he was a senior registrar. One of the other senior registrars used to refer to him as "an inky clerk." But in the years between Raymond Langton had gone up in the world. He still had the same eager-to-please, over-friendly way with him, but now sported a Rotary badge in his button-hole and wore a smarter suit. He would be the new man the consultants would have to deal with when they wanted money for their units, new apparatus, ward alterations, and all that sort of thing. But luckily, thought Jim, he was lower in the pecking order than Dr Durrant.

On went the life of the hospital. Nurses came and went. House doctors came and went. Registrars, usually from overseas, came and went. And senior staff grew older: Allan Berrill was noticeably getting bald, Pollock fatter, Garretts more stooped, Andrew Morton more withdrawn and silent. He was taken over by Dick and the ebullient Patrick Joseph Healy, and looked tired and unhappy.

Jim's hair had grown grey in the years of conflict.

But Sister Helen Billings never seemed to age. Her fair skin and hair perhaps needed a little more attention than formerly, but her face remained so youthful. By now she and Jim were fast friends.

"Mr Burdon's very quiet these days," she said at their afternoon tea session. "I saw his family the other day, with Mrs Burdon. They're fairly growing up. His daughter's very like him—she walks the same too."

"But he's not nice to the nurses. He's very critical, Mr Baxter. He's very jealous about his cases. He wants to be the surgeon who does the most work. He's a bit like Mr Jones used to be."

"Yes." Jim knew that David Burdon now saw as many cases as he did. He was very keen on sending for patients even though he hadn't beds for them—this upset the nursing staff, and the medical staff if he pinched a bed as he did sometimes—but this made him popular with practitioners. If there was one thing G.P.s liked, it was getting their patients in quickly.

"He gives a good service. There's no doubt his vascular work is good, and it's something we just didn't have here before."

"It's a pity Mr Berrill and he don't get on."

"Oh?" Jim was careful not to say anything which could be repeated, though he knew that nurses were not above quoting a doctor to improve their story if they felt like it. But he knew that Allan had now become jealous not only of him but of David also. At least they had their own wards and their own patients and could keep apart. When the new hospital came along, they might have to share. But that was still a long way off.

CHAPTER 12

Jim still went to see Charles Collinson from time to time. Charles liked to hear all the news—how Maurice Garretts had looked at his retirement presentation, how the food supplied to the theatre staff was (it had taken a sudden deterioration before Charles had retired himself, after the administration had decided to rationalise the catering services), how Sister Hoddie was recovering after her stroke, who the new anaesthetist replacing Garretts might be, and how Jim himself was doing in his endeavours to become an even better endoscopist. Charles had missed all these happenings recently because he had been away having his prostate removed, and had made rather a slow recovery. He had very sensibly gone far away for his operation, to have it done in Leeds by one of his old house surgeons now an acknowledged expert in the field. At last, he said, he felt he was making progress.

"How's Pollock getting on as the clinical tutor?" he asked.

"Well, I think," replied Jim, "but you would expect him to. He's an able man. The postgraduate centre made all the difference after it opened. We just had nowhere when I came first."

"I never felt like going to postgraduate meetings after I retired," said Charles. "You don't go all that often, do you, Jim?"

"No, I don't." It was some time since Jim had given up the local postgraduate clinical tutor's job. It was 1979 since his Royal College of Surgeons tutor's post had run its time also. Not long before David Burdon was appointed, in fact. Jim's successor was a younger consultant who worked in the Teaching Hospital. The ending of the College job had removed a large part of Jim's surgical political activity and responsibility, but though he had missed it at first, he no longer did so. Now he was 53 years old, and was full of his new interest. Quite expert with the gastroscope to diagnose and treat surgical disease of the stomach and duodenum, and to remove snips of tissue for examination under Charles Pollock's microscope, called biopsy, he wanted to move to the next step and extend his skill farther.

The next step was to look inside the bowel farther along, to where the bile duct from the gall-bladder came to join the duodenum. Gallstones often stuck here, and tumours of the pancreas nearby could block the duct as well. There was a tight circular muscle around the lowermost end of the bile duct, and surgeons were now trying to divide this sphincter, as it was called, to let impacted gall-stones fall through. Dye could be injected into the duct to show on an x-ray film all its branches and the branches of the pancreatic duct also.

"So you can actually *see* the lower end of the bile duct?" asked Charles.

"Yes. You can see it quite easily with practice. Once you can pass a tube into it, you can take X-ray pictures after you inject the dye along the tube into all the small ducts. This shows any gall stones. Once you cut the sphincter muscle, you can either let the stones fall out or you can pull them out."

"It sounds a big advance."

"It certainly is. It's called E.R.C.P.—short for endoscopic retrograde cholangio-pancreatography."

"Sounds a mouthful. Is it very difficult?"

"It's more difficult than ordinary gastroscopy. You have to have special apparatus."

"But you haven't got one of these yet, Jim?"

"No, I haven't. But Simon Durrant's the new D.M.O. and he's put in a bid for money for one."

"You do gastroscopy regularly now?"

"Yes. I do a session a week, as well as ones on the general lists." Jim had used his extra 10th session for an endoscopy clinic and the work had increased steadily over 1982. Berrill and Burdon both tried their hand at endoscopy as well as Jim, but he had the bulk of the direct referrals from the G.P.s. While Andrew Morton and especially Patrick Healy referred him patients from the medical wards, all Dick's went to Mr Berrill. Dick's Dale chip showed no sign of diminishing in size.

"Is it dangerous?" asked Charles.

"Yes, and it's potentially dangerous when you divide the muscle. You could do damage if you weren't trained."

"Or if you didn't do it regularly."

"Or if you didn't do it regularly. It's like everything else."

"Are you going to do a course, then, Jim?"

"Oh yes, I'll have to. There's a good one in Leeds. I'll get study leave to go on that."

What with one thing and another, it was 1983 before money became available to buy the instruments Jim wanted. He had a bit of luck in having an Indian registrar who had more experience of the technique than he had. He was a great help. Jim begged a spare 'scope from one of the more friendly departments in the Teaching Hospital, but this wasn't satisfactory. It was a half-day's journey to fetch and return it.

At long last the shining scope plus its accompanying wires and instruments arrived. Jim had done his course in Leeds; he was all ready to start.

A couple of cases went off successfully. The telescope was passed, the dye to show up the stones safely injected, the sphincter muscle divided, and out came the gallstones. Jim, his registrar, and Sister Billings, were delighted. Sister Pickering showed genuine interest. Sister Samira was congratulatory.

He had some trouble with the next one, however, and had to do a major operation to get the stones out. Full of gloom he reported the failure to Anne.

"Is the patient all right?" she asked after he had told her all about it.

"Yes. But she's had to have a much bigger operation, and she's not a good risk."

"You'll get better, love."

"Yes, I hope so. But this'll be all around the hospital." Jim had always been jealous of his reputation. And he knew full well that there were two pairs of unfriendly eyes watching him—five if you counted the Dale sisters less Samira.

But he persevered. One or two more cases came along. He was supported loyally by his registrar, who guided him through once when he was a little unsure about how far to cut, and his morale improved again.

Then one afternoon, and for no particular reason, Jim

went to theatre when Berrill was operating. It was a Wednesday, which Jim usually took as his afternoon off. He noticed an extra locker used in the changing room, and a pair of shiny black shoes outside it. He went out and looked into the theatre through the window.

There was a consultant from the Teaching Hospital, using an E.R.C.P. instrument, with Berrill looking on. Jim turned and left.

Back to Anne, he poured out the story.

"There's nothing you can do about it, love," she said. Then she added: "The others do *know* you're using the E.R.C.P. 'scope'? Did you tell them?"

"I did tell them. *And* they know I've been away on a course. Of course they know. Of course I told them."

"Well, Allan Berrill's a consultant. He can refer patients to whoever he likes."

"I know he can. But it's not very friendly."

"If you think Allan Berrill's going to be friendly to you, you've another thought coming."

It was a new hurt. Jim knew of Berrill's animosity in the past, but had told himself for some time now—since David Burdon arrived, in fact, that it had lessened and that at last they were getting on better.

He had a chat with Simon. They had struck up a good friendship, and Simon knew well how things were amongst the medical staff.

"I didn't know anything about this, Jim," Simon said. "But it looks as if they want to prevent you getting this technique off the ground here. You remember they were a bit glum when you got the money allocated."

"What do you think I should do?" asked Jim.

"I'll enquire at the Regional Headquarters if they made any formal approach," said Simon helpfully. "Did you know Dr Hubbard's leaving?"

"No!" said Jim. "That'll be a blessing. Where's he going?"

"He's going to be a Senior Medical Officer at the Ministry in London," replied Simon.

"Life's full of surprises," Anne agreed that evening.

Jim thought long and hard, discussed the latest problem with Charles Collinson, and decided to go to the Teaching Hospital and ask the surgeon there what was going on. He had appeared for three weeks running now, and Jim had had no more cases.

The Teaching Hospital man was younger than Jim. He had worked as S.R. in a unit specialising in just the sort of work he was now being invited to do at Reidham. As he was the newest appointee in this new field he was already collecting the private work in the centre, and it soon became evident that this was what he had his eye on at the periphery.

He was matter-of-fact, told Jim that Mr Berrill and Mr Burdon had seen the R.M.O. and told him they did not think the Royal Reid required an E.R.C.P. service, but asked that he be available to do cases for them as the need arose. He expressed surprise that Jim was trying to set up a local service.

"I'm afraid we are both in a difficult position, Mr Baxter," he said politely. "If I am asked to operate on a patient of Mr Berrill's when he says there is no local service available, I can hardly turn him down."

"No, I see that," replied Jim. "But *I've* got money for an instrument, *I've* taken the course in Leeds, and I know the

G.P.s—and the patients—are looking for a local service."

"That's what they're getting already," he answered.

"Do you advise me just to give up?"

"You'll have to do what you think best, Mr Baxter."

It had not been a helpful interview.

The impasse was put temporarily to one side by the admission of Mr Rollands, now aged 82. He had become ill with abdominal pain and his own doctor had asked Jim to admit him for investigation. Sadly, Jim found he had inoperable cancer, and nothing could be done for him. Hearing the diagnosis, Mr Rollands died quickly, telling Jim he would "pray for the end." Mr Charles Collinson, Mr Charles Wilson, and Maurice Garretts—now due to retire on his sixty-fifth birthday—talked with Jim at the funeral.

"He had a good innings," said Garretts.

"Yes, he had a long happy retiral," said Charles.

"I wish I'd known him better," said Mr Wilson. "I always liked him."

"Did you notice," said Garretts to Jim one day later on, "how his old theatre staff were all in tears? I told Allan Berrill that *he* wouldn't get that sort of affection." He laughed.

Once again, fortune seemed to be smiling on Mr James Baxter. Over the next year, his referrals for upper abdominal cases requiring his new apparatus surely and steadily increased. The G.P.s had tried their local man and had not found him wanting. Alan finally conceded the contest by referring cases. And one day Charles Pollock said to Jim, when he looked in to see him at the lab, "Allan Berrill told me that your E.R.C.P. cases are doing well—better than those he had treated by his expert friend. And for Allan Berrill, that's high praise." He smiled to Jim. Jim was pleased. Things *were* going along all right now, he thought.

The 1983 General Election took place and the Conservative Government was again returned. The "Falklands War Factor" was believed by many to have boosted their vote. The B.M.A. were as ever critical of the party in power, but then, Jim was by now old enough to realise, they were critical of whichever party was in power. "While Mrs Thatcher laid great emphasis on the National Health Service being safe in our hands," the B.M.J. declared, "she went nowhere in the three weeks of visiting places relevant to her policies." Following the Election, it was announced that Mr Roy Griffiths, the deputy chairman of Sainsbury's, was to investigate "value for money in the N.H.S.," and report by the autumn. Allan Berrill had taken over administrative responsibility from Jim Baxter in 1982, so was half way through his three year stint. But it was Jim who was approached by the senior lecturer on the professorial unit about the possibility of rotating a senior registrar to the Royal Reid from the Teaching Hospital.

This was exciting. It was something Jim had hoped for for years. He spoke to Allan about it. With a scowl Allan said:

"Why did he speak to *you?*"

"*I* don't know, Allan. But he did. The main thing is, they're offering us an S.R. It would be great if we had one on rotation."

It was true. Senior Registrars had been asked for several

times to cover summer holidays as locums, but had always been refused on the grounds that they could not be spared.

"Do they have someone in mind?" asked Allan.

"I don't know. But what do you think?"

"I'll ask David B." That was as much as Allan would say.

It soon became clear that David Burdon was even more antagonistic to the proposal than Allan Berrill. Jim was puzzled. He could understand their antagonism to *him* developing a specialty—even though they both pursued their own. "But why be against this, for God's sake?" he said to Garretts. "A senior registrar is a status symbol."

Garretts was just about to have his retiral presentation.

"Don't you understand? It's the old Dale chip again. Those two are fearful he'll be a rival."

"A *rival*? But he'll be a senior registrar. He won't be a consultant."

"Haven't you learned *anything* while you've been here? Jones' ghost still haunts, you know."

However, the Teaching Hospital and the Professor—a new one, that was perhaps the reason—were serious in their proposal. They wanted to rotate a senior registrar to the Royal Reid, as they'd rotated them to District General Hospitals elsewhere for some time. There was no doubt about their intentions.

A young man was produced, called Douglas Roy. He had the reputation of being a "flier." Jim found himself receiving telephone calls from the professor, while official letters went to Berrill. The other two kept trying to stall, raising every kind of difficulty. It was David Burdon who remained the more vociferous. The seniors in the centre wanted their trainee to do a list a half day a week, plus a small outpatient session where he could follow them up and see a few new patients. Berrill said to Jim that he had "grave reservations" but seemed to be giving in.

By ill-luck the senior registrar was unable to do the first list of four patients due to be brought in for him to operate on. At the last minute he had work he apparently could not leave, and at the Reid the anaesthetist had to be somewhere else.

Jim got a copy of Berrill's letter a couple of days later.

"Dear Professor,

Your senior registrar did not appear for an operating list yesterday which had been arranged for him. A great deal of upset was caused to the ward, the staff and the patients. This proves that the suggestion of a rotation of such a trainee to this hospital is unlikely to be useful. It is, in fact, likely to be totally useless, especially if this sort of cancellation is to happen repeatedly.

The suggestion that such a registrar have an outpatient session of his own is also unacceptable. We require our patients for the teaching of our own registrars, and they will not wish to see teaching material given to an individual with no loyalty to the surgical unit in this hospital.

We do not feel that the rotation of a senior registrar, therefore, should be proceeded with."

David Burdon completed the destruction of the proposal,

telling Jim: "We don't want an S.R. here. *I* certainly don't want anyone taking cases from me." Jim made it quite plain, on the telephone to his friend the senior lecturer at the Teaching Hospital, that the project was dead. "The other two just won't have any senior registrar. They say he will take cases from them."

"Well," said the senior lecturer, "he's very bright and very competent. He's an excellent surgeon. It's a pity."

It may have been no coincidence, as far as David Burdon was concerned, that Mr Roy had just completed a year on the Teaching Hospital vascular unit.

But Jim obtained a concession from his colleagues; they kindly agreed that Douglas Roy could do Jim's locum of two weeks while he and Anne were taking a winter holiday. But as far as the next summer month or six weeks one was concerned, they said, it would be an overseas man. All the nursing staff—Sister Billings and even the Pickering brigade—agreed at the end of Mr Roy's fortnight how good he was. "And a very quick operator," added the kindly Sister Samira.

1985 saw the Department of Health for Social Security implement the recommendations of the Griffiths enquiry they had received from Sainsbury's manager the previous year. The big new concept was "managers for the Health Service"—part of the overall Mrs Thatcher ethos of applying the principles of good business to the nationalised industries. Mr Norman Fowler, the Secretary of State, had insisted he was not creating "jobs for the boys" while implementing the Griffiths plans for general managers. The B.M.A. Central Committee for Hospital Medical Services—

their senior hospital staff committee—argued against giving enhanced powers to an individual general manager, saying the unit management teams were now working quite well. Any suggestion that the general manager would have line management responsibility for consultants they insisted was unacceptable.

Inevitably the profession's arguments were ignored. General managers were in post very soon at Regional and District level, and were to be at unit level by the end of the year. So the Royal Reid and Avondale, plus their nearby mental hospital, were to have a unit general manager.

The appearance of a non-medical general manager at Region followed the disappearance of the bad-tempered Dr Hubbard to London. His successor had been another ray of light for Jim. He was a community medicine specialist who had been in the university year behind, and who was well known and well-liked over many years. An evangelical Christian, he would, Jim thought, work well with Simon Durrant with his medical missionary background. Jim had for long liked and respected Dr Arthur Holliday, and the friendship had been returned. Dr Holliday was perhaps a surprise choice, as he had always been a quiet and charitable member of the community medicine department. He had a son married and living in Reidham. After the aggressive style of Dr Hubbard, his appointment was widely welcomed.

"It is the government's intention to introduce management budgeting into the N.H.S."—this was the cry of the time. And from 1985 would begin the chain of events which would destroy Jim Baxter.

1985 was the first year of Mr Burdon's three-year stint as consultant in administrative charge. On the medical side of the hospital, Dr Morton had been in nominal charge since the Dale men arrived in 1979, but had progressively retreated. Healy was the cheerful new-ideas man, but it was the efficient William Dick who by his chairmanship of the local medical advisory committee was the more powerful. Though he was never more then coldly civil to Jim, Jim respected his abilities as a committee chairman. Charles Pollock, though several years older, had teamed up with him as his vice-chairman, and the two had now been in post for six years. Dick had of course been on the Regional Medical Advisory Committee, and was angling to be its chairman next time round.

Like Andrew Morton, Jim Baxter was deliberately taking a back seat. He turned down the offer to be chairman of the Medical Staff Club, and refused to go on the Regional Advisory Committee. Berrill had taken over the nominal position as chairman of the surgical division when he was doing his three years as administrative head.

At the Dale there were big changes. The neurosurgery department had closed. The plastic surgery carried on; all their staff were pleasant and friendly. There had been a clearance out of the older orthopaedic surgeons. Fleischman had died, and the new professor no longer visited. The three new orthopaedic men at the Dale were cheerful and co-operative; now there were no difficulties over casualty and minor broken bones, and the Reid casualty officers were actually encouraged to visit the Avondale orthopaedic clinics and meet their opposite numbers. It was a complete transformation, brought about by the happy and helpful personalities of the new generation of orthopaedic consultants. *That* Dale antipathy had vanished. So Jim was happy at the prospect of their moving over in due course from the Dale, as they were to when the new hospital was completed.

Two sadnesses came along the next year. They were inevitable ones. Mr Armsworth died in Devon, of heart failure. Jim would never forget him. But Charles Collinson also died—like Mr Rollands he had suffered from a bowel cancer which he had sensibly gone away to have treated. All too soon he had a recurrence, and finished like Mr Rollands in Jim Baxter's surgical care. To the end he tried to say his pain was due to something else—back pain he insisted was due to kidney stones—and Jim just could not make up his mind whether Charles really believed this or was putting on a brave face. Even his widow told Jim she couldn't be sure either. Neither Berrill nor Burdon came near Charles' funeral. But many others did, among them young Joseph Healy. He had a kindness those others just didn't have. Said Maurice Garretts: "Well, it's our turn to fall off the pole next."

CHAPTER 13

Some time after David Burdon's period as surgeon in administrative charge began, a memorandum came from the new general manager at Region. While Dr Hubbard in his day had been a new animal when the post of Regional Medical Officer was created, he was at least a doctor. *This* one was a business man and not a doctor at all. His power seemed enormous. Dr Holliday's authority was much less—the R.M.O. no longer ran the Health Authority as most of them had done, no longer ran the Regional Advisory Committees, no longer dealt directly with the Teaching Hospital. The whole thing seemed to be run from the general manager's office.

The memorandum was stated to be for all hospitals in the Regional Authority and it concerned bed occupancy—the percentage of beds actually occupied by patients from day to day. The Royal Reid retained a good supply of beds, always with some spare capacity. And because the geriatric service was better than average, there were fewer beds blocked by elderly people who had nowhere else to go. Over the past five years the policy of sending patients home earlier and earlier after their operation, and of doing more surgery on a day care basis, had meant that the surgical service of the Reid remained very adequate for the workload. But this meant, of course, that the occupancy was lower than the Health Authority required.

Of the three surgeons, Mr Burdon had the least chance of increasing his day cases—Berrill and Baxter had a large proportion of patients who could be examined through a telescope, and so only needed to be in hospital for part of a day. He had tried to overcome this by filling his beds very efficiently and turning them over quickly. So David was not pleased when threats of reductions in bed numbers, if the Authority's occupancy target of 75% was not met, appeared in not one but a series of memos.

At first only information was asked for. Simon Durrant was helpful, but as he was the letter-writer who passed on policy of the Board, he appeared to be personally responsible. Burdon became more and more angry as memo after memo arrived. He claimed there were insinuations that the surgeons were not using their beds efficiently. His short temper, which had resulted in a succession of secretaries leaving his employment quickly, became even shorter. He had outbursts in the wards, in theatre, and most of all in the record office.

Jim saw him seldom. But one day he put in a couple of cases after David's list, letting theatre staff know. When he arrived to do them, he experienced for himself the full force of the Burdon temper. The violence of the voice and the hot anger of the eyes, impressed him so much that he said to Anne that evening:

"I wonder if David Burdon's ill. It's not normal to be angry as that."

David Burdon created so much trouble for the nursing staff that he was called in by Miss Shields' successor Miss Anderson. Miss Anderson was not the District Nursing Officer—that title had gone—but the Director of Nursing

Services. She was, by her own account, a nurse manager. Their meeting had not been a happy one. Burdon had raised his voice more than once. He had insisted that he feared for the future of the surgical unit and its capacity to give a satisfactory service for the people of the district. In reply, Miss Anderson had told him that he was not the only one with worries in these hard times. Her nurses, she said, were trying their best to nurse his patients and were not going to be helped by constant criticism and bad temper from him. "You have no shortage of nursing staff, you have only a shortage of attitude," she told him. Both Berrill and Jim listened sympathetically when he told them about it all later. "She sounds totally useless," said Allan.

The information sent to the Authority about the unit's workload did not seem to be what they wanted. They wanted more details. Anger increased when William Dick came back from a committee meeting at Region with the information that the bed occupancy of the units in the Teaching Hospital was not to be investigated, even if they were below the magic 75%.

The three surgeons discussed the letter form the Authority at some length. It told them bluntly that their bed occupancy was not adequate. It was only 68%. The letter ended with the announcement that a meeting with the Unit Management Team would be arranged.

The meeting took place on 4th December, 1986, in the unit Office. Dr Simon Durrant led for the Board. He was accompanied by Mr Raymond Langton and the unit treasurer, and by Miss Anderson.

"Thank you all for coming along," said Simon. "I know how busy you are."

"We are here," he went on, "to discuss the decision to reduce the number of surgical beds here. The Board decided on this step, after lengthy consultation with all concerned, because of first, concern at the relatively low occupancy—around 67%—of the adult surgical beds, second, a marked increase in the proportion of surgical cases being dealt with, in recent years, on a day-case or short-stay basis, and third, an anticipated reduction in running costs of £60,000 per annum.

"The proposal is that ward 9 will become a 5-day ward, being available from 7.30 a.m. Monday to 5 p.m. for short-stay patients, on a weekly basis. There will be 15 beds available. Ward 10 will become a ward for day cases. It will have 14 beds available from 8.30 a.m. till 5 p.m. on a daily basis from Monday to Friday."

"What about the 15th bed in ward 10?" demanded Burdon.

"That bed will be lost in the conversion process," was the reply from Langton.

"What we will need to agree," went on Simon, "is how to allocate the remaining 7-day beds."

"I notice," said David Burdon, "that it's *my* beds that are being lost."

"Not lost, only converted," said Langton.

"Isn't the real reason for this," said Allan Berrill, "just to save money on nurses?"

"There are more than enough nurses for the bed numbers in this hospital," said Miss Anderson. "I have done a survey of strict requirements, and we have in fact many more nurses than are justified. We can reduce the number by almost 10%."

"That's a huge reduction," said Jim.

"It just shows how overstaffed the hospital is" returned Miss Anderson. "We have to make savings and that is an eminently safe way of doing so." Jim's mind went back to the meeting of more than 10 years before. To say that reducing the number of nursing staff was a safe way of saving money— he just could not follow the reasoning. Saving money perhaps, but to say "a safe way?"

All the surgeons made the same point: there could be an increase in the waiting list. Simon Durrant listened. He said:

"If there is, we may have to think again. But I'm afraid that the Regional Authority is not going to change their decision. We will have to make the best of it we can."

Jim wished that Spiers had been as helpful those years ago. At least he was trying to soften the blow, was Simon.

"We need more male than female beds," said Allan. "I have a clear preponderance of men in my line. So has David. Jim's about 50-50."

"Is this really a money saving exercise?" asked Jim.

"It is part of the new emphasis on efficiency," said Mr Langton. "It is about time the Health Service was run on proper business lines."

"It was run on business lines when there were Boards of Management," said Jim.   Langton looked at him witheringly.

"Local input like that may have pleased the locals, but the present situation demands *professional* management."

The meeting ended with the three surgeons agreeing to co- ordinate their waiting lists, something they had not done before. Burdon was insistent that if *he* wanted a patient in, he would "jolly well bring them in." Jim and Allan Berrill looked at each other. This time, funnily enough, they felt closer together; they were both a little worried about the belligerence of their third colleague.

After more discussion, they agreed that they would use the 7 day beds in the remaining four wards in the ratio of 42 male beds to 18 female. Miss Anderson asked for their co-operation in being prepared to restrict list admissions.

A minute of the meeting duly arrived. The new arrangements were to start, allowing for "re-structuring of the ward areas," on 1st March.

As long as anyone could remember, the Christmas parties in the Royal had been the happiest affairs. The Avondale, too, had had its own tradition. But this Christmas an edict from the Health Board decreed that there were to be no parties on the wards. Instead, there was to be a staff dinner the week before, held in the recently enlarged staff canteen. All the old fun—the side rooms full of cheerful friendship, the sisters out-doing one another with their culinary fare, the turkey carving on the wards, the residents' own Christmas meal—all was to disappear. Sister Billings saw this as another sign of decadence. She was of a generation of nurses who were finding it difficult to live in the new world where money seemed all-important.

"I'm glad I'm due to retire in three years, Mr Baxter," she said at one of their afternoon tea sessions. "What is it, nurse?" she asked one of the staff who knocked at the door of her office. Sister Billings left her office door open, but insisted that nurses knock if they wanted to ask anything. She was still the disciplinarian, and nurses sent to her wards knew that they would learn high standards not only of nursing care, but of ward appearance and cleanliness. Coming in on an afternoon, her sharp eye would quickly notice an messy bedside table top, flowers not properly arranged in a vase, a bed untidy, an unclean pyjama jacket or nightdress. She knew how to make people feel better. The older people loved her. She was well known by so many people in the town and the district. The young nurses all knew they would get a proper training on Sister Billings' ward.

So did Jim. By now he had come to know her well. He knew her strengths and her weakness as she knew his. Although they held many confidences, he had never forgotten Mr Armsworth's counsel to be careful what he said to even a long-known member of the nursing staff. "Never forget nurses like to quote you, Baxter. Never forget they have long memories. Tales remain in their mythology for years and years." How he wished he could have Mr Armsworth's advice now. He saw the future as bleak. These bed reductions would lead to nothing but trouble. The three of them would be thrown together, with not enough beds. Even if they had been the best of friends, it would still be difficult to compromise. With relations as they were, it would be hardly possible.

Sister Billings deplored the new reduced hours of work for the nursing staff. She felt it did not allow continuity of care, and said she wished each of the surgical firms could have another sister. This looked unlikely, in the present climate of staff reductions. Miss Thomson, the "Nursing Officer" who had come from the Dale, was due to retire just before the new surgical plan came into effect, and she feared that whoever came would have a hard time. Like Jim, she knew only too well the personalities of the three surgeons and past animosities.

Another symptom of the progress towards cost reductions was the move to rationalise the system of case records. This had been rolling along over Dr Hubbard's years in office. But a new edict from the new general manager accelerated the process. Dr Dick, who had a large say in the local medical executive, was an enthusiastic supporter of rationalisation, and as a result was a favoured member of the staff in the eyes of the Regional Authority officers. A medical records committee was set up, with Charles Pollock as its chairman.

The first weeks of the new surgical arrangements was a disaster. This was to a great extent because the consultants did not keep their word about co-ordinating their waiting list admissions. Inevitably they had a flood of emergency female admissions, and some ended in medical or gynaecology wards, to the anger of their staff. There were not enough beds available anywhere, and Miss Anderson refused to re-open ward 9 at a week-end. The new Nursing officer went again and again to Miss Anderson's office in a state of alarm, and one evening Miss Anderson actually came to the wards to see for herself. They had to stop admitting female list cases. David Burdon got angrier and angrier, and one day Jim went along to have a talk about him with Allan Berrill

"Allan, I'm a bit concerned about David Burdon. I had the records officer on to me yesterday, saying he had enough of being shouted at. He isn't willing to reduce his admissions, the man said. He says that his responsibility is to the patients, and if he wants someone to come in, the hospital will just have to find a bed."

"What does the records man say?"

"He says he thinks that David is trying to wreck the new system. He says he complained to Simon Durrant."

"I've been worried by David Burdon for a while. Sister Pickering's complained about him to me. She says he loses his temper in theatre. I spoke to Charles Pollock about it. Dick knows about it. I had a word to Andrew Morton as well."

Jim was surprised. Allan had been complaining all over the place.

"When did you speak to Andrew Morton?"

"Oh, about a couple of months ago."

Jim could understand Berrill's going to Charles Pollock. They were pretty close since Allan got Charles interested in squash. They played together regularly. But he wondered why he had gone to speak to Andrew. Perhaps Andrew had taken up squash! Jim was not the least surprised Allan hadn't spoken to him; they had no confidences between them and never had.

"I think we should have a word with Dr Durrant," said Allan. He always spoke of Simon as "Dr Durrant"; *they* were not close.

"It's really what Sister Pickering keeps saying," Allan went on. "She says he's upsetting her staff." It always fascinated Jim how two people as unlike as the handsome Londoner and the blunt Yorkshirewoman were as apparently close friends as Allan Berrill and Sister Pickering were.

"I'll speak to Charles Pollock," offered Jim.

"You do that."

Jim didn't share confidences with Dr Pollock as a rule, at

least, not this sort. Since the David Jones years, Jim had learned to keep to himself, and only share his thoughts with someone like Charles Collinson whom he knew he could entirely trust. He didn't have Charles any more. But he found the pathologist very sympathetic, as he listened, smoking his pipe as usual.

"Yes, Allan Berrill spoke to me some time back. He was very critical of Burdon. He said he was out to wreck the new surgical thing. He thought he was angry that it was his wards that had been changed to 5-day ones. He's been rude to patients, too, according to Allan. I wonder whether he's not ill with something."

"What do you suggest?" asked Jim.

"Go to see Dr Durrant. If he strikes a nurse, there'd be all hell to pay."

What Jim should have done was to see David Burdon himself. But he remembered the blazing anger of that afternoon in the theatre and thought it wouldn't help. Berrill and Pollock were thoroughly involved, and Allan had already spoken to the unit medical officer.

Then a day or two later Sister Pickering told him, in an almost throw-away line, that Mr Burdon was getting in a patient and was going to use the E.R.C.P. instrument on him. "He did use it once before," she said in a matter-of-fact tone.

Jim was really annoyed by this news. He looked at the printed list on the theatre wall, and there sure enough was the patient's name, the diagnosis "gallstones in duct—for E.R.C.P." for Mr Burdon's list the next day.

Simon Durrant listened as quietly as usual.

"David is not trained in the procedure. He could get into trouble. If anything went wrong, we couldn't defend in court."

"What do you want me to do?" asked Simon.

"Write to him and say he's not to do it," replied Jim. "What about all this complaint about his losing his temper?"

Allan Berrill and Charles Pollock have already asked me to write and tell him about the complaints," said Simon. "And I have told him to come and see me."

Jim was relieved. At least it wouldn't go outside the unit. He was genuinely sorry for David. Certainly he was still apparently determined to try his hand at everything, but he couldn't be allowed to run the risk of a court case.

Then Jim remembered. "He's going off on holiday this weekend," he said.

"He'll get my letter before he goes," said Simon.

Jim could not but notice how unpleasant Allan Berrill had become about David Burdon. He told stories about how bad his temper had been, but did not leave it at that. His insinuations about how unhappy his wife was, how poorly his post-operative patients did, and how he was being unhelpful over the waiting list, were repeated over the hospital. Jim had to listen and say nothing. After all, he reflected, he himself had been the obstructive one in the past. But he had never been as rude and angry. But it was clear that Berrill was very clever at character assassination, implying at the same time that he was the reasonable and sensible middle man.

When David came back, Jim thought he should go along and see him to try and help. He found him remarkably calm.

"You and Allan certainly spoiled my holiday," he said.

"I want to try and help you if you'll let me," answered Jim.

They talked the whole thing over. Jim explained that they had been concerned for him. But instead of listening, he became angry again. He had gone to see Sister Pickering, he said, and she had denied that she had ever made any complaint about him. Dr Durrant had told him that Dr Pollock had also complained. But when he asked him what he had said, he had replied that he hadn't said anything. Jim was taken aback. He had certainly heard Charles Pollock say that he had complained, but Sister Pickering had not, he had to admit, said anything in his presence. But Sister Billings was the witness he knew he could believe, and her staff nurse, a male nurse, had given Jim chapter and verse of Burdon's behaviour while in their wards. Pollock, Pickering and Berrill were the ones he wondered about. They had all shown themselves happy to lie.

David Burdon said nothing about the E.R.C.P.

Poor David Burdon. He was the one who had to write the letters to the administration. His frustration was all too clear:

> Dr Charles Pollock
> Chairman of Medical Records Committee,
> 20th February 1987
>
> Dear Dr Pollock
>
> Further to the decision at the Medical Executive and at the Medical Records Committee, as you know we had our discussion about fluid balance charts. I must say I found the letter from Dr

Durrant dated 14th February, 1987 somewhat intimidating, but I feel this is typical of the reaction of the Unit Medical Team.

In the current state of surgical disarray when we can hardly admit patients into the Unit, and when the standard of nursing care in charting of fluids is deteriorating, certainly the point that if we use anything but the recommended Health Board forms then the Board are not going to support any mistakes that may be made, makes me feel there is little point in arguing to try to keep up the standard of care in this hospital.

With the poor charting of fluid balance that is taking place, one would be as well using Andrex or something similar to write the fluid charts on. As the Authority wish to spend more money in providing forms which we do not want, yet not spend money on services which we do want, I feel that we should, nevertheless, use the recommended Authority forms...

Jim said nothing. He thought the new form was an improvement, but by now he was beginning to take the line of least resistance with David Burdon's antagonism to everything the administrators came up with. He agreed with his antagonism to the bed reductions because they were a cover for the insistence that a large sum of money had to be saved. In this antagonism the three surgeons were of one mind.

Inevitably there were instances of patients being sent for

operation and then finding when they got to hospital that there was no bed available. For the first time in the history of the Royal Reid hospital, the older general practitioners complained, patients were being turned away. David Burdon went so far as to tell patients to complain. Jim and Allan Berrill had many telephone calls with family doctors angry that a patient could not get admission, and enlisted their aid to write to the local management and complain. To their annoyance, they got no change from the Unit Management Team. Dr Dick, who was virtually a member of it now, was unhelpful. To Jim's disappointment, Simon Durrant was unhelpful also. Raymond Langton was now the District Manager and he was now the boss. Again, it was Burdon whose frustration boiled over:

20th May 1987

Dear Dr Durrant,

Further to your letter to Mrs Bell, 30 Lyndford Gardens, Reidham, I really feel you were trying to shift any responsibility for the introduction of the five-day ward back on to the consultant surgeons.

In the last paragraph of the first page of your letter, your comment that the three consultant surgeons are understood to have cancelled all admissions, is really a bit fatuous as you know perfectly well that the admissions were cancelled because there are not enough male beds in the hospital since the introduction of the five-day ward.

I see that you blithely stated that 'I understand that arrangements were made for your husband to be treated in Leeds and therefore arrangements for admission to the Royal Reid have lapsed'. Yes—this man was treated in Leeds, he should not have had to go out of the area to get treatment, and the only reason he had to was because we were unable to admit him here i.e., unable to offer him the service for which the Health Service was set up in this area. Don't you think it would have been more honest of you to have that the five-day was being set up on the advice of the Board, and that is why there is not enough male surgical beds, and that is why Mr Bell could not get in, and that a decision was made in the presence of the Unit Management Team that the only patients who would be admitted were malignant patients or day patients, and stop trying to, as I say, always shift the 'blame' to someone else?

Yours sincerely,
David Burdon
Consultant Surgeon.

David made a good job of it—he sent copies to the general manager, to Dr Holliday, to the other surgeons—and to the secretary of the Community Health Council. He wrote several letters in the same vein, and glared at poor Dr Simon Durrant whenever he saw him in the corridors of the hospital. Had Langton been there, he would have glared at him too.

Things improved a little when the surgeons agreed to reserve Berrill's wards of 30 patients for female patients, and Jim's of 30 patients for male patients. They agreed to admit their smaller operation cases, and their day patients, in rotation to the 5-day ward—open from Monday to Friday but not at weekends—and to the day ward. But now all wards were admitting every day. It was back to the days of 1974. The nurses were angry and unhappy.

The birth of a grand-daughter brought a new dimension into Jim and Anne's lives. They were delighted as all grandparents, and a new interest in small clothes, disposable nappies, feeding bottles—all the things a new baby needs—followed the baby's arrival. But there was no sign as yet of marriage for their daughter. She was wedded to her job as a community nurse in the north east.

But another sadness came with this happiness. Anne's brother David's multiple sclerosis had worsened. After several years of little change, the disease had suddenly accelerated, and he now had difficulty walking. Anne and her older doctor brother decided to share his care—he had become so restricted he had had to give up his job. But he was no trouble. He had always been a quiet and uncomplaining man, and disability had not changed him. His presence made their lives more anxious; his need for help added another component of exhaustion to their days and nights. He was not going to improve this time.

The way the hospital world was changing, Jim found hard to accept. Nurses no longer stayed in theatre as long as the operation they were assisting at continued; when their "time was up," they would say: "I'm off now, Mr Baxter. Nurse so-and-so is taking over." And off they would go. Registrars and even house surgeons thought nothing of disappearing a 5 o'clock and expecting another to take over, even an ill patient's care. On Fridays, they disappeared at half-past-four and were not seen till Monday morning. General practitioners came out less readily. They did not routinely visit the old people, or the post-operative patients, as the previous generation had always done. The younger consultant anaesthetists refused to do more than their minimum, and seemed to take longer and longer to put the patients asleep. And Mr Armsworth's words to Jim on his appointment were coming true; the younger family doctors allied themselves to the younger surgeons and the younger physicians. Dr Healy was much in demand, and David Burdon was starting to get more referrals than Jim and Allan Berrill. But it was still Mr Baxter who got the private work, and he knew well how much this made the others resentful of him.

Anger over the bed shortage spilled over into the general practitioner world. Finally Dr Durrant was forced to acknowledge that there was a problem, and at a meeting with the surgeons plus Miss Anderson the nurse manager, Mr Langton being away on a managerial course, he agreed to examine other options.

The surgeons asked that wards 9 and 10 go back to being a 7-day wards. Miss Anderson countered this at once, saying it would require a further 4.586 whole-time-equivalents of nurse time—in terms understandable to ordinary mortals, an extra £45,000 a year.

They next asked that ward 9 stop being a ward open only from Monday to Friday—a short stay ward, and revert to being a 7-day ward, open every day of the week. This she said would cost an extra £33,603.

Finally, a request that the surgeons use Saturday mornings for extra day cases was also refused, on the grounds that it would be prohibitively expensive of nurses' time. The idea was the surgeon on call over the weekend could do a short Saturday list. The young anaesthetist in charge also rubbished this idea, saying his staff would not co-operate. Langton backed him up.

But Dr Simon Durrant showed that his first promise when the new arrangements were ordered would be kept. His letter to the general practitioners of the Reidham district ended:

> "While emergencies are being brought in and dealt with as expeditiously as usual, and the overall through-put of surgical patients appears to have been maintained, the surgeons have represented that it is much more difficult than formerly to arrange for the early admission of waiting list patients who are not suitable for the 5-day ward, yet who require early treatment for e.g. gall-bladder or prostate disease.
>
> Accordingly, two alternative options which could increase the number of 7-day surgical beds have been costed and discussed with the consultant surgeons.

As a result, representations are being made on their behalf to the Regional Medical Officer, and I shall keep you informed of the outcome.

Yours sincerely,
Simon Durrant.
Unit Medical Officer."

"What a difference it is having Simon here," Jim said to Anne that evening as he showed her the letter. "He's so reasonable. What a mercy Langton's away. Do you remember Bill Spiers?"

"Yes. The whole story would have been different if *he* had been more understanding," she replied.

"The trouble is," went on Jim, "we're all caught in the trap. I've told Simon that the others think nothing of me (what he'd actually said to Simon was that the others thought he was a shit, but Anne did not allow four letter words in the house or anywhere else) and that there's nothing I can do about it. I'm due to take over the administrative charge thing next month, and that'll make things worse. They know Simon and I are friends, and they are suspicious. But at least David Burdon's doing it for the last three years must have made him realise how difficult it is to be the representative surgeon. He may not be so ready to criticise now—he used to say when I did it when he first came here that I never told him anything. *He's* never told me anything half the time while *he's* being doing it."

"You'll have to be very careful with him," said Anne.

"I'll try," said Jim.

Now re-installed as surgeon in charge, Jim had to prepare a memo for the RMO's visit. Sadly, Simon Durrant had lost what power he had had to influence events—as a result of the report on management in the N.H.S. by Mr Griffiths of Sainsbury's a post of District manager was created. In this further "concept of management" by the government, the various services were to be divided into units. Unit 1 was acute medical services, and the other units were to include community, geriatric and psychiatric services. So the Reid and Avondale were to have a Unit General Manager, and applications were invited. Simon applied, asking Jim if he would act as a referee for him. But he was not appointed. Instead, Mr Raymond Langton was preferred, and became the person all staff would now have to defer to.

The summer of 1987 saw another Conservative victory in the General Election, with a bigger majority. The government claimed that it had put a very large amount of money into the National Health Service in its last term, and would continue to increase its funding during the life of the new one. "Management" remained the key word; increased efficiency, better use of resources, less waste. But the next six months saw worsening shortages, press agitation over patients not very far from the Reid being refused heart operations, angry words from the surgeons, local government politicians, and the ever-nagging Community Health Councils.

Mrs Thatcher, the Prime minister, alarmed at the intensity of the complaints, promised a review of the whole Health Service. It was on television that the Prime Minister first floated the idea of the review, advising the House of

Commons of it in the form of a written answer only three days later. On 25th January 1988, on B.B.C.'s programme "Panorama," Mrs Thatcher said "the most far- reaching reform of the National Health Service in its forty year history" would be carried out, in response to the many and varied complaints about financial shortages leading to clinical distress. "Now we shall look at the future—John Moore (the Secretary of State for Social Services)—and myself and the whole of the cabinet—as thoroughly as we have in other subjects. And when we are ready, and it will be far quicker I believe than any Royal Commission, we shall come forward with our proposals for consultation, and should they meet with what people want, then translate them into legislation," Mrs Thatcher told Mr David Dimbleby.

Back in Reidham the previous summer, Jim thought his memorandum was not a bad one. He worked carefully on it for a long time. Putting words together had never been something he had found easy. He showed his draft to the others before sending it off to Dr Holliday. They did not comment beyond saying "O.K."

The meeting was something of an anti-climax. He put the case for the others, who listened in silence. He mentioned the fact that the Teaching Hospital had not had to suffer any bed reductions, even though several of its firms had a lower bed occupancy that those of district hospitals. He stressed the offers the three of them had made to alternate week-end operating and that these had been turned down because there was not enough money to pay the extra time of nurses. It was shortage of beds, they insisted, which curtailed their through-put of patients, not shortage of theatre time, between Mondays and Fridays.

Allan Berrill said very little—he never did at these meetings. David Burdon became angry as usual. Simon Durrant murmured soothing words. But the man who spoke against the clinicians was Mr Raymond Langton. Jim gave him a very long and very hard look, and he shut up.

Dr Arthur Holliday raised no objections at all. "I agree we will need to return ward 9 to 7-day status," he said. "I will arrange for the extra funds to be provided for the extra nurse staffing. I will inform the general manager and Miss Anderson."

And that was that. When the administrators had left, Berrill said: "It shows you what a good case we had. It's that Miss Anderson we'll have to watch, though."

In no time, things had improved markedly. David got what he felt were his own beds back. Baxter and Berrill got their ward mix restored. They agreed that David Burdon would have male patients in his ward 9, and females shared between the others' female wards. The nursing officer no longer had to rush about from ward to ward, looking in vain for a bed. The crisis seemed to be over. And Jim got a notification that he had been awarded a merit award.

CHAPTER 14

Soon after the happy result to the pleas of the Royal Reid surgeons, the summer holidays came along. The Baxter grandchild was progressing well. When Jim asked after the family of Allan Berrill and David Burdon, he was told they too were doing well in their schools. Jim was delighted when a new consultant anaesthetist arrived at the beginning of the summer. He was from London. At once he and Jim got on well—it was reminiscent of the good days of Bobby Sugden. Peter Holmes was an expert in the fast- moving new subject of intensive care, and unlike the other younger consultants, could put people to sleep and waken them up again quickly. The new generation of anaesthetists was more and more dependent upon machines, monitors, chemistry results than their predecessors had been. They were slower, too, and this meant that an operating list took longer, and so fewer cases were done. But this was difficult to explain to the new general manager, Mr Raymond Longton. He was becoming harder and harder to please—he kept producing figures of what Jim felt was factory production. His constant cry was "more through-put." He meant by this more patients put through the wards in a unit of time—a week, a month, three months, six months.

Because Jim Baxter was now nearing 60 years of age, he was approaching the age when in former times a surgeon would be allowed a little consideration, as far as the length of lists he did was concerned. This had always been so; Mr Collinson had reduced his lists but no-one had criticised him. He was by now the senior surgeon, and he was beginning to feel tired at the end of a long list in a way he had never been before. He was seeing fewer patients at his out-patient clinics because his referral rate had gone down. But he was still the surgeon who was asked for by the retired doctors, other professional people, and nurses who had a child with a surgical problem.

He was very lucky with his registrars. It was now 5 years since he had finished his time as the College tutor, so his days of having a degree of pull were long since past. His registrars were, as was normal in a district hospital, from overseas. His present one was an Indian who had been rather dishonest, and Jim did not extend his contract to a third year. Alan Berrill had an excellent Pakistani at the same time, and he was extended beyond the usual period. David's registrars somehow did not ask to be extended; several came to Jim and asked if they could transfer away from Mr Burdon.

The new registrar was not the first choice on the appointment day. The first choice said he wanted time to consider. The second was an Iraqi, who had been working at a professorial unit, and had done a Master of Science degree. His unit had specialised in the very form of gastric disease which Jim now had as his special interest. On paper he sounded he seemed ideal. But there was just something about him which made both Jim and Alan Berrill hesitate. He seemed just a little too confident. But the degree was something extra, and the reference from the professor was excellent. So they decided to appoint him; Mr Abdul Aziz thanked them and assured Jim of his devotion in the years to come. This sort of effusion though not unknown amongst Arab registrars was also just a little disconcerting.

Jim soon found that his doubts had been realised. It was soon apparent that Mr Aziz, although well qualified on paper and having a glowing reference from a professor they all knew, was a most unlikeable person. He had a profound knowledge of theoretical surgery, was entirely capable in the out-patient clinic, but was not a good practical surgeon. Jim consoled himself that this was not really so unusual in an overseas registrar, and that he could cope.   The real problem was that Aziz really was very clever. He could catch people out. His reading was wide, his confidence considerable. In no time he had pointed out an error in one of Charles Pollock's reports; the fact that he was right made him even more unpopular with the pathologist. He was always polite to the consultants, but was often nasty to the house surgeons and senior house doctors. But he was full of ideas, and this made him an interesting person to talk to and discuss patients with. And after an initial near disaster, his operating settled down into a very adequate pattern.

Allan Berrill and especially David Burdon disliked Aziz from the outset. Sister Pickering soon found things to complain about. "I am a broad-minded woman," she said to Mr Baxter, "but I draw the line at Mr Aziz's language." When taxed by Jim, Abdul blithely said the surgeons in the prof's department had used those sort of words, and so he didn't think they could be bad ones! Sister Pickering's Yorkshire accent broadened markedly as she gave her opinion on this excuse.

Aziz claimed that like many Iraqis he was a political exile

and did not dare to go back to his own country. He said in fact that his father was under house arrest by Saddam Hussein. Jim went so far as to make enquiries at the unit where Aziz had worked and the story was confirmed by the senior lecturer on the firm. "We were rather sympathetic to Abdul," he told Jim, "the poor chap's got nowhere to go. He's lost his passport."

But Jim was worried. He realised that this man had the potential to be a trouble-maker. He also was well aware that the others were clearly out to catch Aziz if they could, especially Burdon who disliked intensely any registrar questioning a decision of his. Jim had long since become aware that David Burdon had an inferiority complex—this was why he could not admit that he could not do the entire range of surgery and why he always chose rather subservient house surgeons. This was why he got so angry; his shouting masked his underlying insecurity.

He realised, too that if he had refused to confirm Aziz's post at the end of his first year, Aziz would have taken him to an industrial tribunal, claiming unfair dismissal, and would probably have won his case. He still kept feeling sorry for the man; he seemed so very lonely and often said he feared for his father's and his brothers' lives.

Troubles never came singly as far as the Baxters were concerned. David, Anne's brother, became progressively more ill with his multiple sclerosis. It was all too obvious that his disease was entering its final phase. David stayed with his older brother for a while, but Anne was very keen to take him; they were very close. So he came to the Baxter's home and Anne nursed him over the second half of the year. Although both Berrill and Burdon knew about David's illness—because Jim told them—they never once asked after him and made no comment when he died in July.

Jim felt whacked after the death, totally drained of strength. Anne was even more drained; she loved her young brother dearly.

Just before David died, it happened that Jim was telephoned by the surgical tutor of the College of Surgeons. He was finishing his 5-year term, and was looking for a successor. He asked Jim's advice: "They want someone from the periphery this time," he said. Jim said he would think about it and let him know.

The very next day after the funeral, Jim slipped and fell on the path while walking towards his garage and fractured his right wrist. It was quickly set and a plaster-of-paris applied. He was philosophical about it, saying to Anne:

"Well, this gives us both a rest for a bit. We can go away while the plaster's on."

The others were sympathetic. A locum soon came along, a particularly nice man from the Teaching Hospital whom Jim knew well—he had remembered Mr James Clark arriving as a new consultant when he had been a senior registrar. And here he was, recently retired but still the same nice and extremely capable man.

"Don't even come in, Jim," he said. I'll stay here for a month—no problem. You have a break—not meant as a pun!—I know the bad time you've both had. There's no point you seeing outpatients. I'll keep things going for you."

So Jim and Anne went off for a holiday in Scotland, where they enjoyed the autumn colours, but not before Jim had decided to ask Allan Berrill if he would like to be put up for the College tutor's post.

"Allan, would you like to do the College post, the one I used to do?"

"I'd like that very much." There was not a moment's delay. "Thank you for asking me." Allan looked genuinely pleased. Jim had no doubt he would do the job very well.

"I'll ask them to put your name in to the College. Of course I don't know if it will be accepted, but we'll just have to wait and see."

When Anne and Jim came back after nearly three weeks, they were surprised to find that Mr James Clark had apparently decided to leave before the month was up. They also heard that Mr Berrill was to be appointed as the Regional tutor for the Royal College of Surgeons. Jim went to see him and congratulated him.

"I'll go with you to the College and introduce you, if you'd like."

"Thank you. I think I'll manage all right."

It was in fact another four weeks before Jim got back to work. When he did get started, in early September, he was glad to find that Aziz had been working well. And then Aziz went off for three weeks' leave. The locum failed to appear. Allan Berrill at once offered the loan of his registrar, who was quite senior in his post and could do a good range of operating—to help with the backlog and while Aziz was away. He was competent and Allan let him do major cases on his lists. He was a cheerful Pakistani whom Aziz got on with; Aziz did not get on with everybody.

Jim felt he could take things a bit more easily. He was still tired after the stress of Anne's brother David's illness and death, and the silly break in his wrist had somehow taken more out of him than he had expected. His waiting list went up, partly because of the break after Mr Clark had left when there was no consultant, but partly because he shortened his lists. And Aziz was now beginning to apply for jobs—Jim felt he would be glad when he got one. He knew how difficult he could be, and he knew the list of people he had offended. But he felt that if the man really *had* no passport and nowhere to go, it would be unfair just to tell him he had to leave when his year was up.

David Burdon had no doubts: "Allan and I consider you should not extend Aziz," he told Jim. Jim made the excuse that Aziz was improving, and told David the tale about him being a political refugee. From the look on David Burdon's face, Jim realised that his attempt at kindness cut no ice. "Allan and I consider him dangerous," he said. Jim noticed that this was a regular expression Burdon was starting to use about all sorts of things: "Allan and I—" but also noticed that Allan did not use it in reverse. Berrill still habitually criticised Burdon, but after many years of hearing Allan's habitual criticism of people and things (and being *very* aware of Berrill's habitual criticism of *him*), Jim did not pay a great deal of attention any more.

The end of the year came along. There were no Christmas parties. Jim did not extend Aziz' contract for a third year. The government's Health Service proposals were awaited by the medical profession. The theatre food had deteriorated another rung; they all paid £1 a month for coffee which the nursing staff bought, but food was no longer supplied. They all had their own sent along—a roll and butter, a bowl of soup, something like that. Jim and Allan had theirs sent along, and ate together on the day they shared the two theatres. Jim didn't know what David Burdon did; he never went into theatre at lunch times on his operating days, because they coincided with his private sessions at home. But he did make a point of going in to have a morning coffee with them both every week to discuss the latest reduction or threatened reduction in service.

Monday afternoon was outpatient letter time. Jim dictated these, just like Mr Armsworth had always done, at the end of the morning clinic. Only now he put them on tape. And Paula, just like Auntie Betty of old, always had his letters typed for him by the later afternoon, after his ward round, so that he could sign them and have them put in the 5 o'clock post. Over the years he had prided himself on always keeping his consultant service to the town and country doctors as prompt as possible. If there was anything special about a particular patient, he would telephone the doctor at afternoon surgery time, as well as writing.

This January Monday was no different from any other. There were always several odd letters which came in the afternoon post, and today there was one from the internal mail system—so it must have come from the Health Authority, or the university, or another nearby hospital—addressed PERSONAL and CONFIDENTIAL. These were not unusual. They were about a range of matters—about a house doctor or member of registrar staff, and in his capacity as surgical tutor Jim had received very many. But this letter was different. Jim sat and read it in amazement.

Regional Health Authority
Headquarters.
6th January, 1989.

Dear Mr Baxter,

I regret very much having to write this letter, but now feel I have no other option.

Over a considerable period, colleagues of yours have been dropping hints to me that you have not been pulling your weight so far as your clinical responsibilities were concerned. The comments were usually non-specific and could not be regarded in any sense as formal complaints. There was little I could do, therefore, but make a mental note of what had been said.

Over the past three months, however, I have received more positive complaints from consultants in several medical disciplines and from senior non-medical colleagues in the Reidham unit. All are implying that your work output is at a level which can no longer be considered to satisfy the terms of your contract with the Health Authority.

I imagine that you are probably aware of the recent initiative by the British Medical Association to introduce an informal professional review machinery as a first stage in the exploration of the kind of advice I have been receiving. Within the past few weeks, senior officers of the Association have encouraged Regional Medical Officers throughout England to adopt this sort of approach in the hope of avoiding more formal procedures.

I am very reluctant, however, to select as a test case for the new review procedure, a consultant who has been in the service of the Health Authority for over 30 years. While it may yet come to that, I would prefer to have an informal discussion with you in the hope that it may be possible to avoid any of your colleagues, or indeed independent assessors, in what would be an embarrassing situation for all concerned.

I should be glad if you will telephone my secretary to arrange a suitable appointment. I shall be away from the office between Monday 16th and Wednesday 18th January (inclusive).

Yours sincerely,
ARTHUR HOLLIDAY
Regional Medical Officer.

Jim read it again. This time his feeling was of horror and fear. He could not believe this was happening to him. He kept thinking: who were these people? He read the letter a third time. Had there been only two, they must surely be the other two surgeons. But there were several, from different specialties. One was non-medical, and a senior one.

But who? Another, he was fairly sure, must be William Dick. He had carried his all too obvious dislike of Jim with him since he had arrived from the Dale, along with D.G. Jones. And of course as chairman of the local medical staff committee would be involved. Yes, thought Jim. Dr Dick had probably been the one who had fed in criticisms—he was constantly at the regional Headquarters, talking to the RMO and his community medicine administrative officer colleagues. He was also a leading light on the Regional Medical Advisory Committee. Yes, Dick could well have been criticising him over several years now. Ever since he came over from the Dale.

But others? Jim thought over the whole range of his consultant colleagues. The frightening thing was, it could be any of them. There were some it could hardly be, though—not the obstetricians, nor the X-ray people. Of the two lab. people, Pollock was a likely one, on the other hand. Certainly not his friend Simon Durrant. *He* had been on the receiving end of angry letters from Burdon already—Jim had seen two in particular which David had had no compunction in copying to him, and had listened to his absurd paranoia. The latest had been an outburst: "Durrant passed me in the corridor yesterday. He didn't even say good morning. Who does he think he is?" Jim had always put down Burdon's hatred of Simon Durrant to the fact that it was he who had cautioned him over that ill-fated E.R.C.P. scope.

He thought for a few moments on end, the open letter in his hands. Would he show it to Paula? She was so loyal, so much his confidant, and so aware of how Berrill and Burdon thought, spoke, and behaved. No, thought Jim, this is for me to go through, and I will have to do it alone.

On the way home he came to another decision. He would not show Anne the letter. She had enough on her plate just now. Since her brother's death she had been on sleeping pills. He would go along to the Health Authority and find out just how bad things were. Before then, he would find out just who his would-be destroyers were.

Happily, Monday was the night Anne was out at her pottery painting class at the local Tec college. She was out for three hours. So as soon as he got home, Jim telephoned from his bedroom one G.P. friend he respected and trusted. Frank Marples was one of the best G.P.s in the town. Only about five or six years older than Jim, he was a good friend and had just had a most successful piles operation. While he had been in, he and Jim had talked a good deal. Frank had just retired.

"Frank, are you free this evening?"

"Yes, Jim."

"Frank, I need your help and advice. I've a serious problem about the N.H.S. It's a complaint against me."

"A patient?"

"No, other consultants. Could you possibly spare me half-an- hour or so? I could come to see you."

"No, Jim." Frank could clearly sense the anxiety in the younger man's voice. "I'll come and see you. What time would suit you?"

"Seven o'clock. Anne is out at her pottery painting class."

"Of course, Jim. I'll be along. I'll help if I can."

He talked in as cheerful a voice as possible over supper. Anne's class began at half-past six, so she was soon away.

After she had gone, Jim telephoned another family doctor friend. He was from a small town called Lenning, ten miles out from Reidham, and he was another—though younger—friend of many years. His practice looked after the many retired people who lived in Lenning. Cameron Wallace was an excellent G.P., well known in B.M.A. circles and a shrewd but kindly medical politician. He was an examiner for the Royal College of General Practitioners, and as he was their local tutor for the region, he and Jim had had common interests. Cameron referred his private patients to Jim. Cameron was one who what was going on in the medical world.

He told Cameron his story. Cameron's voice sounded concerned.

"I think this is serious, Jim."

"I'm beginning to think so, Cameron. What I don't know is where it has come from."

"I think it's appalling. You have always given excellent service. You're a gentleman. The G.P.s in this area rate you very highly. This must have come from higher up, I'm afraid. Someone—some people—have it in for you. They want to destroy you."

"Cameron, do you know if there's been any criticism of me in the Regional Committees? Or in the G.P. Local Medical Committee? Or in the Regional Authority?"

"I'll ring around and make enquiries. Believe me, Jim, the more I think about this, the more appalled I am. I fear this is a set-up. I'd advise you to waste no time—consult your Medical Defence, and consult the B.M.A."

Frank Marples arrived promptly at seven. He had been at the same medical school as Jim, and this was another bond. He looked as friendly and kind as he invariably did. He hung up his overcoat and they went into the sitting room.

225

"I'm more than grateful to you for the first-class job you did on me," said Frank. "I'm a changed man. It was so easy afterwards, too."

Jim told Frank his story. Frank's kindly eyes narrowed.

"Who do I think's behind this? I think it's Allan Berrill."

"But he's been helpful recently—lent me his registrar after I came back after my fracture." Jim did not add "And he's been a bit friendlier too."

"This isn't you. The town G.P.s all know you give good service. That's why we refer you our patients. That's why I went to you for my operation—and my son's, you remember. But we know all too well that the general surgeons here don't get on."

"That's so. But I've tried to get on with the others, without success. No matter what I do, it doesn't seem to help."

"Why not think of asking Allan Berrill? If there is a problem you can air it between you, and it may solve this. Or it may help."

"I hope so."

"I do not think you'll get much out of Burdon. I don't think I can suggest anything much more. But if it does lead to trouble, Jim, there are plenty of people who'll speak up for you."

Frank had not added a great deal, but it had been helpful to talk to an older, sympathetic person. Once upon a time, Jim would have gone straight to Andrew Morton. But Andrew had deserted Jim long since, and he had been retired for a whole year. Had George Bell been alive, he would have gone to him. But George was dead. He had no one to turn to in the hospital world. No one at all.

That night was one of the most miserable—perhaps the most miserable—of Jim's whole life. It was much worse than the sadness he had felt on his father's and his mother's death—that was natural bereavement. He lay awake, going over and over the contents of the letter—especially the threat of a public tribunal—until six in the morning. After an hour and a half's sleep, he got up and was off as ever by eight fifteen for his Tuesday list.

Luckily the list was straightforward. Luckily too Jim knew that David Burdon was coming to see him before he started, so he did not need to make any special opportunity to raise the subject.

Along came David. His query about a registrar's holiday was quickly answered. Then Jim said, in as level a voice as he could:

"I've had a letter from the Regional Medical officer saying that people here have been saying I'm not doing my work. Have you been complaining to the Health Authority about me, David?"

David Burdon looked at Jim. So often, he tended to look sideways. But this time, he looked Jim straight in the eyes and said:

"If I'd any complaint to make about you, Jim, I would say it to your face."

He seemed very sure; very open.

"I'm glad to hear you say that, David. Thank you."

Jim felt genuinely relieved. David Burdon, he felt, was the more likely of the two to have set this attack going.

Jim found the early operations so hard. His feeling of isolation was complete. To make matters worse, it was Sister Pickering who was taking his cases and assisting him. He knew her so well by now. But he kept talking politely, carefully, as time passed.

Berrill was operating in the next theatre. Baxter asked him to come into the changing room during a break between cases. This time he showed Allan the letter, saying:

"Have a look at this, Allan. Did you have anything to do with this?"

Jim watched Allan's face as he read the letter, and saw him frown, then look angry.

"No, I didn't," Allan Berrill said. "But I think some of the agro directed against Aziz has rubbed off on to you."

He looked up, his eyes angry.

"That fellow Holliday's a fool. He's just gone over the top with this. There was no need to take this so far."

Jim was relieved. He felt that Berrill really *was* sorry for him.

That afternoon he confided to Paula what had happened.

"I'll have to phone Holliday's secretary and arrange an appointment."

"Yes." She was truly sympathetic. If anyone knew how things had been going, she did. She said:

"But they can't say this about you, Mr Baxter. It's just not true."

"This is really serious, Paula. It might come to a public hearing thing at the Health Authority." He smiled. "You might have to give evidence on my behalf."

"I'd certainly do that. So would a lot of others."

He telephoned Dr Holliday's secretary. He did not know her. Her voice was neutral and flat. She obviously knew why he was phoning, though she pretended not to.

"Dr Holliday has no time tomorrow, except half an hour at nine o'clock. Would your business require more time than that?"

"Oh, I believe so," said Jim, continuing to play the game. "What about Friday? I have operating in the morning, but could manage to get away in the afternoon later on."

"Four o'clock on Friday onwards Dr Holliday is free," said the voice. It was almost hostile. But Jim realised that in his present state of mind he could read anything into a tone of voice. Friday was the 13th of January.

The evening at home was a long one. Still he said nothing to Anne. But he felt more desolate, even lonelier and more frightened, even sorrier for himself. That night in bed Anne put her hand inside his pyjama trousers, trying to excite him, but he pushed her hand away.

Overnight he lay awake again. He saw himself marched before the Regional Health Authority. He saw his career in ruins. He saw newspaper headlines. He tried to think there might be another side; he went over his recent past, trying to think if he had been neglectful of his work. The only thing he could think of was one occasion when he had been away at a meeting of the university postgraduate department and returned to find an ill patient whom he had had to operate on urgently in the evening; Aziz had called Burdon who was on call. Well-chosen remarks had been written on the case-sheet. Perhaps these five were right? Perhaps he had been backsliding and just been unaware of it. But as he thought and thought, the more he realised that he had not been doing anything less than before. He had seen his outpatients promptly. If he *had* put any more new patients on to Aziz, it was to give him more experience—he was always asking if he could see new patients. Any which sounded difficult he always made sure he saw himself. Perhaps he had gone around the wards more quickly recently. He had in fact been working hard to get his waiting list down, and he had certainly concentrated on the endoscopies and the E.R.C.P.s, but this was because they were specially referred. Perhaps Aziz had complained about having to do more cases. But Jim was very aware that *Berrill* gave his registrar more cases and more major cases too. And then who was the "senior non-medical person?" It could only be Langton. There was no-one else.

Another night of misery ended and in he went on Wednesday. Today he sent Aziz off and did the list of minor cases—the registrar list—himself. Today he had Sister Turner. She was her usual glum and fault-finding self. It was a trying morning.

Later on he went along to X-ray and spoke to Arthur Neil, the senior radiologist.

"Has anyone here been complaining about me?" he asked.

"No." Dr Neil looked genuinely surprised. "Mind you, I've rung Aziz and your present houseman once or twice about request forms for X-rays not being filled in properly."

Jim groaned to himself. For years he had insisted on writing or initialling all pathology forms from theatre himself, as an insurance against Pollock's likely bad temper and criticism if these were incomplete. He hoped he wouldn't have to start doing the same for X-ray.

Off he trudged to the maternity. The consultants there looked at him in some amazement when he asked his routine question. None of them knew of any complaints at all, and it was crystal clear by their faces that they were telling the truth.

Back at the ward, he had his regular cup of tea with Sister. She was by far his oldest colleague in the Royal Reid. Many times now she had been full of angry complaint about Burdon's rudeness and had gone to the nursing manager's office about him. But although they had both lived through the years after the Dale staff had descended upon them and set out to take them over and had both told their complaints of all sorts to each other over those same years, Jim knew her well enough to be sure that this was not a confidence to share with her. For her dislike of the other two surgeons was now so intense that she could not have resisted the urge to spread it about that it was they who had attacked her chief. And that could not happen, because there was no evidence that they *had* attacked Jim.

Thursday was next day. Sister Begbie was on duty in outpatients, cheerful and smiling as ever. When he asked her if she knew whether any of the nursing staff in outpatients had complained that he was not doing his work, she laughed out loud:

"Not *you*, Mr Baxter! Somebody must be joking, if they ever said that about you!"

Along the outpatient corridor went Jim, to button-hole Dr Healy. Ebullient as always, he became serious when Jim asked him directly if he had complained to the Regional Medical Officer about him. Interestingly, he made a rather similar reply to Berrill's.

"You must know that Aziz has made himself unpopular as he's been rude to senior staff. The fact he is sometimes right when they are wrong just makes him more unpopular.

You've been a bit too trusting over that fellow. But *I* haven't complained—there is nothing to complain about."

The succession of denials hadn't really helped Jim's anguish of mind. The people he had asked over the past two days had done no more than confirm his own instincts about two people. He had certainly not gone to speak to Dick or Pollock, knowing how close they were and sensing, instinctively, that they were active members of the anti-Baxter group. Also, he recalled Pollock's lie—or so he had been told by Burdon, when poor David had questioned him, a year and more earlier. At that time Pollock, according to David Burdon, had denied uttering any word of criticism, when Jim had heard harsh words from Pollock's own lips only a month previously.

Thursday afternoon had no private consultations. In his present state of mind he felt sure this was significant. So he used his free time to telephone both his Defence Union and the British Medical Association. The Defence Union man he spoke to thought the complaint was one from a patient. When he explained it was a complaint from colleagues about his failing to do his work, he was asked to send any details and his *curriculum vitae*—his record of qualifications and career.

"Are you a general surgeon?" asked the voice at the other end.

"Yes," replied Jim. "But I have gastro-enterology and E.R.C.P. as an interest."

"Can you say anything about your work—how long have you been in post?"

"For over twenty years," said Jim. "And I've a merit award—I got it nearly two years ago."

The other voice laughed. "Well, Dr Baxter, if you've a merit award, *someone* must think you do your work all right. Perhaps the B.M.A. might be of more help than us, for this sort of difference between colleagues. But if you like, by all means write to us and send all your details."

Jim next rang the regional B.M.A. office. The British Medical Association had over several years appointed industrial relations officers. These were full-time, non-medical people who undertook any sort of query about terms and conditions of service by doctors, very often if the N.H.S. employer was trying to evade paying a part-time doctor, especially a woman doctor—what she was due. He had no experience of the service, although he had once asked its help in the aftermath of the Dale episode.

The industrial relations officer, the I.R.O., sounded helpful and pleasant.

"Don't worry, Mr Baxter. As a matter of fact, we've had a spate of these recently. Are you part-time?"

Jim said he was.

"Do you have a good private practice?"

"Well, yes, I'm the only general surgeon here who is part-time. I always have been. The others do some now, of course, since the new government regulations came in."

"How old are your colleagues? How many are there?"

"There are two of them. They are half a generation younger than me. The younger one graduated the same year as I was appointed here."

"That figures. This is just what we've had elsewhere. I'm sure we can help. Can I come over and have a talk with you?"

Jim felt extremely heartened. "Would you?" he asked.

"Of course. It's the service we offer."

"I have to see the R.M.O, tomorrow."

"That's all right. You will know more about it. So next week will be time enough."

They agreed on the next Wednesday afternoon. Between three and four. Jim blessed the B.M.A.

CHAPTER 15

The drive to the Regional Authority Headquarters was a long one. Jim had seen to it that the list for that day had not been long, so he did not have the fear of having to leave Aziz to finish and then be terrified that his foes were watching. He consoled himself that at least he knew Arthur Holliday of old, and that he was always the straightest of men. Jim had known him as a clinician, even though as a community medicine one. But Arthur had been R.M.O. for a good 2 or 3 years now; he could have changed. He recalled Bill Spiers. He had changed overnight when he became district medical officer from the local medical officer of health.

He was ushered into the large and impressive office. He did not have long to wait. Arthur came forwards, his hand outstretched.

"I hope you're not going to give me the sack, Arthur," said Jim, with a forced smile.

"No," replied Dr Holliday, but a little over-cheerfully. "No, certainly not. This is not a disciplinary interview."

Jim stared. There was a certain pomposity about Arthur Holliday he had not known before. But then, Jim had not met him in the flesh for 2 years. If they had communicated it had been over the phone—apart from the one occasion when Holliday had come to the Royal about the bed closure disaster.

"Who have been saying these things about me, Arthur?" asked Jim.

Arthur Holliday looked formal and severe.

"There is no point my telling you. In any case, it would not be helpful."

"But it would help *me* to know. I just don't understand who they can be. I asked Allan Berrill and David Burdon directly, and they both denied it was them. So who could it be? Who has been looking at me and what I'm doing?"

"Your colleagues are the ones who would know most about your work, of course."

"But they both deny it. Your letter said," went on Jim, "that I'd been criticised in committees. Is this the Health Authority?"

Arthur Holliday pulled himself up into his already grand Regional Medical Officer's chair. Again he spoke in a pompous tone.

"It is unfortunate for anyone, especially someone as senior as you, to lose his self-esteem. But I have received complaints about you, and it is unfortunate that you find yourself so unpopular that four of your colleagues are prepared to go to the length they have." He paused. "There is only one surgeon in the whole of this Region who is more disliked than you. That is the new professor." He paused again.

Jim couldn't help smiling inwardly. Arthur Holliday had certainly learned how to speak for effect since he had become a medical administrator.

"But at least *he* works."

Jim was genuinely distressed now. He said:

"But Arthur, I just don't understand these complaints. I'm doing my work as hard as I've ever done. Every night I think to myself how I have to think of my patients and do my best for them. I know my waiting list went up last year, but that was because I broke my wrist and couldn't work for a time. And I didn't get any fewer referrals, either. And then, my endoscopy work—I'm the only one who does it at the Reid. You must know that. So I've had to concentrate on that, to keep the local service going. I assure you, I've not been neglecting my work. You can ask the G.P.s. You can ask my secretary. You can ask my ward staff."

Holliday's face softened. But not enough to matter.

"You made a request recently to go full-time. When this came to the Health Authority, you were criticised by a member from the northern district. So you're unpopular throughout the whole of this region."

"Well," returned Jim, "if I have been remiss over my work, I can only say I am very sorry. But I assure you again that I haven't been, and I can bring witnesses to support what I say. And if I have upset my colleagues, I can only say again I'm very sorry. But they're not the easiest to get on with. I have asked around the Reid, and I really believed the people I asked when they said they hadn't complained about me. This is what really puzzles me, Arthur."

Dr Holliday's face was beginning to look like its normal serious but kindly self. Jim was speaking from his heart. It was all too obvious he was speaking the truth.

Jim went on: "Were there complaints about me from the Staff Medical Committee? And who was the senior non-medical person? Was that Mr Longton?"

"Jim, I've said I was not going to tell you who the complainants were. Of course the office bearers of the Staff Medical Committee were aware of them. Whether it was Mr

Langton or not, I'm not prepared to say. It would not be helpful for you to know who they were. Besides, they said they did not wish their names revealed."

Arthur was signalling now. It was clear that Dr William Dick, Dr Charles Pollock, and Mr Raymond Langton were part of the team. Jim followed up quickly. He was a little more confident.

"I wonder how people in other parts of the hospital know so much about it, for example, exactly how many clinic patients I see and how many I ask my registrar to see. How do they find this out? I can tell you that Sister Begbie, the senior out-patient sister, will confirm that I see the bulk of my new referrals myself and only give straightforward ones to the registrar. This is no different from what's done everywhere. I've certainly been away at times in connection with College business, but this isn't often. And I've been off much less often in recent years than I was 10 years ago.

"You said that G.P.s had changed their referrals because of my not doing my work. But that's not true. I've asked two whom I know in the southern end of the district and they say the G.P.s who refer me patients have not changed. In the northern end I've not had any referrals, at any time—at least, not since a new generation of G.P.s arrived there, and that is a year or two ago now.

"Allan Berrill has actually been very helpful. When Aziz was off he lent me his registrar for my Friday list and that was good of him. I'm sorry about all this."

"And I'm sorry about it all too, Jim," Arthur replied. "We've known each other for a long time, and I know how much service you have given the Royal Reid and this whole Region for so long now. But I *had* to write to you the way I did, because I could not allow this to go on and run the risk of it going public. That would have been much more unpleasant. If I can keep it confidential, I will do so. I promise you that this will go into your personal file, which I keep here, and there will be no reason why any successor of mine or anyone else will have access to it. And meantime, do try and communicate better with your colleagues. They've complained about that, too."

"If I've been unhelpful to the other two, I can only say once again that I'll try to do better," said Jim.

They talked for a little more. Jim elicited the information that the local administration had complained that he did not work on Tuesday afternoons; Jim explained that because he was paid for only ten sessions and not eleven, this was his free afternoon. But as often as not, he was in the hospital, in spite of this.

"It is in my power as R.M.O. to take no action on these complaints, or take them further," said Arthur Holliday finally. "Now that we have had this talk I propose to take no action. I will write to the people involved and tell them what I propose. And if you want to come and see me again, Jim," (at last he smiled—in fact, he positively grinned to Jim) "come any time you want. You may want to write formally to me—that would be helpful— now we have spoken."

"Could I ask a last question? Has there ever been any complaint that I have been unkind or rude to a patient?"

"No, there has not."

Jim got up. He said: "These aren't happy times for anyone in the Health Service."

"No, they are not. If I can take early retiral I'll certainly do it."

"Thank you."

"Thank *you*, Jim. Thank you for making this interview so much easier for me—for both of us."

On the way home, Jim could not convince himself that he felt mollified. He was relieved, certainly, but mollified, no. The emotion that now gripped him was anger. He tried very hard to control his emotions as he drove along. He went over and over the ground, puzzling who these complainers could be. His surgical colleagues had given him assurances that it was not them. So who was it? He decided it must be the community medicine people locally. He even suspected Simon. Every sort of permutation went through his mind. He felt very tired and yet felt he must fight and not let himself be beaten.

The next person he felt he must see was Mr Raymond Langton, the unit general manager. Jim had gone specially to see him, as senior surgeon, when he was appointed. He had honestly expressed concern about the bed closures and policy in general, but had gone on to say that he would certainly support him in his new post.

Perhaps he might help. He was a keen member of the local parish church and Jim had seen him on occasions when he had passed by on a Sunday morning on his way back from hospital smiling and chatting to the vicar. Surely he would help; a church member and all that.

As he got nearer home, he began to feel sick with anxiety again. He hoped Anne would not notice. But Anne had grown so used to his complaints about the bed shortages, the unhelpfulness of the administrators, and his colleagues, that she did not notice. Or if she did, she said nothing.

On the Saturday and Sunday, Jim went in twice each day, and spent a wholly unnecessary amount of extra time with his patients. He habitually went in on Saturdays and Sundays. He always had. But now it was fear of his position, not concern for his patients, which was driving him. And as he walked in the front door, along the corridors, up to his wards, he felt totally alone and totally isolated. He felt sure people were staring at him. As ever he was polite, friendly. But now his politeness was more forced, less natural. He even felt the porters were watching him.

By Sunday afternoon he could stand it no longer. The feeling of loneliness he had had first in David Jones' day had never left him, but it had faded. Now it was intense again. He burst out to Anne:

"I've had a complaint made about my work to the Health Authority."

"A complaint? Who's complained?"

"I don't know. But there are four different people. They say I've been neglecting my work."

The whole story poured out—the visit to the headquarters, and what Dr Holliday had said. But still Jim did not intend to show Anne the actual letter. He felt he wanted to protect her. As ever, Anne was practical as well as sympathetic.

"It must have been the other two."

"But they said they'd nothing to do with it."

Anne ignored this. She went on:

"The main thing is that Dr Holliday says he will do nothing about it. He must know that they cannot say you have been neglecting your work, because you don't neglect your work. Everyone here knows how much you work.

241

You're never out of the place. He knows about your wrist, too."

"But it's awful to have an attack made on you like this."

"Well, you did complain about David Burdon, you know."

"But I never complained to the Regional Authority. I never wrote letters. I only complained to Berrill. I was worried about David Burdon. I thought he was ill. And you remember that Berrill complained much more about David Burdon than I ever did. I found he had been complaining to Charles Pollock months before I said anything. And he had all those stories about the nursing staff complaining. And he complained to Simon Durrant."

"So did you," said Anne.

"That was just once. I said I was concerned. I didn't say any more. I was as much asking his advice as anything."

"I think the more important thing is who has been dropping hints about you over the years. That won't have done you any good."

"Oh, I think that's Dick. I'm quite sure it was him. He's always been antagonistic since the days of D.G."

Anne sighed.

"Jim, you were in such a state over D.G. Jones. Don't let yourself get like that again."

"How would feel, Anne? It's most unpleasant. And I don't know for sure who they all are."

"I know, love, it's awful. But try and think that whoever they are, they're just small jealous people."

"I'm going to see the B.M.A. about it."

"What about the G.P.s?" asked Anne. "You said you'd spoken to Cameron Wallace."

"Yes. He was a big help. But *he* said this attack has come from high up, from someone in the General Manager's department."

"I don't believe that. Think. How could *they* know how many new outpatients you see and don't see on a session?"

"Sister Begbie knows how many I see. *That* part of it I could certainly refute."

"*I* think," said Anne, "that Aziz may have complained. You know you've never really been able to trust him, and I wouldn't trust these Arabs one bit. Not him, anyway."

"He's due to finish in a couple of months."

"Exactly. He probably wants to be unpleasant before he goes."

"I'm going to see the B.M.A. about it."

"How do you think they can help?" Anne was never very impressed by the B.M.A. She said they always talked more than acted.

"Well, they may have had other complaints like this. They will be able to advise me what to say. And what to write. Arthur Holliday said I should write a reply of some sort."

Jim felt much better for having told Anne. She sent him to bed, made him read a funny book, and brought him up a cup of tea.

On the Monday morning Jim saw all his outpatients—nearly all the returns as well as the new referrals. Aziz got fed up and excused himself, saying he had patients to see in casualty.

Monday afternoon was his interview with the Unit General Manager. Mr Langton had moved into the largest office in the building, formerly occupied by two secretaries and a junior assistant.

"Please sit down, Mr Baxter."

Jim viewed the boss for a moment. He looked a little stouter, a little fuller in the face. His bright eyes were cold and unfriendly.

Jim told him his story. Once again, he asked:

"Did you complain about me?"

"No. I knew your problems with the waiting list, of course."

"Well you would know it wasn't because I was slacking over my work that I got behind. And I've more or less made it up now."

"Yes."

"Mr Berrill has been very helpful. He lent me his registrar, to get through the cases when I had extra outpatients to see on those extra days." Jim had done a number of extra outpatient sessions, much to the anger of the nursing manager but with every help from the outpatient nursing staff, to get his outpatient referral times reduced after his accident.

Langton remained as haughty as could be. Jim sensed he was relishing the chance of taking down this senior consultant now so totally at his mercy.

"There is no question of disciplinary action against you, Mr Baxter."

"I'm glad of that. Dr Holliday told me that."

"Yes." (So he *had* heard, thought Jim.)

"But there is one thing. Dr Holliday told me you had said that I had a session—a theatre session—on a Tuesday afternoon which I didn't use. But I've never had an afternoon session on a Tuesday for years. It was always my spare one as I was part-time."

Raymond Langton was not prepared to concede any mistake on his part.

"Dr Holliday told me you have applied to go full-time. When the Health Authority accept your request—if they do—you will be able to operate on a Tuesday afternoon also."

"But I don't have enough beds now. That's why I went for a Wednesday morning—do you remember? That was why you agreed to Wednesday."

Langton was clearly wrong-footed. His face fell. Then it resumed its rather superior expression.

"Can I help you in any other way, Mr Baxter?"

"No, thank you. But I'm glad you didn't complain to the Health Authority about me. I'm still not sure who it was."

"The Staff Medical Committee office bearers were aware of the waiting list problem."

Another slip. So it was certainly Dick and Pollock.

Jim's interview had not been time wasted.

The week carried on. Allan Berrill was as civil as ever on Tuesday. Jim went specially to see David Burdon to talk about the bed closures, about holidays—anything to try to make contact. Berrill was as civil as ever on Wednesday.

On Wednesday morning Jim spoke to the telephonist:

"There's a man from the B.M.A. coming to see me this afternoon, Joe."

"That's all right, Mr Baxter. When's he coming?"

"I don't know exactly. Between three and four. The name's Mr Fenner. When he comes, could you give me a bleep and I'll come and meet him."

"Right-O, Sir."

Mr Ian Fenner was a pleasant, short, dark-haired young man with spectacles and a moustache. He showed Jim his card. They went to Jim's office. He asked Sister to get them tea.

Mr Fenner listened to Jim's story and read the letter from the R.M.O.

"I don't think it's too bad. I told you we have had several similar troubles of this sort, over the past six to nine months. We've had two from the Teaching Hospital. They are a bit the same—a number of members of staff have ganged up on an older colleague—and it's usually someone who has a large private practice."

"Have any of them come to a public investigation?"

"No, but there's one where the complainants seemed determined to have one, and then withdrew at the last minute."

"It's very hurtful when you realise that your colleagues are prepared to gang up on you to this extent. It makes it worse when you don't know who they are. I've spoken to two of my G.P. friends about it—they were helpful. But one of them worried me a bit—Dr Wallace."

"Dr Cameron Wallace from Lenning?"

"Yes."

"We know him well. He does a lot of B.M.A. work."

"What do you advise?"

"Well, you need have no worries that you won't have our full support. If you can assure me that there's no real weight behind these allegations..."

"I can get my secretary, the ward staff, the outpatient staff—even the cleaners," replied Jim with a smile. "I'm sure the G.P.s would support me."

"Have you spoken to your own G.P. practice?"

"No. The reason I didn't was that the senior partner—an awfully nice man—has just retired. We've transferred not to the next senior but to the one after that. He's a good deal younger. But he's a nice man too."

"Are there any practices who may have disliked you and stopped sending you patients?" Ian Fenner was candid but so pleasant and obviously on your side that you didn't mind at all, thought Jim.

"Yes. there's a group—two group practices in one small town who have never sent me any patients. They always referred to the Avondale Hospital. The previous, older doctors used to, certainly private ones, but that was ten years ago. These are all new. And then there's another practice in Stonleigh where I was very friendly with the senior partner and he used to send me almost all his work— N.H.S. and private. His younger partner used to as well. But since the older man retired eighteen months ago, I haven't had one single patient—well, perhaps the very odd one— from him or his new junior partner. He's a very keen squash player and I think he sends stuff to Mr Berrill. The new senior one uses Mr Burdon. I've just accepted this. I remember my chief, Mr Armsworth, warning me that this sort of thing happens. I just accept it."

"But not the others?"

"No. I wouldn't say so. You see, since I started this endoscopy service, I've tended to get a fair bit of that."

"Do your younger colleagues refer you cases for E.R.C.P.?"

"They didn't at first. They wouldn't accept me doing it at first. Now Mr Berrill does. But Mr Burdon never has. I don't know where he sends his. He refers them to the Teaching unit, but I don't know."

"Who do you think has been making complaints against you over this long period the R.M.O. talks about?"

"Well, again, I don't know. But I think it could be a Dr William Dick. He was a very close friend of a surgeon who was at the Avondale Hospital and who came over here in 1975 when the units were amalgamated. Dr Dick has never made the slightest pretence of having any respect for me—he's always looked at me or talked about me, as a half-wit. He was on the staff of the Avondale too, you see."

"Were the other surgeons on the staff of the Avondale Hospital?"

"Mr Allan Berrill was. Mr Burdon was Mr Jones' successor. Mr Jones was an older surgeon there. They do outpatient sessions there. I've never been on the staff there. I was appointed here."

"Well Mr Baxter, I think you should write a reply to the R.M.O. refuting these charges. If there is anything you feel you should offer to help this disagreement—for it is like the others, a case of disagreement between consultant colleagues—do so. That's always a help. I suggest very strongly that you should let us at the B.M.A. see your letter first. Or, we can discuss its content before you send it."

"Can I put in the letter that you're prepared to support me?" asked Jim. He was warmed by the reassurance from this sensible young man, and at last felt some others were on his side.

"Of course. And by all means say that you have been in touch with us. Say that we are concerned about this, and that we will help you to the utmost."

"Thank you very much. I am very grateful, I really am. I'll send you a copy—no, would you mind if we met again, so that we can discuss it a bit more?"

"Not at all. Remember, it's better not to rush this, Mr Baxter. It is always better to get our side thoroughly prepared and all eventualities thought out."

That evening he had a telephone call from Cameron Wallace.

"Jim. How are you getting on?"

"I've had a session with Arthur Holliday. It was a help. And I've spoken with Mr Fenner, the B.M.A. industrial relations officer."

"He's very good. He sorted out a G.P. quarrel very well not so very long ago. Now, Jim, I've made enquiries discreetly to people I can trust. No-one has complained about you in the town, and no-one here. The new practice at Stonleigh may have, about a patient having to wait a long time to get in. No-one on the Regional Advisory or Local Medical G.P. Committee has complained or even discussed you. As far as the Health Board members go, all I've got is that some woman queried your wanting to convert from part-time to whole-time (how on *earth* does he get to know all this, wondered Jim. *That* was supposed to be very confidential) but just on financial grounds—she had nothing against you personally."

(So Holliday had, if Cameron was correct, been a little economical with the real content of that Board member's remarks, thought Jim. Fancy that.)

"Thank you very much, Cameron."

"I still think it's disgraceful. It's damned disgraceful. There is a gang who are out to harm you, but they are not G.P.s. Have you been in touch with your Defence Union?"

"Yes, but they thought the B.M.A. would be more help. I told you, I've seen Mr Fenner."

"I'll do what I can to get this quashed, Jim. But I hope I've helped. I hope you sleep better tonight."

CHAPTER 16

Although he had had such strong support, he still felt frightened. Going into hospital had become a nightmare. He felt more isolated than ever, if that were possible. But the ward staff, the cleaners, the porters, the telephonists, the patients, were all as friendly as ever. His private referrals continued to come in. Because of the way the wards were now shared, David Burdon appeared regularly to see his own patients on either Jim's male or female ward. Jim sighed when he heard him angrily finding fault with the nurses. Paula was his best source of strength, because she knew all that was happening. She remained loyal and could see the funny side. "I'm keeping my head down just now," she said laughing. So was Jim.

The next day a letter came from Jim's trusted friend Cameron Wallace, addressed to his home. It said:

"We decided we would write directly to Dr Holliday to support you. If I get a reply I'll let you have it."

A couple of days later Jim made an appointment to see his own G.P. When he arrived at the surgery he found he was off for the day, so saw the senior partner instead. Jim had known him since he came to Reidham and had operated on his wife when he was married first. Jim showed him a photocopy of the R.M.O.'s letter.

"This is very unpleasant. I'm sure you don't want this shown to the younger partners."

"No. But I thought since you are my doctor I should let you see it. Have I in fact been neglecting my work?"

"Not at all. We've never found you other than extremely helpful, and always courteous and gentlemanly. But why have your colleagues made these accusations against you?"

"They haven't. They both say they had nothing to do with them."

"Do you believe them?"

"I've got to, if they say they haven't."

"I'm very sad about this, Jim. All of us in general practice know about the troubles there were when the Dale staff came over to the Reid, but we hoped they were a thing of the past. But if I can help you, I'll be glad to. Remember that no matter how unpleasant this must be for you, they will never be able to make charges like these stick."

"But the other trouble is that I've only had vague charges, and Dr Holliday wouldn't say any more."

"Have you consulted the B.M.A.?"

"Yes, I've seen the I.R.O.—a man called Fenner. From the Regional office. He was very helpful. I've to write a reply to him and I'll see him again before I send it off to the R.M.O."

Another week passed. Jim was never out of the hospital. He could not sleep. Anne looked helplessly after him; he was much worse than in the Jones era. He carried the letter in his pocket. Aziz was due to leave in the middle of March; this was some consolation. He had kept Aziz on, in spite of the all too evident anger of the other two. But he was well aware that there was nothing concrete against him to merit his being forced to leave before his two years were up. And form his previous experience while doing the College job, he knew well also that Aziz was quite capable of taking them all to the Health Authority and claiming unfair dismissal.

And then, in the afternoon internal mail came another brown N.H.S. envelope, marked PRIVATE AND IN STRICT CONFIDENCE. Paula looked anxiously on as Jim slit open the envelope and read its contents.

20th January 1989.

Dear Jim,

Herewith, as promised, a copy of the letter I have sent today to the several people to whom I referred in our recent conversation. Please note the apology in the final paragraph; I owe it to you more than to any of the others, but I am afraid it was simply not possible to get this letter off earlier.

Since returning from London, I have had a letter from the Lenning practitioners. It appears to have been written by them following contact with yourself. I think that the easiest way to comply with their request is to let you have a copy of their letter and my reply. These are also enclosed.

I am sorry if anything I said led you to believe that I was referring to the Lenning practice. I was trying not to identify 'third parties'. I certainly did say that practitioners in three towns had been mentioned in the complaints made to me, but I can assure you that Lenning was *not* one of the three.

Yours sincerely,
Arthur.

This letter in Arthur Holliday's normal style certainly contrasted with the earlier one Jim had received. The other more bulky one was to his attackers:

PRIVATE AND IN STRICT CONFIDENCE
20th January 1989

Dear
Mr James Baxter, M.S., F.R.C.S.

You will recall that within the past three months, we have discussed matters relating to concerns that have been expressed about the colleague named above. I am sending this (identical) letter to all those with whom I have had such discussions; it is being copied to Mr Baxter but without any indication of those to whom it is being sent.

Mr Baxter and I met on Friday 13 January. I shared with him most of the points which had been raised in discussions and correspondence by several colleagues and, in particular, concerns that:

His operative throughput was considerably less than his surgical peers

He was not making as full use as he might be doing of theatre and outpatient clinic time available to him, with a resulting (unnecessary) increase in waiting lists and waiting times

Junior staff were being left to handle a level of responsibility that was inappropriate to their status and responsibility

General medical practitioners in some parts of Burshire were referring patients to other surgeons (within and without the Royal Reid Hospital), indicating a possible dissatisfaction with the service offered

Personal communication with clinical colleagues was unsatisfactory and leading to difficulties in maintaining high standards of practice and good working relationships.

We had a very full and frank discussion of these points which Mr Baxter has noted.

I do not intend to take any further action on the basis of what has been reported to me to date.
May I apologise for the fact that it was not possible to write this letter immediately after my interview with Mr Baxter. I had to go to London the following day and have been on leave since then.

Yours sincerely,
Arthur Holliday.
Regional Medical Officer

The letter from Cameron Wallace and his three partners was straightforward and forthright:

> Dear Dr Holliday,
>
> Mr James Baxter has been in contact with us with an inference by you that we are using his services less through dissatisfaction. We all feel you should know that this is entirely untrue and referral to our referral practice would substantiate this.
>
> We have always had an excellent relationship with Mr Baxter who has been most helpful to us and our patients.
>
> We hope you will inform Mr Baxter that you have had this letter of support.

Arthur Holliday's reply did no more than express surprise that the Wallace practice should have heard about the Regional Medical Officer's contact with Mr Baxter, and insist that there had been no direct reference to them in what he had said.

Jim did not show Paula the letter. He said: "It's all right. It just says he is not going to take any action."

But he was immensely relieved. These details in the new letter Arthur Holliday had not in fact listed when they had talked. He had talked only in much more general terms. Now that Jim had seen precisely what was alleged, he knew he would have had no difficulty in defending himself. Some, such as the charge that he was slow in seeing outpatients and not filling up his clinic, were absurd. There was a good answer for all of them. But the worry, that four of the other consultants had been in touch with the Health Authority, had not gone away. Who were the four? And who was the senior lay person?

About ten days later, Jim had to go away to the Teaching Hospital to a meeting of surgical trainees called by the Postgraduate Department. It meant his having to leave before lunch and be away for the rest of the day. He had checked that Alan Berrill was on call for emergencies that day, and mentioned his absence to Paula as he always did. His ward was quiet. In the present climate he had become afraid to go anywhere, but he had had this meeting arranged for several months.

Next morning there was a letter in his mail. It was not marked PERSONAL, so Paula had opened it. She showed him it when he came into the office.

"More trouble, I'm afraid," she said.

The letter was a blistering attack from David Burdon, with copies to Alan Berrill and to the Community Medicine specialist who was filling in for Simon Durrant. It was complaining that Mr Baxter had gone off duty without telling him, and he had had to see one of his patients.

This needed to be sorted out at once, thought Jim. So he went along that afternoon—it was a day Burdon did a clinic at the Dale in the morning—to see him in his room.

"Can I come in?"

"Yes, Jim." The voice was as usual, but the eyes were hostile.

"You wrote this letter yesterday. But Alan was on call, and I told him I was to be away. In fact, I told him a couple of weeks ago, so that he could put it in his diary."

"But you never told me."

"I'm sorry."

"You might well be. You think you can come and go as you please." The face was angry now, the hot anger Jim had seen only once before directed at him.

"Oh, that's not true. I let you know if I'm to be away at meetings or registrar business. I ask you if I need cover."

"That's as may be. But you should let me know whenever you are away from duty."

(That was quite amusing, thought Jim. Alan Berrill was regularly away playing squash—and not next door either.)

And then the dam broke. His eyes glittering with hatred he burst out:

"Why did you not speak to me about that endoscope? Why did you go to Durrant? We—I—know he's a friend of yours, of course. So he'd always do what you wanted."

"Oh come now, David." Jim was sorry for the man. "You'd never have accepted for a moment if I'd tried to speak to you about using that apparatus. But just think for a moment. You never used it. You were never trained in it. I knew you had used it two or three times, but what do you think would have happened if you'd tried again and run into serious trouble? You'd have been asked how often you used it and if you'd had any formal training—and what could you have said? I *had* to try and get you stopped from using it."

There was no reply. Then he said:

"Well, I suppose I could have damaged someone. But that was no reason for you to complain to Dr Durrant about me."

258

"It wasn't only me, David. Alan Berrill complained about you long before I did. *I* thought you were ill."

"That complaint will be on my personal file for good. You've always been against me." His eyes were wet with temper. "You've never made any effort to help me ever since I came here."

Again Jim felt more sorry than angry.

"That's certainly not true, David. When you arrived I took you to the golf club and introduced you around. Don't you remember? We invited you to our home, and to people we thought you might like to meet. Did you ever ask us to your house? Never. When you were setting up your garden, Anne offered to give you plant cuttings—did you ever take us up? We offered more than once to take your boys to the scout camp. You never even answered."

There was a pause. The answer was lame in the extreme:

"I don't suppose we've ever been very good at inviting people to our house."

Then his eyes burned again.

"You may think you can lord it over us. You can't. I've waited for years. But now we've made sure you know what it's like to suffer. From this room."

So that was it, then. David Burdon *had* been involved in this attack. He had lied, that man whose eyes were bright with shining goodness when he was speaking to the vicar or when he saw the vicar pass in the hospital. And he had vowed vengeance on his wrongs. In a flash, Jim saw him as a second D.G. Jones—bitter, inadequate, and above all jealous. This is a re-run of the last time, he thought. His confession was made before he could stop—his inability to control his temper had let him blurt out too much.

And then the telephone rang. Burdon picked it up. Jim could hear as clearly as if his ear had been to the receiver Berrill's voice:

"Have you seen our colleague?"

Those five words told Jim that Berrill, too, had lied, even though perhaps not so blatantly as David Burdon. Their tone had the sarcastic inflexion Jim had heard him use so often over the years, but in addition they had a hard and pityingly hatred coming out of each of them. Alan Berrill, the man who had pretended so convincingly that he was doing his best to help, that he was on Jim's side, was no different from poor David Burdon whose temper had got the better of him and caused him to blow the gaff.

"Yes, he's with me!"

The tone at the other end of the line changed at once.

"Oh, it's all right then, David. I can get you again."

"Well," said Jim, thinking of his reassurance to Arthur Holliday, "I'm sorry, I'm genuinely sorry, David, if I've not let you know exactly what I'm doing. I'll promise to do better from now."

"You never speak to me anyway. You just ignore me."

Jim felt that nothing would break this man's determination to see insult where none was intended.

"That fellow Simon Durrant. That friend of *yours*. He ignores me, too. The other day he walked past me in the corridor. He just passed me by. What does he think he is? He's not the boss now. Raymond Langton's the boss."

Another slip, thought Jim.

Now that the mystery was solved, Jim was able to think on his feet for the first time in many days. He said:

"Aziz is leaving very soon now. I hope very much the new one is a pleasanter and more honest man."

"Just as well. He was so two-faced. He lied to everybody. You should have fired him when Alan and I told you to."

"You're right, I admit," Jim conceded. "But it would have been difficult, you know. There wasn't anything definite, and he could have had us for unfair dismissal." But this card drew a blank.

The interview ended, with Jim assuring David Burdon that he would not fail to inform him of any time, no matter how short, he was to be away from the hospital.

He felt so much better as he walked away. He knew they had both lied. Berrill he realised at once was the worse, for he had been quite happy to destroy Burdon's character to Jim a year and a half ago, and then transferred his support to David against Jim. Well, they are not going to destroy me, if I can help it, was his determined answer to himself. As he walked back to his own room, he repeated the words again.

The next Monday afternoon was the monthly meeting of the Group Staff Medical Executive Committee, when they were to discuss the round of bids for money to buy equipment as the end of the 1988-89 financial year approached. So Jim, as the current chairman of the surgical division, had to go. Every year the nonsense of the system angered consultant staff. No money was available for months on end. And then there was a rush to spend money before April 5th, so that funds left in hand were used up. If they were not used by that date, they were lost, and could not be held over to the next financial year. This year was going to be an extra important one, because the government's proposals for the National Health Service were about to be made public.

Also, it was to be the last meeting of Dr William Dick's chairmanship of the committee. He had proved an excellent chairman, all agreed. The chairmanship carried considerable power and with it membership of the unit management team. So the chairman had the ear of the unit general manager, and through him, an entrance way to the general manager himself.

Jim had not seen Dick for some time—their paths had seldom crossed since he came to take over the medical side of the Reid those years ago. But although he never asked Jim to see a patient on his medical ward except in the most unusual circumstances, Jim had, at least at first, held him in regard. When early on he had had a cartilage operation at the Dale, Jim had gone over to visit him. And he had once, on Andrew Morton's suggestion, written confidentially to the Health Authority recommending him for a merit award. Jim was well aware of Dr Dick's dislike of him, instigated by Jones those nearly twenty years ago and never softened since.

Jim was not looking forward to this meeting. Not only was Dick in the chair, but Charles Pollock, his vice-chairman, he now suspected of being the fourth man in the gang of four who had written to the R.M.O. about him.

Although Jim arrived at the boardroom with its unhappy memories very early, William Dick was already there, sitting in the chairman's high chair and with one of the administrative assistants beside him. There was the usual pile of paper between them. One look into Dick's eyes, as he said "good afternoon" very politely, was enough to tell Jim that he indeed was another. The look was normally of cold dislike. Today was added the disappointed anger that the hunter shows when he sees that his prey is going to elude him. Like Berrill's voice on the telephone, it told everything in a moment of time.

Various other members came along—the eye man, the gynaecologist, the X-ray man, the lady geriatrician, the community medicine specialist. Simon Durrant always attended, but the unit manager did not. Late came in Pollock, smoking his habitual pipe, and sat down in the last seat. He and Dick nodded to each other. They were an unusual combination, Jim thought, a pathologist and a physician.

The first item on the agenda was a carry-over from the last meeting and concerned a suggestion that senior medical staff have name tags on their white coats as a means of identification. There had also been a suggestion that name boards be put up at the front door. It was all part of the "new look" being encouraged by the management.

"Has anyone got any comment?" asked Dr Dick.

"I think it's a good idea," said Jim. "I remember when I came first in 1966 there were name plates in the front hall for the consultants with in and out bits on them. The residents had theirs too, on another wall. Dr Spiers took them all down when the place got called a district. They were good. You could see who was in and who was out."

From the other end of the room came Pollock's voice:

"*You* may have had one of those. But *I* never did."

Another moment, another eyeblink, told the whole sad history of the hospital service in their area. Pollock had been primarily on the staff of the Dale. He, too, had only moved over finally with the others in the mid-seventies reorganization—when the N.H.S. began to go wrong. In spite of all his ability—his pleasant manner, his helpfulness over cases, his time spent overseas, he showed in this moment that he too had a chip on his shoulder over the Royal Reid and the Avondale. This blink had shown him with his guard dropped. He was probably the fourth man.

The talk went back and forwards over the various bids. Jim supported the request for a new electrocardiograph for the accident Dick wanted, and Pollock's request for new analysers for the pathology department. Though they might plot against *him* in Burdon's office, he was very sure that he would continue to support *them* in trying to improve their specialist services. His own bid, for a camera to fit on his E.R.C.P. apparatus, had gone in *via* Simon Durrant and had not come up for discussion today.

A vote of thanks to Dr Dick for the outstanding service he had given to the district during his years as chairman was given a short hand-clap. The meeting broke up.

The next Monday came round and Anne was off to her china painting class. Jim spent the evening composing his letter to Dr Holliday. He had told Anne about his talk with the B.M.A. man, and she had approved very much of getting his help. He had told her, with a mixture of relief and anger, of his session with David Burdon and of the telephone call by Berrill. As ever, she was practical and seemed matter-of-fact, but he sensed she was less upset about the whole business than he was. She never asked to see the "complaints" he spoke about, and Jim thought she did not want to see them. There was almost a conspiracy of silence between them.

"You've known for a long time what they were like," she said.

"I suppose I have."

"Try and not let yourself get into a state like you did over David Jones. He was jealous of you. That was all it was. They're both jealous of you. Especially David Burdon. He sounds just a poor inadequate man."

"But it's awful to feel that they hate you so much they'll go to this length."

"Well don't worry about them. Poor love, you should be sorry for them."

"You must admit they're strange."

"People know they're strange."

"I had all this before over D.G. Jones. I'm having it all over again now. It's not fair. I'm sorry to go on about it, especially just now." He knew she was still fraught since her brother's death and tired out with nursing him. So was he.

Another session with Mr Fenner, and the letter was complete. Jim thanked him heartfully for his help, and gave him a copy of all the letters—the first one, Holliiday's reply, and now their joint reply in turn. They decided he should arrange to see the R.M.O. and take the letter with him.

Ian Fenner showed no surprise when Jim told him that David Burdon had let slip that he had made the complaint to Dr Holliday.

"I was pretty aware from what you told me the last time that it was your colleagues who were responsible," he said. "That's the usual pattern, you know. The other is a senior man who writes letters of complaint about his juniors. Either way, it's an expression of pent-up jealousy.

Sometimes of course they have a case, but if that is so they don't write and say they don't want their names mentioned. They go and speak to the person. If they do it anonymously, there's always an element of malice, I'm afraid. If they were to be foolish to try and bring this to a public hearing, our barrister would soon be able to make that obvious to all concerned."

"We have had a rush of these, I was telling you that."

"Why do you think it is? Is it because of bed reductions? I think that was the start of our troubles," said Jim; "when we were all fighting our own corners to keep our patients coming in and there weren't enough beds."

"Hospital consultant staff have always been riddled with jealousy. But it's usually in Teaching Hospitals. We think this recent spate is certainly a symptom of the recent government changes—just like the state of gloom amongst the nurses is certainly the result of this re-grading exercise when they've to justify what they are doing to claim the salary they think they merit—plus the activities of the nurse managers. These ladies who sit all day in their offices and do not go on the wards are bad enough. The re-grading is just another straw. I'm afraid it will get worse. From the waves we're picking up about what Mrs Thatcher has in mind for the N.H.S., we're all in for a bad time."

"I'm very upset about this, I must admit," returned Jim. "I've always worked hard here. From the way that Mr Burdon behaved, his hostility was frightening. When I spoke to the district medical officer about him a year ago, I didn't make anything up. The nursing staff were all saying the same thing about him, that he was shouting at them. So was the records officer, I remember. I thought he was ill, and that was why I spoke to Dr Durrant. And when I spoke to Mr

Berrill, I found he had already spoken, a good time before to a Dr Morton who used to be the senior physician here, and to Dr Charles Pollock—they are great pals. He had in fact said a lot more criticism than I ever did."

"Another thing which is coming out of all this unhappiness is the number of consultant staff who are desperate to take early retirement," said Fenner.

"I know that," said Jim. "It never used to be like that, but it certainly is now."

"Would *you* think of putting in for early retirement?"

"I've been unhappy for a year already. This just makes me want to get away from it all."

"If you can get your pension made up, it's got a lot going for it. But your first aim is to see your Regional Medical Officer again, and see what he has to say."

He shook Jim's hand and went off.

Jim and Paula got the letter typed, looked at it together, and decided it would do,

"It's very good," said Paula. "You write good letters." She was nice.

Another appointment was made to see the R.M.O. Jim made it personally.

This time, Arthur was more of his usual self.

"You'd get a copy of my letter," Arthur said.

"Yes, thank you. It was very helpful. Now I've brought a reply I've put together. I went to the B.M.A. and asked for their advice. They said they'd help me in any way they could. They've been a great help."

He gave Dr Holliday the letter and sat and waited while he read it.

Dear Dr Holliday,

You wrote me on 6th January explaining that written complaints had been made against me by hospital staff and a lay administrator, alleging that I was not fulfilling my contract with the Health Authority.

When I came to see you, you listed a number of complaints. You said that because of my poor service, the doctors in the Lenning area had altered their referral patterns and did not send me patients. I was informed by Dr Wallace and later by other doctors there that this allegation is untrue.

You also told me that the Stoneleigh doctors had complained against me and had ceased to refer patients. This is however not recent, but began as soon as Dr Patrick Ward retired. His successor has never referred patients to me, except occasionally. If you wish a fair commentary on this change, could you please speak to Dr Ward. (It was perhaps not a coincidence, Jim was aware, that the new doctor in the practice was a personal friend of Alan Berrill's!)

You also told me that complaints had been made against me in the Medical Advisory Committees. Dr Cameron Wallace has informed me that he has made careful enquiries about these, and that there is absolutely no foundation for this allegation.

My recent alleged failures seem to have included the period when the waiting list initiative was enforced in Reidham. Last year I fractured my right wrist and was unable to get back to full work for three months. During this time my waiting list for gastro-intestinal procedures increased, and I was never able to get it satisfactorily down. This was mainly due to bed shortage and shortage of operating time. I offered Mr Langton that I would operate on a Saturday morning when I was on emergency call so that the list could be got down with no extra expense. This was refused both by him and by Miss Anderson, the nurse manager.

During October and November last year my registrar was off and no substitute could be found. I am grateful to Mr Berrill for offering me the help of his registrar. But it was impossible for me to get through my large referral clinics with no help other than a Senior House Officer. So if it appeared I was not seeing an adequate number of patients over this period, it was due to external factors and not due to idleness on my part.

When I tried to arrange extra operating, this was always refused by the nursing management on account of shortage of nurses following the cuts made last year.

I understand from Mr Langton that it was generally believed I had an afternoon list on a Tuesday, but never carried it out. This was untrue, and I am sorry the accusation was made.

I certainly admit that I have not communicated as freely with my surgical colleagues, particularly Mr Burdon, as I might have done. I am sorry for this, and will see it does not happen in the future. But I deny that I have been idle or uncaring in carrying out my work over the past three months. If you ask the ward staff, the outpatient staff, the cleaners, the telephonists, and the very large number of general practitioners who have given me solid support against these charges, I hope you will get another side of the story.

I am writing this letter following professional advice and strong support from the British Medical Association. Although I am fully appreciative of the kind way you have handled these complaints, I am sure you will understand my concern about the suggestion that one individual has allegedly complained about me over a number of years. I have worked very hard here, have set up an E.R.C.P service, and before that I was a local tutor for the Royal College of Surgeons for ten years.

If, as a result of our previous discussions and after reading this letter you are satisfied that the allegations made by this individual are without substance, I would welcome any assistance you might be able to give in persuading the person concerned to send me a written letter of apology. In the meantime, I hope you will find the above comments helpful.

He looked up and said:

"Thank you, Jim. This is very helpful. I'm glad you have said all you said. I'm glad you've said you will communicate better with your colleagues."

"I did try, you know. But I must admit I gave up after some years, when they didn't reciprocate."

"There is one thing," said Arthur. "You say that if someone has been criticising you for several years, you want an apology. But no-one has been criticising you for years. It only began last summer."

"But you said for some considerable time," replied Jim. "I thought that meant years."

"Well, perhaps I wasn't really correct in writing *that*. It was only last year. I cannot give you an apology. There's no benefit in you knowing who the people were. I don't think that would be useful. Mind you," he went on, "you won't find it too impossible a task to work out who the people were. Obviously, the people who would be bound to know most about your work are your two colleagues."

Jim thought. Then he said:

"But they both denied it."

"People are very often unwilling to admit to something like this if they are asked directly. I've had to deal with other complaints like this. Yours isn't the only one there's ever been."

"I had a copy of a letter which David Burdon wrote about me last week and I went to see him. I'm sorry he was very angry, and he let it out that he has had it in for me for a long time."

Arthur Holliday looked sharply at Jim. He paused for

several seconds. In fact, Jim wondered if he was all right. Then he said:

"Well, Jim, since he said that to you there's no point me still saying nothing, because you know. Yes, it was David Burdon. He began this. He was the one who was dropping hints and he was the main protagonist against you."

"What about the others, then?"

"You most have realised that the medical staff committee office bearers would be aware of what was being—what was happening."

"All right, Arthur," replied Jim. "But you must know yourself that I complained to Simon Durrant—in words—about David Burdon before. It was when he was behaving so badly on the wards, and shouting at the nurses, and so on."

"Yes, I heard about that. Cameron Wallace was through and told me." This was a surprise, but a nice one. That a man of Cameron Wallace's stature was willing to drive all the way to see the R.M.O. on his behalf, well, that was quite something.

"And when I spoke to Alan Berrill about it, I found he had been complaining already about him, unknown to me. He said very hard things."

It was clear that Berrill's complaint was unbeknown to Dr Holliday also.

"When I was through to the registrar training meeting and was away—this is what David Burdon wrote the letter about—the new prof told me that he had a complaint from students about Burdon, They complained he had been very unpleasant to them at a clinic."

Arthur Holliday sighed. "Poor David," he said. "He does seem to have his problems. When I see him, he always strikes me as a very unhappy man."

"Well," he went on, "I will file your letter away, as I said I would. It won't be seen by anyone. But I told you there is nothing to do about your request for an apology. Now you know why, I'm sure you'll agree. This has been a grudge, basically."

"Yes, Arthur. I do see."

Arthur Holliday was back to the person Jim had known before. The rather formal, unhappy manner of their last interview had gone. Never an effusive person—rather a shy, over-conscientious one; in fact, he was obviously feeling much better and his speech was more relaxed. They passed some pleasantries about people they had known from the past, Arthur told Jim how tired he was with all the pressure from the Ministry of Health, and they parted.

They shook hands. "Thank you for making this much easier for us both," said Arthur. "I hope you can put it behind you now."

CHAPTER 17

As he drove the miles back home, Jim's tiredness came back. He felt so deeply hurt—that a group had disliked him so much that they had gone along with the two who, as he saw it, had never shown him any kindness or made any real attempt at friendship. Berrill he could understand, because he was a disappointed man who had become even more disappointed at the Dale. He saw himself as Teaching Hospital material, his merit unrewarded. Not once but several—many—times Jim had tried to befriend him, work with him, and had been repeatedly rebuffed. There was nothing to be said about Burdon. His succession of secretaries told his tale eloquently. His outbursts were known by everyone. His outburst at Jim had gone all the way to the Health Authority.

Jim thought, as he drove along, that this was effectively the end of his career. If those four, or five if the non-medical one was included, disliked him to that degree, then there was no doubt they would not stop belittling him now. In fact, they could very well redouble their efforts. As ever, the no smoke without fire syndrome would apply. But he managed to cheer himself by remembering the kind help he had received from doctor friends—Frank Marples, Cameron Wallace, the others he had spoken to. Cameron Wallace had been a real Good Samaritan—he made a special journey all the way to speak to Dr Holliday. He would write and thank him when he got home, he thought. He felt better. Perhaps it wasn't so bad after all.

He could not help thinking of the four of them. First was Berrill, the smooth featured, apparently helpful, who had been prepared to accept a favour of a prestigious College job while at the same time working to destroy him. He was the nastiest, because of his outward appearance of reasonableness and moderation. But Jim told himself that Allan Berrill was the stereotype of the clever man who thought himself too good for a district general hospital. There must be many like him. It was just bad luck that he had been appointed to the Dale, where the majority of the original staff had the same sort of life reaction.

Then there was David Burdon, the leader of the pack, whom Jim and Anne had tried so sincerely to help and welcome on his arrival—his outbursts were there for everyone to see and hear and he had railed against many others besides Jim. Everyone knew his temper: said Patrick Healy, "Short fuse? He's got no fuse at all!" His eyes glittered with the same jealousy of David Jones'.

Dick the physician had never made any secret of his smouldering antagonism over the years since coming from the Dale—he had been true to form.

Langton the administrator Jim decided was not really important enough to matter. Yet his new-found status could make him a more powerful foe than his ability or intelligence would ever have in normal circumstances.

Pollock was the one Jim could not understand. He had been so obviously friendly over the years, so kindly and helpful. He was, or Jim thought he was, too big a man to add his signature to the malice of the others. Perhaps he had been more influenced by Berrill than appeared on the surface. Charles Pollock was the real disappointment.

This had to be put into the past, if possible. As he kept driving along towards the periphery where he belonged, Jim realised he had gone through the whole range of emotions from despair to confidence. Although he knew, and had been reassured by the B.M.A., that he would have won a public hearing, his final emotion was heart soreness. He could not get out of his mind the hurt of being disliked and attacked. Burdon's admission, and Arthur Holliday's confirmation, did not make it any better. He *must* try and put it behind him.

He soon found he could not. He slept badly, waking in the early hours. His bowels ran loose. He was as near impotent as made no difference. He spent more and more time in the hospital, fearful of another attack. He thought of Peter Millard and of how he had solved his anguish all those years ago by hanging himself. If Burdon had aimed to pay him back, he had succeeded. He kept more and more to himself, yet had to maintain public friendliness and courtesy towards Berrill and Burdon while seeing the look of hardness every day in their eyes. Private patients still came; Mr Baxter was still the consultant the people who mattered used.

This was the small local scene. On the national level, the N.H.S. Review was now public. The proposals for hospitals and general practice were attacked from their first appearance in February by the British Medical Association, especially by their chairman, Dr John Marks.

"Working for Patients," as the White Paper was called,

was divided into detailed papers giving the government's proposals. There were eight of these, beginning with one on self-governing hospitals, going on to budgets for general practitioners, medical audit—comparison of the usefulness of various treatments—to the last two, on contracts for N.H.S. consultants and implications for family practitioner committees.

The first of these was the one which concerned the Reid staff. Because the government wanted decision-making to be "at local operational level," they proposed allowing N.H.S. hospitals to become self-governing. "Self-governing hospitals will remain firmly within the N.H.S. and there will be safeguards to ensure that essential local services will continue to be provided locally," said Working Paper no. 1. "But they will have far more freedom to take the decisions on the matters which affect them most without detailed supervision from above. This new development will give patients more choice, produce a better service and encourage other hospitals to do even better in order to compete," it went on.

The idea was that self-governing hospitals would be separate legal entities within the N.H.S. and be known as N.H.S. hospital trusts. They would be run by a board of directors and have "a range of powers and freedoms not available to existing health authorities and hospitals." Hospitals would have to volunteer, to "bid," to Mr Kenneth Clarke, the Secretary of State, to be accepted as trusts.

In the same way, G.P.s could apply to become "budget holders"—to take their own responsibility for purchasing health care for their patients, within their budgets, of course, and if they were of a certain size. They would enter into a "contract" with their hospital trust to "buy" services for their own patients from the hospital trust.

The outcry from the B.M.A. was the loudest since the days of Mrs Barbara Castle fifteen years before. It was alleged, at once, that the new system would produce a "two-tier" health service, with the trust hospitals providing services which would bring them a profit and neglecting the less obviously marketable services, such as geriatric medicine and geriatric psychiatry. The insistence by the government that "core" or essential services would have to be provided locally did not allay these fears. But the first G.P. budget holders and self-governing hospitals were not to be introduced till April of 1991 and the "bids" did not have to go to the Department till the later part of 1990. So from the B.M.A.'s point of view, there was time to try and reverse the proposals.

The Labour opposition not surprisingly threw its weight with the B.M.A. against the proposals. Mr Robin Cook, their spokesman, spoke chillingly of the evils they would bring. The spectre of the privatisation of the whole service was raised and fostered. Urgent B.M.A. conferences were called, a video challenging the government's scheme was watched at B.M.A. divisional meetings rather larger in participants than usual, and a press campaign launched. Mr Kenneth Clarke spoke scathingly of doctors "reaching for their wallets." He went on to ridicule their opposition as no more than a repetition of previous form, when "The B.M.A. had always resisted changes, every time they were proposed."

In Reidham the foundations for the new hospital were now being dug. The initial plans had, inevitably, been modified and reduced to save money. Months had then passed, while the modifications remained at the Department, until when they eventually came back the new cost was relatively little less than the original. But now tenders having been accepted, the work had begun. When the new District Hospital was completed, the old Royal Reid and the Avondale would both be demolished.

Mr Raymond Langton was enthusiastically in favour of the government's proposals. So were Mr David Burdon, Dr Patrick Healy, and some of the new orthopaedic unit. But the others were doubtful. A new grouping of friends and enemies appeared, as one or two of the larger town practices said they would consider becoming budget holders. Those in favour were all of the younger age group. Birrell would make no opinion. Dr William Dick had failed in his aim to become the chairman of the Regional Medical Advisory Committee and was not taking it well. He was also glum and silent. Jim as the senior member of the consultant staff in both the hospitals felt that this was the last straw. He had no sympathy with the increasingly finance-orientated N.H.S. he saw appearing. He just wanted to get on with his work and see and treat the patients referred to him. His request to go full-time had been accepted, so he would be reducing his private work. He feared for the future of the new hospital, too. It would be a square, box-like building, with shared ward areas and cramped consulting in pairs with a tiny office between—to let the consultant see patients quicker and so more efficiently. In the meantime, there would be all the mess and dirt of contractors' lorries and builders' materials. Sister Billings, his last remaining prop within the hospital, was due to retire that Spring.

Sister Billings had become rather like Jim—a staff member who did not enjoy or fit in to the new scheme of things. She had been in trouble with Miss Anderson, who had a sarcastic tongue, because of her lack of enthusiasm for the new era in nursing. Whereas it had been Jim who had made most of the complaints at their cups of tea sessions in her duty room, it was now Sister who looked for comfort and support.

"This job's difficult enough, Mr Baxter, without them harrying you the way they do."

Jim agreed.

"If they even knew what they were talking about. Miss Anderson just sits in her room or goes to meetings. She never comes to the wards the way matrons used to."

Jim agreed again. He felt the same. During a meeting to try to settle yet another complaint by Mr Burdon, she had said tartly to Jim:

"I am a nursing manager, Mr Baxter. I do not have *time* to go on to the wards." He had repeated that remark often. It epitomised the new attitude of the senior nursing staff.

Sister Billings got more depressed as her retiral date came nearer. Jim tried to console her by telling her she would be away from it all. It didn't seem to help.

"I'm so upset my doctor's given me tranquilisers," she confided one day.

Jim sighed. He passed on the news to Anne that evening.

"I'm really sorry for Sister Billings. She's such a good sister. I wonder who we'll get when she leaves."

"She must be very upset, if she has had to get tranquillisers," said Anne. "Has she any financial worries?"

"I hadn't thought about that. She has two married sisters.

She'll have her pension. And her state pension. She's sixty."
"I know she's interested in music," said Anne, "and gardening."

"Jim," said Anne suddenly, looking at him, "do you think you'd like to retire?"

"Wouldn't I just. But I've four years to go."

"Yes, but you've done nearly forty years in the N.H.S.— since you graduated. You're full-time now, so you can put your whole income for this year towards your lump sum." The lump sum was the other half of the pension package for hospital staff—it was three times the best income of the last three years if service, and complemented the pension which was paid monthly. This was the reason Jim had changed his contract to a whole-time one. It meant he was paid for eleven sessions and not ten. So his N.H.S. income rose.

"Yes, love, but remember I've been part-time all these years. So I've not done forty years by next year. I need four years to make my full pension."

"But you've got your private pension to mature next year—no, 1991. If you retired and paid the premiums over next year, you could cash that pension and re-invest it. You might even be able to get early retiral under this achieving a balance thing."

The "achieving a balance" was a government announcement of 1986 that new consultant posts would be created—but there seemed little evidence of how widely it had been applied.

Anne had always been the practical partner. While Jim over the years had been immersed in his work, and lately immersed in all his unhappiness, she had made the suggestions about what they should buy, whether they might invest, what they ought to ask their accountant about. It had been her idea, ten years before, that he should start to pay for a personal pension to mature either before he retired, when he could stop paying the premiums but not take the money, or continue payments for longer to increase the final cash further. Now she was putting into words what his subconscious must be telling him. He ought to get out.

"I really do love you, you know," Anne said. "I know how bad things must be, because you're not yourself and I know you are unhappy. *I'm* not going to see you go on this way and have a coronary or something."

As a rule Anne would laugh Jim out of his fears of illness and of the heart attack which had removed friend and non-friend over the years. He realised that for her to talk like this showed she was in earnest.

They talked it out, as they had done so often in the past. Almost tearful, Jim finally said:

"Even if it meant losing some of my pension, I'd go early. I'm fed up, I'm fed up. You don't know what those two are like."

Sister Billings' retiral presentation was to be in the nurses' home. There was the usual array of cakes and tea, and chairs for the guests. She was led in, looking very tense and unhappy, by Miss Anderson. Miss Anderson made a rather standard speech, referring to Miss Billings' years of good and faithful service. Then she asked Mr Baxter if he would like to say a few words "as you have been so closely associated over so many years." The staff gift was a painting and a cheque. "I am very happy to thank Sister Billings for her service here," he said. "We have worked on the same wards since I arrived here over twenty years ago. Over those years I've learned to respect her more and more. She has never lowered her standards over the years. I know that at one time she was asked to become an assistant matron, but turned it down after a short time because she wanted to be a ward sister. She and I have seen many changes in these recent years, but we've both believed that our first duty was always to the patients and not to targets for numbers. I know that Sister Billings has been one of the best trainers of nurses in this or any other hospital, and I know how much a succession of nurses in training have looked back in gratitude to what she taught them. The patients loved her.

"I've looked back in gratitude to what she had taught me, many times. If Sister said a patient was ill, she was always right. The present you've so kindly got for her is a token of your real affection. I have a present of my own to give her, and here it is."

He gave her a combined radio, tape and C.D. disc player—something he knew she would like, as she had often told him that she was looking forward to listening to music in her retirement. The alternative was something for her garden, but Jim and Anne both agreed a music player was more lasting and more personal.

Kisses accompanied presentations these days, thought Jim as he gave her his gift. But he made no move to kiss Sister Billings. He knew she would not like it. She was not a modern.

The doctors' doubts about the new government proposals were not, as ministers declared, just emotional. They feared the time-table was too hasty, especially since the programme was being imposed on a service that had barely got over its third restructuring in 15 years and was still struggling with the nurses' re-grading exercise, where nursing staff had to justify their own skill and experience within their own job. Langton had left no-one in any doubt about his position and his intentions—he was determined that their new hospital become a trust. Those opposed to him—and these were the great majority of the hospital staff—consoled themselves that he couldn't do very much while the new hospital was building. Or so they hoped.

Jim and Anne had never lost their friendship with the Macgregors, but what with one thing and another, hadn't seen them now for a good six months. Ken was always good value when medical politics were in the public eye and there was any extra controversy. So when they went through one Sunday, both Jim and Anne were looking forward to his usual forthright opinions being expressed. Ken had become much less socialist in his opinions over the years, as he too grew older and approached his retirement, and had supported Mrs Thatcher over the miners' strike and even the Falklands war.

"This is going to set a new style for the N.H.S.," he told them. "But this idea of an internal market to improve efficiency through competition I've my doubts about. Competition can't be equated with consumer choice whether it's hospitals or G.P.s. If your local—what do you call it—district health authority—contracts for services with you lot, it can't be on anything other than price."

"And quality," said Jim.

"Well," replied Ken, "I can't see much difference in quality around here. You all seem to do the best you can in spite of the troubles you've got. Does the government offer any extra cash?"

"No," said Anne, "it doesn't. There's actually less. The nurses have had a terrible time over all this re-grading. You have to prove that the amount of responsibility you have is enough to earn you your grade. But there aren't enough places in a grade for all the nurses doing similar work. For example, there are four theatre sisters, apart from the one they call the nursing officer, but only three senior grade posts. So one of them will have to accept a lower grading. But they all do the same work."

"What annoys me," went on Jim, "is that they've put this forward without any consultation, and without any pilot schemes to see if their ideas actually work."

"You've a hope," returned Ken, sucking his mouth as ever. "The government aren't daft. If they'd consulted the B.M.A. they'd never have got anything done—you'd have just argued and argued."

"Well I don't know," said Jim. "I think the B.M.A. could have been very helpful because doctors actually work in the N.H.S. and know the difficulties first-hand."

"An odd thing," said Ken, "is that these two ideas about fund holding G.P.s and trust hospitals are to be introduced only if volunteers agree to take part. If no-one volunteers to form a trust or hold a budget, what happens then?"

"That's no problem, Ken. The managers are pressurised to push people into volunteering. It's in their interest to do so. Remember they get a bonus on top of their salary if they make their target to save money." And then he told them about Raymond Langton, who had already circulated a memo extolling the virtues of the trust system.

"Worst of all," said Ken, "is the loss of influence of you doctors. I used to think you had too much, but now I think you've too little. If these opted out hospitals can pay their medical staff what they like, where's your national agreements and your pay review body? And if the opted out hospitals cream off good staff by paying them more, what's that other than the road to a two-tier N.H.S? These managers seem a dangerous lot. They've tasted power, and you doctors are there for the taking. They'll soon push you around. You wait and see."

Ken was much more sympathetic at Jim's personal problems with his colleagues. He listened to the tale of recent woes, sucking his lips quietly.

"I've never met either of these characters," he told Anne, "but I know you and Jim well enough to know that if they said he wasn't doing his work they must be an odd pair. They sound a couple of jealous wee men."

"They've certainly upset Jim, Ken," said Anne. "I wish he'd retire."

As the months passed, the hope of retiral loomed larger and larger for Jim and Anne. 1989 was full of medical politics, and the B.M.A. ran a large and expensive campaign against the proposals, urging caution and the setting up of pilot schemes to test how they worked. But the bill became law, and a few of the larger Teaching Hospitals began to show an interest in becoming trusts.

Langton and Burdon became closer brethren as this year progressed. David was the only consultant who was keen on the new ideas, so Raymond Langton favoured him increasingly, to the annoyance of Berrill and the amusement of Jim. Burdon's requests for new equipment were agreed by the unit general manager, Berrill's requests were pencilled out.

David Burdon showed himself increasingly determined to take the leading part in the planning of the new hospital. The general ward layouts, the arrangement of clinics, had all been long since imposed at Regional level. But as the building went on, there were inevitably queries of every sort. It was here that Burdon insisted on putting his oar in. While Jim was still the consultant in charge till the end of 1989, when his three year stint finished, and Allan Berrill was next to follow on, David Burdon had no hesitation in insisting that *he* represent the general surgeons—and the orthopaedic surgeons also, if they would have let him—because he said he was the youngest and so would have the most time in the new building. He conveniently forgot that he was only three years younger than Allan. Jim quietly agreed. He was filling in his time now he was on a full-time salary, and was trying to reduce his private practice. He had made his decision about leaving. The others could fight it out between themselves.

By the Autumn, further new alignments of hospital staff relationships were emerging. Dick was now taking a back seat; he had never got over his failure to be elected chairman of the Regional Medical Advisory Committee. Healy had moved into the medical chairmanship, where his flamboyance was much more entertaining than Dick's steady but rather boring efficiency. Pollock, too, had retreated. He was becoming more bad-tempered and frustrated at the regular refusals by the administration for new apparatus for his lab. He attacked bitterly the all too obvious favouritism of Mr Langton towards Mr Burdon. The other departments were not interested in politics or power.

Sister Billings' successor was a very young, quiet girl who had been appointed from a thin list of applicants with nursing administration approval and no particular enthusiasm on Mr Baxter's part.

Sister Pickering had at last got her come-uppance. Because the plastic and orthopaedic surgeons were to form the larger element in the new surgical division, and were to be, of course, in the new hospital, a new overall supremo nursing post for all the theatres was created, and it had been won by a young and very determined lady from elsewhere. Sister Pickering had been passed over.

Jim had no sympathy for the tough Yorkshire lady. She had behaved spitefully towards Sister Pope, pushing her out as Jones had pushed out Jim Baxter. Now *she* was being pushed over, but by someone legally appointed above her. And she did not like it. "I think I'll take early retirement," she told Jim!

For several years now, the surgeons had suffered decreasing standards of comfort provided in their coffee room in theatre. Sister Pickering had collected their monthly money for coffee, and biscuits, after the administration had refused to provide them free. Now, in her pique at being passed over for promotion, she announced that she would no longer do this but would make other arrangements. In triumph, she told the surgeons she had got the main kitchen to provide coffee free again.

The result was depressing, to say the least. In the coffee room, where the surgeons and anaesthetists, both junior and senior, met, the old table was removed, as well as the cups and saucers. A plastic table was substituted, with a plastic sock of disposable plastic mugs. The free coffee was a 250Gm industrial size tin. The sugar appeared in a 1Kg paper bag and the milk in a plastic pint container. Water was boiled in an electric kettle on the floor. No-one looked after the room during the day. Sometimes the new contract cleaners the management team had engaged did not even clear up in the evening. As Jim surveyed the table, awash with cold spilt coffee and with its tin, sugar bag and milk carton, he thought wistfully of the splendid luxury of his first days at the Royal. The coffee table summed up for him the new alien hospital service; plastic, cheap, and undignified. This was Raymond Langton's brave new world.

As 1989 wore to a close the B.M.A. campaign looked less effective. Mr Kenneth Clarke's rude confrontational style won him no friends among nursing or medical staff. Sister Pickering returned full of condemnation from a theatre nurses' conference in Liverpool where he had spoken.

And as local opposition waned, so the confidence of Langton and Burdon increased. When Jim told Burdon and Berrill of his wish to resign David Burdon said at once:

"That's fine Jim. When we are a trust Allan and I will carry all the work here between us and will each have half your salary, because Raymond Langton says we can set our own rate of salary." When he had gone, Jim couldn't help laughing.

CHAPTER 18

Work on the new district hospital was going well. The project team monitored progress. Langton and Burdon were now the two men out, because they were the minority viewpoint. They were not bothered. But it soon became apparent that the Reid and Avondale hospitals were *not* the Regional Authority's first priority. This was the Teaching Hospital. Here the bulk of the senior staff shared the B.M.A.'s official suspicion, but again there was a sizeable minority in favour of seeking trust status.

Arguments went back and forth. Meetings were held. The unions—C.O.H.S.E. and the B.M.A.—warned in their different ways of a two-tier service. Having stronger and more capable personalities in post than the former office-boy Raymond Langton, the managers worked very hard to make their arguments acceptable. Mr Langton was sent packing by the R.M.O.'s staff. His early bounce sagged sadly. With it sagged the enthusiasm of Mr Burdon and to a lesser extent of Dr Healy.

Mr Langton did not however slacken his determination to create a unit run on better and better business lines. Nurse numbers were reduced further, Miss Anderson dutifully producing tables of fractions of nurses and hours of work which she insisted were totally adequate for her workload targets. Mr Langton then trotted them out before the ward sisters who were suspicious, and the doctors, who did not understand them.

New rosters were drawn up for the porters and their numbers reduced. The engineers were told they were not efficient and to do better. Even the hospital gardeners, whose work gladdened the eyes of everyone each year, had their numbers cut and found themselves running after their mowers from one hospital to another. Mr Langton marched round the theatre sterile supply unit and said he would put it out to private tender. The cleaners had been privatised long since. Night staff in the hospital kitchen disappeared; free soup and tea and coffee vendors appeared in their stead. This was a clever move; the night staff then brought in their own sandwiches, so the hospital food budget went down. The C.O.H.S.E. secretary wrote angrily to the local press. The Unit General Manager wrote angrily to the local press.

His tables for surgical through-put were his star turn. This was not to his credit, because numbers of operations, days before discharge after operation, as well as the inevitable waiting list times, were very easy to quantify. It was less easy to make a table to illustrate the way the psychiatrists or geriatricians got through their workload. It was to Mr Baxter's disadvantage that he kept his patients in longer than Mr Berrill and Mr Burdon and that his lists looked shorter because he was a faster operator.

Mr Langton's public relations policy was to inform a clinical division that he would visit them on a certain date. At first he was full of consideration not to upset their working schedules, but as time passed and his arrogance began to increase again after his snub by the Health Authority, he began to insist that the clinicians suit him rather than the other way round. At such a meeting for the surgeons he would follow a prepared pattern. He would start by telling them how well he was handling the unit budget, and how return on money spent was more and more in accord with sound business. He next told them of his meetings at Headquarters with other unit managers and the general manager, and as he spent much of his time at these meetings, there was plenty to tell. Finally he told them their performance figures were satisfactory but showed room for improvement. Mr Burdon was always warmly applauded. Mr Baxter was described in terms at best coldly polite, at worst snidely offensive.

Dr Simon Durrant had lost his former status. He was by now just a member of Mr Langton's team. He and Jim talked together about the way things had gone and where they might be going. They had a trust in each other which helped. Simon spoke of the general picture that was coming out—everywhere there were lay managers appointed who were ruling the doctors because they were supported by their own superiors. The doctors had no such support; in spite of the often-repeated claims that they must take a more active interest in management their views counted for less and less.

"I think that's why they're not bothering," was Simon's opinion. "The way they are pushing forwards at Region to make the Teaching Hospital into a trust in spite of the opposition of the bulk of the consultant staff doesn't exactly encourage the consultants."

"It just makes the older ones want to take early retirement," said Jim. "Which reminds me," he went on, "I've definitely decided to put in for early retiral myself, Simon."

What about your pension, Jim? You can't retire on health grounds. You've four years to go, haven't you?"

"Yes, but I really don't want to go on beyond next year."

"When did you start here?"

"1966. So by 1991 I'll have done 25 years. I've had enough. So has Anne. She's had a job with all my complaining and she's been marvellous. But I'll see about trying to get my pension made up for as long as the Health Authority will let me. If they won't, I'll still retire. I'm going to write to the superannuation now to find out exactly where I stand."

"What about your operating? How are things going these days?"

Simon of course knew all about the affair with Burdon and Berrill.

"That's all right. Since that man Aziz left and my new registrar settled in, it's been much less of a worry than it was. And Peter Holmes is such a nice anaesthetist. He reminds me of Dr Sugden, who was here when I came here first."

"When does Allan Berrill take over the chairmanship of the general surgical division—it must be sometime soon, isn't it?"

"Yes. The end of this year. So I'll have a year to earn a full-time salary to help my final pension and retire in 1991."

"I'm not exactly sure," said Simon, "what the present position is about getting your pension years made up. All I seem to have thought about in the last six months is all this talk of trusts and the new hospital here."

"It certainly seems to be getting on well—the hospital, I mean," laughed Jim.

"Yes," said Simon. "It's supposed to be 1992—late 1992—when it is due to open. It'll take a good six months after that before it's fully commissioned and working. Wouldn't you like to hang on for the move in?"

Simon laughed to Jim. They both knew the answer.

"Don't I just wish I could retire too," said Simon.

Spring of 1990 and the Teaching Hospital was confirmed as a volunteer for the first wave of trusts. It was well known locally that the majority of consultant staff were against, but the number in favour had risen remarkably. The managers, encouraged by new Health Authority members who happened to support the government, had simply gone ahead. The efforts of the B.M.A., the local Trade Unions, and the member of parliament, had been in vain. When he heard the news, Jim wondered if trust hospitals' surgeons would get coffee out of cups with saucers again.

The atmosphere in the Reid had changed, even in the past year. There was a constant flow of paper from Raymond Langton, and most people tried to ignore it. "There's no shortage of paper in this new N.H.S.," said Simon Durrant sadly. The biggest irritation was the constant exhortations to process more and more patients, to "keep the figures good." In the past consultants had admitted patients depending upon their needs; people with tumours at once, then the rest depending upon the severity of their illness. People with less serious things wrong waited longer, but everybody knew that. Acutely ill patients came in at any time, with no delay.

In the Royal Reid, compared to most hospitals in England, the waiting times had never been long. This was one of the reasons why the original staff felt proud they were doing a good job. But now the very fact that staff were being ordered to hurry patients into hospital was an irritation, and the fact they were being ordered to send them out again before the consultants felt they were really ready, was another.

New also was the demand that clinicians do what the majority had taken for granted throughout their medical careers—to be "polite to patients." They were exhorted to explain, to warn, to call patients "clients" or "customers." Nurses, too, were bewildered at demands to detail all their nursing procedures, procedures the older ones had done for years without having to write it all down. Now they had to write down even standard items of nursing care. There had grown up an atmosphere of sullen resentment.

Costings were in everyone's minds. Certainly the past had seen a great wastage of every sort of item, because the staff took it for granted that there was an inexhaustible supply. Certainly, too, the high cost of drugs the great majority of medical and nursing staff neither knew nor worried about. So care in drug usage was worth-while, and most staff realised this. Unfortunately the government's policy had led to a fear that necessary items might run out if a trust or general practice exceeded its budget—in spite of Mr Clarke's reassurances to the contrary.

Litigation was another new fear. Doctors had always made mistakes, and every doctor had had his tragedies. But now the fear of litigation was very much in the forefront of clinicians' thoughts. The fear was made worse by the exhortations by Mr Langton for patients to complain. Complaint cards appeared in every ward, in outpatients, at the front door, and there was a huge pile in casualty. There were no cards in the administrative block.

The time had come to make definite arrangements for his retiral. Jim had an interview with the superannuation department at the Regional Headquarters and found that if he retired in a year's time he would indeed be two years short of his 40 years. This was the number of years a doctor had to work for the National Health Service to earn his full pension. It was worked out on the principle that if you started at age 25, by the time you had done 40 years you would be 65, and so eligible for retiral. But this was only if you had worked on a full-time contract. Jim had always been on a part-time contract, and so although he had bought five added years of service by putting money aside in the past out of his N.H.S. salary, and had "bought" himself some of the shortfall, he was still a couple of years short. This would reduce his final pension.

He went to see Arthur Holliday, to ask if he could help.

"Glad to see you, Jim."

"Nice to see *you*, Arthur. How are you enjoying the new-look N.H.S?"

"Don't talk about it. I'm against the trust hospital idea, but I'm a back number now. It's going to go ahead, I am sure of that. The only way it'll be stopped is if we have a change of government. And even then, I doubt if a Labour Government would do away with the buyer and provider idea altogether."

"*Your* new district hospital's coming along very well," Arthur went on. "You'll be looking forward to its opening. At the moment it looks as if you'll be in time for the opening." He smiled. He was as nice as ever, thought Jim.

"I have decided to take early retirement," said Jim. "I want to go next Spring. You can understand why. In any case, I'll have completed two years full-time by then."

"I can understand. But how are things going?"

"As well as can be expected, as the saying is. I'm not doing any more and certainly not any less than I ever was. Things are a bit better. We've no trouble with registrars just now—that's a help. But I've no illusions, Arthur. The only consolation I have is that the others are critical about everything and everybody. They haven't changed. But I've had enough."

"You said you were short of time towards your pension?"

"Yes. Two years. Is there any way I could get this made up?"

Arthur Holliday paused before he replied.

"I know just what happened and I wish we could help, Jim. But this is 1990 and the general manager has decreed that anaesthetists and physicians may retire a year early and have their pensions made up. But not surgeons. Surgeons were last year. It's silly. But that's what he has decided. It's to do with this policy of making more posts available—you know, achieving a balance, they call it. Apparently it's anaesthetists here this year, not surgeons. What about staying on for another year?"

"No, I've had enough. My wife's had enough, too."

Arthur gave him a sharp glance.

"Is she unhappy about things too?"

"Of course. She's always been a great help. She's always tried to show me that things aren't too bad as I've thought, and told me when I've been being silly. But she's never known about that last trouble. I kept that from her, Arthur. She's quite reconciled to us having to lose pension. Her older brother—he's a doctor—he's retired and says he loves it. But then he's a G.P. and I think it's different for them."

"What about your private work, Jim? I know you do a great deal of that."

Jim laughed. "If I get anything and I hope I do I'll have to do it in the nursing home in Reidham. But that place is more or less a geriatric home now. It has been for a while. I would come here to the new B.U.P.A. place—I've used it a bit, but for bigger things it's too far from home to be safe. The fact that there are no private beds in the new hospital hasn't affected my decision."

"What do you think you'll do? Have you anything in mind? Everyone I've seen retire finds themselves busier than they were when they were working."

"My trouble, I must admit," said Jim, "is that I've no outside interests apart from a bit of golf and a bit of gardening. So I'll have to find something. The sad thing is," he went on, "I've seen so many hospital consultants retire and have no other interests, and yet I've never done anything to get any outside interests myself."

"Well, you have made a big contribution in Reidham, Jim. That endoscopic service you set up was much needed and very worthwhile. Whoever succeeds you will have to have an accreditation in E.R.C.P. work."

They chatted. When Jim rose to go, Arthur Holliday shook his hand warmly.

"You haven't had the easiest of lives in your neck of the woods. But if you knew about other places, they have the same. It's perhaps not much consolation, but it's true."

"I'll send you a formal notice that I'm going to retire next year, Arthur."

"Mind you tell David Burdon and Allan Berrill!" Arthur Holliday laughed.

"I'll do that."

Paula was not surprised when she heard Jim's news. Nor, he suspected, were his two colleagues when he told them. There was the usual non-committal response and coldness of eye. Never a flicker of a hint of wishing him well. Burdon had already informed Jim—by letter—that he intended taking his holiday at the time Jim had planned to leave. There was no question of *David's* coming to discuss things with Jim when *his* wishes were involved! Simon Durrant, who knew already, was cheerful and optimistic:

"You'll be much better off now you've got your decision made, Jim," he said. "And you're giving us plenty of notice."

The weeks after the advertisement appeared in the *British Medical Journal* and the *Lancet* were quite amusing for Jim. At first Berrill was fiercely critical of the response. The new appointee had to have a special interest in the specialty Jim had developed, in the teeth of the others' opposition those few years ago. At first there seemed to be very few candidates, who were dismissed by him as "totally useless." Jim had as always happened in the N.H.S. no part in the appointment; the others not unexpectedly told him nothing at all about the field. He did not fail to notice that there was no obvious rush to see over the hospital.

One day Jim thought he would be bold enough to enquire of Allan how things were going. Allan looked annoyed. Then a couple of days later he told Jim: "We're overwhelmed with candidates." Jim made no comment.

Although the others did not let Jim know, he heard from Paula the day the interviews were to be. That afternoon as he was leaving the hospital at half-past five, Jim met David Burdon coming back in. He knew where David had been.

But there was no word spoken, only the now familiar insincere smirk of friendliness on Burdon's face. Nor did Berrill even once say anything about who had got the job. By now it was more funny than annoying. Jim's release was coming closer and he felt better as the weeks passed.

Jim was surprised at the response to the news of his impending retirement. Doctors from all over the district wrote him. A letter came from Tom Stone—how had he found out? Frank Marples and Cameron Wallace wrote the kindest of letters, both saying "the past two years can't have been easy for you." Old patients stopped him in the street. Most surprising of all, a public fund was started by some citizens of Reidham, and advertised widely. The nurses, porters, cleaners, all stopped in the corridors to say how sorry they were that he was retiring and to wish him good health. Mrs Bell, his great friend George Bell's widow, wrote an especially kind letter. "You'll be able to put your burden down now," she wrote. "I hope you will be happy to know that a generation of people here have admired your work and will never forget your skill and your kindness." It was heart-warming. Many notes from G.P.s apologised for not being able to attend his hospital presentation because it coincided with their surgery time.

The day dawned and rather nervously Jim went in, and went around his patients for the last time. His new ward sister seemed to have managed to have the whole staff on duty—he wondered how she had managed to do it without complaints from the nursing office. In the sideroom sat Allan Berrill, who was in seeing a patient of his. He passed the time of day civilly, but did not say anything about the afternoon's occasion.

In the afternoon, Jim and Anne both returned rather nervously to the postgraduate centre, where medical retiral presentations were held. Jim thought back to his first years at the Reid; his efforts to run a pastgraduate programme before there was such a thing as a custom built postgraduate centre. He—and more so Anne—was a little worried at the rows of chairs that had been put out. They hoped there would not be too many for the size of the audience.

Simon Durrant appeared before 4 p.m., along with Miss Anderson. There was no sign of Langton. But to Jim's intense surprise, not only had Arthur Holliday come from the Health Authority Headquarters, but the General Manager himself had come over with him. Jim could not remember the General Manager or Regional Medical Officer ever appearing at a retiral presentation at the Royal Reid.

They all sat down. Then Simon's secretary hurried in and came straight to speak to Jim:

"Mr Baxter," she said in a rather embarrassed voice, "I've just had a phone message from Mr Berrill. He says he can't come this afternoon because he had to take his son to an interview."

"Thank you," said Jim.

Simon Durrant made a pleasant speech, Jim replied, and thanked everyone for their gift. It was a cheque, he knew. He knew already that the amazing sum of £1000 had been raised by public subscription. But he thought this would inevitably be a small one.

Anne received her flowers.

They were both touched by the turn-out, and most of all by the number of retired nursing staff who had come along. There was Sister Billings, but also Sister Fletcher, old Sister

Hoddie who once ruled the private wing, Nurse Porter of old outpatient days and Sister Begbie and her staff of new ones. Sisters Pickering and Samira came along. But so did Sisters Pope and Oliver, from his golden years. Three members of the Teaching Hospital staff were there, and even some former patients. General practitioners sat in the front row. The new generation of orthopaedic surgeons from the Dale were present to a man. The anaesthetists were out in force. Andrew Morton was there, sitting at the back.

It was almost an epitaph of his life as a consultant surgeon at the Royal Reid—bitter unhappiness within the hospital and respect and affection without it.

By now he had opened his envelope. This cheque was for a further £1200. He showed it to Anne. "I've *told* you people like you," she said.

Cameron Wallace came to speak to him.

"Well, Jim, you're a free man now."

"Yes. Thank you again for all your help, Cameron."

"What will you do with yourself now you've finished with the N.H.S.?"

"I don't know."

"Well," said Cameron, with a twinkle in his eye, "you can always write a book about it."

ABOUT THE AUTHOR

John S G Blair was educated at Dundee High School where he was dux, and at St Andrews University where he was a Harkness Scholar. He served in the RAMC as a National Service officer from 1952-55, and graduated Bachelor of Arts as an external student at London University where he was placed first of 200 in the external examination of 1955. In 1961 he graduated ChM at St Andrews with High Commendation for his thesis on 'slipperiness of human fat'. He was Consultant Surgeon at Perth Royal Infirmary from 1965-1990, Honorary Senior Lecturer in Surgery at Dundee University and examined in Anatomy and Surgery at the Royal College of Surgeons of Edinburgh from 1964-1992. He was in the Territorial Army until 1992 and has carried out surgical consultant locums in Hong Kong, Nepal, Cyprus, and Musgrave Park, as well as in military hospitals in Britain and Germany. He was made an OBE (Military) in 1974.

He took early retirement from the NHS and is now an Honorary Senior Clinical Teacher at the Faculty of Medicine, Dundee University. A former President of both the Scottish and British Societies for the History of Medicine, he was World Vice President of the International Society of The History of Medicine, only the second Briton to have held this position. His work for both British and

International medical history was honoured by the creation in 1997 of the John Blair Trust, available to help those students studying History of Medicine within the UK. He was made Doctor of Letters (*honoris causa*) by St Andrews University in 1991, a Fellow of the British Medical Association in 1993, and a Fellow of the Royal Historical Society from 2000, a unique honour for a medical graduate. From 1993-98 he was Chairman of the BMA Armed Forces Committee.

ND - #0459 - 270225 - C0 - 229/152/26 - PB - 9781861510822 - Matt Lamination